A Deadly
Christmas Carol

by

Sh~~...~~ *ook*

NEPTUNE RISING PRESS

NEPTUNE RISING PRESS

Cover Illustration: Sharon Love Cook

Cover and Book Design: Donnie Light

All characters in this book are fictional and products of the author's imagination, with the exception of Chester, the 95-lb black Lab.

Published in the USA by Neptune Rising Press

For Isabelle Autumn Cook

CHAPTER ONE

"There's nothing like an old-fashioned church fair to get me in the Christmas spirit," Betty Ann announced, pushing her way through the crowded basement of St. Rupert's Lutheran Church.

Rose followed her friend into the warm room, her gaze taking in the tables of home-crafted goods. "I wish they'd do something about the lights," she complained. "Everyone looks embalmed."

"That's part of the charm," Betty Ann said. "Oh, look— sweaters!" She surged toward a display of hand-knit booties, scarves, and garish holiday sweaters. "I've always wanted a Christmas sweater." She flipped through the stack and selected one, holding it against her broad chest. "What do you think?"

Rose stood back and studied the effect. "Are those supposed to be reindeer pulling the sleigh?"

"Of course they're reindeer. What else would they be?"

"Well... dachshunds."

"Dachshunds! What are you talking about?"

Rose shrugged. "You asked my opinion and I'm telling you. It looks like Santa's sleigh is being pulled by a team of dachshunds. It's the legs; they're not long enough for reindeer."

Betty Ann held the garment at arm's length. "Hmm, you've got a point. Maybe they ran out of yarn." Sighing, she returned it to the table.

Rose examined a sleeveless cable-knit sweater. "This red would look great on Chester." She got the attention of a woman behind the table: "Do you think this would fit a ninety-five-pound Labrador?"

The woman's gaze was impassive. "Are you referring to a resident of the island of Labrador?"

"Um—actually, I was referring to a Labrador retriever. You know, the dog?"

The woman snatched the sweater from her hands. "This is a lady's vest."

"Oh, I see. It doesn't have sleeves, and I thought..." Rose felt her cheeks flush.

"I don't make clothing for dogs," the woman said, carefully folding the vest.

When she returned it to the stack, Rose grabbed it. "In that case, I'll get it for my aunt. She's a nun, stationed in China." Before the woman could protest, Rose held out some bills to her, and she took them reluctantly.

When the woman left to deposit the money in a cash box, Betty Ann said, "All the years I've known you and not one mention of an aunt in China. And by the way, nuns aren't stationed, they serve."

Rose shrugged. "She wouldn't have sold it to me otherwise."

"In any event, Chester will look great in it. Just don't go walking him near the church."

After collecting her bag, Rose joined Betty Ann to navigate the busy room."What do you feel like doing?" she asked. "I need to buy a tote for my dad. He carries a beat up old bag everywhere."

"There's plenty of time for shopping," Betty Ann said. "Let's check out the food tables first. I hear Edith Bicknell is making eggnog doughnuts again this year."

"I'm not hungry right now."

"What time did you have breakfast?"

Rose stopped, feeling puzzled. "You know what? In all the rushing around this morning, I forgot to have breakfast."

"Rose McNichols, you 'forgot' to have breakfast?"

"Yeah, what's wrong with that?"

"Forgetting to have breakfast is like… like forgetting to get dressed, and going out in your pajamas. If I ever forgot to have breakfast, it would be because the house was on fire." She patted her belly. "But you've got a point. What am I doing talking about doughnuts?" She took Rose's arm. "Come on, let's buy that tote bag."

But Rose resisted. "Now that you mention it, I could go for a couple of Edith's doughnuts. After all, they're only once a year."

Betty Ann laughed loudly. "You're such a bullshitter, McNichols. That's why you're my best friend."

"Not so loud," Rose said. "The pastor's over there."

In a nearby corner, Pastor Walter Chitwick, in a Santa hat, was filling balloons from a helium tank. Small children clustered around him, watching with rapt attention as he inflated each balloon.

"Do you think he heard me swear?" Betty Ann whispered. "I'd better say hello." She nudged the children aside. "Good morning, Pastor. Lovely fair. Is Mrs. Chitwick here today?"

Pastor Chitwick had pink cheeks and thick sandy hair with graying sideburns. Being a short man, he had to look up at six-foot Betty Ann. "We finally got Hyacinth to work the fair," he said, chuckling. "I credit Dottie Lugo, our new chair, who talked her into it. Hyacinth is running the beanbag toss in the Sunday school wing." He indicated a door against the far wall. "Go in and try your luck. I warn you, my wife's a stickler for accuracy."

"Great. I love a beanbag toss," Betty Ann said. She grabbed Rose's sleeve. "We'll check it out now."

As they walked away, Rose grumbled, "Now who's the bullshitter? You really like tossing a beanbag?"

"Hush. I was trying to be nice. Is the pastor watching? We can slip away in the crowd."

Rose glanced behind them. Pastor Chitwick was distributing balloons to the children. "I'd feel guilty lying to a pastor. Let's go to the beanbags, stay a minute, and leave."

"You bet I'll leave," Betty Ann said. "I'm getting a plate of Edith's doughnuts if I have to storm the kitchen."

The sign on the Sunday school door read, *Godly Play*. Inside were six classrooms, three on either side of a short corridor. Handwritten signs indicating the individual games were posted on each door. The women stopped in front of the first door.

"Look at this: 'Guess your weight and age.'" Betty Ann said. "Who in her right mind would submit to that?"

"It's probably meant for kids," Rose said.

"I hope so. I wouldn't participate even if they offered a free trip to Samoa."

The door bearing the sign *Beanbag Toss* was ajar. From inside came the sound of crying.

"Let's just pop in and say hello," Betty Ann whispered.

Three people were inside the makeshift game room. A sobbing child clung to a frazzled-looking woman while another woman, her hair in a long silver braid, calmly addressed the little girl: "I'm sorry, dear, but if I gave prizes to everyone, the church would have no money for a new roof. You wouldn't want that, would you?" She leaned close, causing the child to wail.

The frazzled-looking woman dropped to her knees and embraced the little girl. "Don't cry, Taylor. Mommy will talk to the nice lady." She gave Hyacinth Chitwick a pleading look. "You can't blame my daughter for being upset. Her bag was definitely inside the circle. Anyone would consider that a win."

"You're correct, it's within the circle," Hyacinth said, "but a corner of the bag is outside. In order to win, the bag has to be entirely within the circle, all four corners. No overlap."

"Most people would call that a win," the mother insisted.

At that, Hyacinth turned to see Rose and Betty Ann hovering at the front of the room. "Shall we ask an impartial party?" She beckoned to them. "Excuse me, will you help us?"

"You go," Rose whispered. "She's your friend."

"She is not," Betty Ann hissed. At the same time, she moved into the room. "Come over here, please," Hyacinth said.

Before her, spread on the floor, were five wooden hoops. Scattered around were dusty cotton beanbags.

Hyacinth pointed to the middle hoop, the one holding the bag in question. "In this game, the bag must be completely within the circle. Close doesn't count." She moved aside. "Examine it carefully, and tell us what you think."

Betty Ann withdrew her glasses from an oversized pocketbook. A silence fell over the room as she knelt to inspect the wooden hoop. Finally, she straightened and nodded to Hyacinth.

"Have you made your decision, Betty Ann?" Hyacinth said, sounding like a game show host.

"I'm sorry, but I can't call that a winning throw," Betty Ann said. "There's a teeny, tiny bit of overlap."

Hearing this, the little girl shrieked. The sound reverberated off the walls of the empty classroom. Grabbing her daughter's arm, her mother pulled her toward the door. "I hope you realize my daughter will have bad feelings toward this church for the rest of her life." Rose stepped out of their way.

"Life is a series of learning experiences," Hyacinth said, her voice calm. "The sooner children accept this, the better they'll be at handling disappointment."

Dragging the shrieking child away, the woman shouted over her shoulder, "You shouldn't be a minister's wife. You should be a prison warden!"

If Hyacinth was annoyed by the comment, it didn't show. Her face registered a bland complacency. She wore a plum-colored tunic and, around her neck, a chunky necklace made of stones and what looked like copper screws.

When the pair had left the room, she said, "Thank you for participating."

Betty Ann shrugged. "You can't please everyone."

Hyacinth nodded. "Ironically, I had another mother and daughter earlier. In this case, the mother was elderly and in a wheelchair. Her beanbag was challenged by the daughter. Again, I wouldn't back down."

"You're just following the rules," Betty Ann said. "The object is to make money for the church."

"That's what I told my husband when parishioners complained. People expect to be rewarded for nothing."

"Don't worry about it," Betty Ann said, edging away. "You did the right thing."

Rose pushed open the door, and Betty Ann quickly followed her into the corridor where people wandered from room to room, sampling the games.

"Look how popular the other games are," Rose said, "yet no one came into Hyacinth's room the whole time we were there."

Betty Ann nodded. "Word gets out."

"She claims she's saving money by not giving away the prizes. But what's the point if you have no participants? People pay to play."

"Good luck explaining that to her. Now let's get out of here. I'm getting claustrophobic. I'm also worried that Edith's doughnuts will be gone."

After leaving the Sunday school area, they emerged into the brightly lit basement.

"Hyacinth won't win any personality contests," Rose said, still mulling over the recent contretemps.

"I've seen more compassion from Boston cab drivers," Betty Ann said.

"Does anyone call her Hy?"

"No one I know. Not even the pastor."

"There should be a law that people with three-syllable names be forced to abbreviate them. Otherwise, it's presumptuous."

"Right. That's why I'm B.A."

Betty Ann led the way, cutting through the crowd like a tugboat in a busy harbor, and they soon arrived at the food court. A half dozen tables, mostly occupied, were set outside the kitchen door.

"Mother of Mercy, I smell fresh doughnuts," Betty Ann said, clutching Rose's sleeve. "There's the Happy Hearth, Edith's venue. Looks like Florence is serving."

"Why does she call it the Happy Hearth?"

"That's the name of her housekeeping agency. You're the local journalist. Don't you know about it?"

"Local reporter," Rose corrected her. "If it's a new venue, Yvonne hasn't assigned the story. If they advertised with our paper, it would be old news."

"Don't wait too long. Edith's been in business three months."

Rose pulled a notepad from her bag. "I'm supposed to be covering the fair anyway. Maybe I'll write up the agency and kill two birds."

"Let's grab a table," Betty Ann said. She scurried over to an empty table against the wall and collapsed onto a rickety wooden chair. Rose followed, and as she sat down, Betty Ann said, "I'm feeling guilty about that little girl, even though she was a brat. Hyacinth really put me on the spot."

Rose hung her peacoat on the back of the chair. "Sounds like you need doughnuts to cheer you up. Let's check out Edith's goods."

They moved to the Happy Hearth display. Standing beside a table, Florence Huke greeted them. Thin and wiry, she wore a long holiday apron that hung to an inch above her battered sneakers.

"Just in time, ladies," she said, whipping the cover off a tall aluminum pot. "There's still some of Edith's chowder left." She stirred the creamy mixture with a long spoon.

"You've talked me into it," Rose said. "I'll have a bowl."

"I thought we were having doughnuts," Betty Ann said.

"Have both," Florence said.

"If you insist," Betty Ann said. "I'll have chowder, doughnuts, and coffee."

While Florence wrote up their order, they examined the neighboring vendor's wares. Under a sign reading *A New Leaf* were two shelves holding flat, dark loaves wrapped in wax paper alongside bowls of rice and grains.

"Whose group is that?" Betty Ann asked.

"That's the vegetarians," Florence said. "Pastor's wife organized it. Matter of fact, that's her lentil loaf on the lower shelf. It's decorated to look like a Christmas tree ornament, but I ain't so sure."

Betty Ann studied the bulbous shape. "It looks like a big tick."

Florence laughed. "A kid in the kitchen thought it was a football. See, the strips of red pepper's the lacing." She shrugged. "Maybe if they said it's an official Patriots' football, someone would buy it."

"They haven't had many takers?" Rose asked.

Florence rolled her eyes. "What would you rather have, homemade doughnuts or lentil loaf?"

"Good point." Betty Ann got out her wallet. "How much do we owe you?"

After handing them their change, Florence said, "You girls sit, before someone steals your table. I'll bring your order over."

They settled themselves at the table, now set with plastic utensils and paper place mats decorated by the Sunday school students. Before long, Florence arrived with a tray.

"Careful, it's hot as hell," she said, placing steaming bowls before them. This was followed by mugs of coffee and a paper plate heavy with doughnuts. "I thought I'd give you extra, 'cause these go like a fart in a hurricane." She glanced back at the kitchen. "I hope Edith didn't hear that. She's always getting after me to talk nice to the customers."

"You don't have to watch your language around us," Betty Ann said. "Come sit a minute. Do you know Rose McNichols? She writes for the *Granite Cove Gazette*."

"Nice to meet you, Rose," Florence said. "I read your articles every week."

Rose thanked her and asked, "Could you tell me a little about your agency?"

Florence scratched her head with a latex-gloved hand. "Sure, but first I gotta get someone to cover for me."

"How about Edith?" Betty Ann said.

"She's rolling pie crust in the kitchen. Her piña colada pies are as popular as her doughnuts." She stood and scanned the room. "Let me grab my niece, Kristal. She's on a smoke break and shoulda been back five minutes ago." She hurried away, zigzagging around the tables.

Rose set her notepad aside. "How do you know Florence?"

"Through the church. I've only been coming here about a year, but that's a long time for me. You know how I feel about organized religion. It was Tiny's idea that we all attend church together as a family. He wanted Jonah to have a 'religious upbringing.' It was fine for about a month— until the kid wouldn't get out of bed. Every Sunday became a battle, so Tiny gave up.

"Strangely enough, I grew to like the services. The pastor's sermons are bland, allowing me to doze, but the people are nice. Florence is a good-hearted soul, always taking meals to shut-ins, whether they like it or not." She bit into a doughnut. Spraying crumbs across the table, she announced, "I'd give my firstborn for a stack of these."

"Does that mean you and Tiny are expanding your family?"

Betty Ann scowled. "Pregnant and forty? No, thanks. Besides, Jonah is all the family I can handle right now."

"I'll bet he's looking forward to Christmas vacation," Rose said, stirring her chowder to let it cool.

"I'm sure he is, but I'm not. It means he'll be at home unsupervised for a whole week. I told Tiny to install one of those nanny cams. You know those hidden cameras that record what's going on?"

Rose nodded. "What did he say to that?"

"He said it's an invasion of Jonah's privacy and an indication his parents don't trust him. I wanted to remind Tiny that I'm not Jonah's parent. I'm a stepmom, and a reluctant one at that."

"What does Jonah want for Christmas?" Rose asked, steering the conversation into less turbulent waters.

"Get this—he wants a Jet Ski and a trip to Vegas with his friends. These are thirteen-year-old boys we're talking about. I told him, 'Your father's a retired firefighter and part-time bartender, not a hedge-fund manager.'" She shook her head. "The kid has no sense. Earlier in the year he wanted to transfer to the voc school. Tiny found out why. A student in their graphics program was caught printing twenty-dollar bills."

As always when discussing her stepson, Betty Ann became loud. Thus, Rose was relieved to spot Florence walking in the door. She was followed by a sullen-faced young woman whose blond hair sported an inch of dark roots. The girl's apron was rolled up high to reveal pudgy white thighs.

After stationing the girl behind the Happy Hearth table, Florence joined Rose and Betty Ann. She plunked her coffee mug on the table and flopped into a chair with a loud sigh.

"Is that your niece?" Rose asked.

"Uh-huh. I had a talk with her, outside. I said she couldn't keep taking smoke breaks 'cause Edith don't like it. The only reason Edith keeps Kristal on is because she's my niece." Florence shook her head. "That girl's got a temper just like her mother. She told me what Edith could do with the job." She glanced around. "Seeing's we're on church property, I won't repeat it."

"Sounds like Kristal needs a wake-up call," Betty Ann said, reaching for another doughnut.

"Kristal's had so many wake-up calls her ears are ringing. Remember the mess she got into with her fiancé?" Nodding at Rose's notepad, she added, "This ain't meant for the newspaper. Besides, you folks already wrote about it in the police section."

Rose gave her a quizzical look.

"It was last year," Florence said. "Kristal shot her fiancé when he took off before their wedding."

"Don't blame her a bit," Betty Ann muttered.

"I remember that," Rose said. "It was right before Christmas. At least he wasn't badly injured."

"That's right," Florence said. "He was running away from her when she shot him. Fortunately, Kristal had been drinking and couldn't shoot straight."

"The judge went easy on her, as I recall," Rose said.

"We hired Spencer Farley. Still paying him. At the hearing, he told the judge about Kristal's mother running off to Louisiana when the girl was thirteen, and her being raised by a no-good dad. That's why when this fella came along and proposed, we breathed a sigh of relief. He had a good job, a troubleshooter with the gas company. We figured she'd finally settle down. Poor kid went to pieces when he ran out on her. She'd put a down payment on the K of C Hall."

"Didn't Kristal get off with probation and community service?"

Florence nodded. "She was driving the senior center van until someone complained." Florence fidgeted in her chair. "You gotta understand that Kristal's twenty-six, but she's really a kid. Takes after her mother—my sister, Honey. You can't tell them anything. I told Kristal not to smoke while driving a van carrying old people and oxygen tanks. She was lucky she didn't blow everyone sky high."

Betty Ann, the activities director at the Green Pastures nursing home, shivered and added, "Amen."

Rose glanced across the room at Kristal. The young woman slouched against the wall, her arms folded across her chest. "How does she get along with Edith?"

Florence pursed her lips. "Tell you the truth, not too good. When Edith insists she wear long sleeves to cover her tattoos, Kristal shows up in a tank top and says she forgot. Edith also doesn't like the way Kristal acts toward the men at the parties we cater. She watches her like a hawk."

"Sounds like Edith runs a tight ship," Betty Ann said. "That's why her agency is doing well."

"I'm used to Edith's ways. She goes by the book. Like cleaning up after a party; Kristal will polish off the drinks people leave behind. Rich folks are wasteful." She shook her head. "They'll take a sip, put the glass down, and walk away. If Kristal didn't finish 'em, they'd end up down the drain. I says to Edith, it ain't like the girl's stealing. She's using up the leftovers." Florence lowered her voice. "To be honest, I don't think she'll be working here much longer. Matter of fact, she'd be long gone if Edith had ever found out what happened at Mayor Froggett's sixtieth-birthday party..." She stared into her cup.

When Florence showed no sign of continuing the story, Betty Ann touched her hand. "You know, whatever you say will go no further than this table."

Florence leaned toward them and lowered her voice. "Near the end of the party, Kristal went missing. I found her in the parking lot in the animal control officer's van. She wasn't alone." She glanced around. "I can't say who she was with, except I voted for him two years ago. He was supposed to be the big family man."

"Your niece sounds... impetuous," Rose said.

"I warn her, but she don't care. Lately she's been working nights at Marilyn's Pie Palace. You know the place, open all night on that godforsaken road off Route 128? Kristal says she's making lots of money in tips."

"Marilyn's Pie Palace?" Rose glanced at Betty Ann, remembering the night they'd visited Marilyn's at two in the morning after Betty Ann had threatened to leave Tiny. "I'm shocked the place is still open."

"There's a new business moved in down the street from them," Florence said. "A paper-shredding plant. Matter of fact, the night manager, Dionne Dunbar, is in my mediums class. I imagine the employees like having someplace to go on break, even if it's only pies."

"I can't see how Kristal's making money serving coffee and pie," Betty Ann said.

"She claims she put a down payment on a Miata," Florence said. "That's why she's been so sassy to Edith lately. She says she doesn't need this job and is only staying because of me. I says, don't do me any favors." Florence drained her cup and got to her feet. "I gotta get back before she takes another break."

"Just a second, Florence," Rose said. "Did I hear you mention a mediums class?"

"That's right. Hyacinth's our teacher. Classes are held at her house."

"What's that all about?"

"We learn psychic stuff, like how to contact those who've crossed over. We never use the word *dead*, we say the departed are *in spirit*. Some of us are naturals. Others have to work at it. You should sign up for the next class. We get some nice folks from the community."

"I don't know about signing up, but I'd love to do a story on your group, providing Hyacinth goes along with it."

"I don't know why she wouldn't. Folks say Hyacinth's one of the best mediums in New England."

"Thanks. I might call her."

"Just remember, we gotta be anonymous. Some members in my class don't want people to know. Me? I don't give a rat's ass." She glanced around, suddenly alert. "Dammit, Kristal's gone. She's had her eye on that big guy who runs the cotton candy machine. I'll bet she's with him."

After Florence rushed off, Betty Ann said, "Why not take Hyacinth's class? You like trying different things. I'll bet you'd be a natural."

Rose shook her head. "I know what would happen. I'd receive messages from my mother, berating me for being forty and single."

Betty Ann chuckled. "Even from the grave, mothers get the last word."

CHAPTER TWO

The office of the *Granite Cove Gazette* occupied the basement level of the old Kirkbride Building, the latter an icon in its day. In the 1950s and '60s, the granite building had housed a popular music store, a quality clothing shop, and a store specializing in "foundations." The latter was where Granite Cove girls got fitted for their first bras. With the advent of the malls, the stores eventually closed their doors. Today the once-proud Kirkbride was home to a Goodwill store, a nail spa, and in the bowels of the building, the newspaper office.

Looking through a long, horizontal window, Rose could watch, from her desk, the citizens of Granite Cove passing by. Owing to the basement location, she saw only their legs. If she stood on the short flight of stairs at the entrance door, however, she could see them in their entirety.

Now she stood on those steps, leaning forward to gaze at the Town Green spread before her. Workers from the DPW—the Department of Public Works—were perched on ladders, stringing lights around the gazebo and surrounding trees. Beyond the Green, St. Rupert's wooden spire rose into a leaden sky filled with low-hanging clouds. Speculations about an early snowstorm swirled, although opinions were mixed. Like many "born and bred" New Englanders, Rose went by her senses. If the air smelled of snow and had a certain "snap," chances were, the flakes would fall.

Yvonne's voice broke her reverie: "Has it started snowing yet?"

"Not yet. I can't tell whether the sky's getting darker. This morning I would have sworn we'd have snow by noon. Now, I'm not so sure." Rose returned to her desk.

"Well, I hope it holds off until Stewart gets back from Boston. Every year that boy forgets to get his winter tires put on until he's stranded in a snow bank," Yvonne said.

"Even if he gets his snow tires on, they're probably old and useless," Rose said. Stewart, the "boy" Yvonne was referring to, was in his midforties, a part-time sports writer and a long-time trust fund recipient who hated to spend money, inherited or otherwise. "What's he doing in Boston, anyway?"

"He's writing about a young man, Otto Mullen, who graduated from Granite Cove High. Apparently he's distinguished himself playing football at Boston College. Do you know him?"

"Nope."

People from outside always assumed that because Granite Cove was a small town of five thousand, everyone knew each other. "I might have a story of my own," Rose said, and told Yvonne about Hyacinth Chitwick and her students in the mediums circle. "People love reading about the paranormal. I'll bet our readers would be curious to know what goes on at one of those classes."

Yvonne wrinkled her nose. "I want nothing to do with Hyacinth Chitwick," she announced, and swiveled her chair around.

Rose waited for Yvonne to elaborate. Instead, she removed an accordion file from a desk drawer and began stuffing papers into it. Finally, Rose said, "I take it you know the pastor's wife."

Yvonne frowned. "That woman ruined our outing. Mother and I like to visit the Lutheran Church Holiday Fair every year. Mother loves playing the games, particularly the beanbag toss. As a girl, she played field hockey at Miss Mossgrove's School. She can still hit a target, although she can't fully extend her right arm, due to arthritis. I managed to maneuver her wheelchair in as close as I could.

"Despite those deficits, Mother did very well. One beanbag landed completely within the circle. In fact, I got quite excited, thinking she'd won. Hyacinth Chitwick, who was running the game, thought otherwise."

"Pastor claims she's a stickler for accuracy," Rose said.

"You'd think she'd have allowed it. For God's sake, Mother is eighty-four years old." She shook her head. "That woman can't have many friends in this town, with that attitude. On the other hand, I don't suppose it matters to her."

"I'm sorry you had a bad day," Rose said, turning to face her desktop computer. "I guess I won't be writing about the mediums class."

"Rose McNichols, do you think I'd be so petty as to allow my personal feelings to interfere with running this newspaper?"

Rose held her tongue and waited.

"On the contrary, I think it's an excellent idea," Yvonne continued. "Chipper Foss, the head of the drama department at the community college, is a member of that group. I had lunch with him last week. He's fascinated with spiritualism and the paranormal." She glanced at the calendar on her desk. "By the way, he's beginning auditions for *A Christmas Carol*, and asked me to codirect. Chipper values my years in community theater."

"Good for you," Rose said. "In the meantime, should I get in touch with Hyacinth about an interview?"

Yvonne nodded. "I'm sure you'll find it fascinating. Chip says his aunt appears to him in spirit. Apparently she was the only member of his family who supported him when he came out."

Rose glanced at her. "You mean he sees her ghost?"

"He doesn't actually see her. Other members of the group do. They relay her messages to Chip. And by the way, spiritualists don't call them *ghosts*. They say they're *in spirit*."

Rose nodded. "I'll have to remember that. You seem to know a lot about the subject."

Yvonne raised an eyebrow. "I've often thought I had psychic potential. I even considered taking classes in Salem. However, I can't find reliable care for Mother." She glanced at the wall clock. "Goodness, I'm late for my appointment." She pulled a zippered bag from a desk drawer. Inside was a pair of clear plastic boots, brittle with age. She tugged them on over her linen espadrilles. Rose remembered her mother wearing similar footwear in the winter.

Yvonne turned her back, removed a bottle of spray cologne from her top drawer, and spritzed herself. Then she hurried to the front steps, where her poncho hung from an old-fashioned wooden coat tree.

"Are you returning?" Rose asked, although she knew the answer. The cologne had tipped her off to where Yvonne was heading.

Lowering the poncho over her head, Yvonne said, "I'll be at the police station. Chief Alfano is holding a press conference regarding the department's plans for public safety during the holidays. If it runs late, I won't be back."

Rose didn't ask why the chief didn't simply e-mail the plans. "Stay warm," she said.

After Yvonne left, Rose looked up Hyacinth Chitwick's number in the big phone book. Fortunately, the rectory had a landline. In fact, there were three separate listings for the Chitwick household: one for Reverend Walter, one for Hyacinth, and one for Nathaniel, no doubt their son.

She dialed Hyacinth's number. After four rings, the machine picked up and Hyacinth's cool voice said, "You've reached the number for Spirits of Universal Resonance. If you are calling about classes..." Here, she listed information about upcoming dates. After thanking the caller, she concluded the message: "Know that the world of spirit is a breath away. Within us lies an innate power to open that door."

In the silence that followed the beep, Rose introduced herself, mentioning that she'd been with Betty Ann Zagrobski at the church fair. She stated her request: to sit in on a mediums class. After leaving her phone number, Rose hung up. Ten minutes later, as she was typing the scores for the senior center's bowling league, her phone beeped.

She glanced down at the number. It was Hyacinth.

"Hello?"

"Thanks for calling, Rose. Sorry I didn't pick up right away. I tend to screen my calls. Lately I've gotten a few anonymous messages."

"Concerning what, may I ask?"

She sighed. "The usual disapproving, provincial Granite Cove citizen."

Rose said she'd be interested in hearing about it, off the record. Then she repeated her request to do a story on the mediums circle. "Florence Huke, one of your members, suggested I visit the class. Our readers would be intrigued. Of course, the members would remain anonymous."

"I'll bring it up at our next class and get back to you," Hyacinth said, her tone brisk. Before Rose could thank her, she'd hung up.

Rose wasn't worried that her request would be turned down. According to Betty Ann, Hyacinth Chitwick wasn't one to hide her spiritual light under a bucket. Other pastors' wives in similar circumstances might keep their ghostly dabblings quiet. Hyacinth, however, refused to be silenced.

Alone in the office, and with Yvonne gone for the rest of the afternoon, Rose decided to go visit her dad. She could finish her housekeeping hints column at home. She shut down her computer, grabbed her pocketbook, and headed for the door. Key in hand, she spotted Stewart approaching on the sidewalk. He wore a long scarf that covered his lower face. His customary loafers, wrapped with duct tape, had been replaced with equally shabby boots.

Yanking the door open, he said, "What, leaving for the day?"

"I'm going to interview someone. Not that it's any of your business."

"Touchy, touchy. Don't worry, I won't tell Yvonne."

"Stewart, I don't care what you tell Yvonne. I've nothing to hide."

"She won't be back anyway. She's at Chief Alfano's press conference." He smirked. "Think they'll go out for drinks afterward?"

Although Rose would love to discuss the relationship between their editor and the police chief, she wouldn't do it with Stew. The man was a weasel, not to be trusted.

"I'll be back if I finish up early," she said.

"I've heard that one before," he said, stepping aside to let her pass.

For a moment the two colleagues stood nose to nose in the doorway. Looking into his beady eyes, Rose had an urge to grab the ends of his scarf and yank.

Instead, she said, "Merry Christmas, Stewart."

Because it was a weekday, Rose found a parking space in the visitors' lot at the Granite Cove Retirement Center. Weekends, she often had to park behind the DPW's storage shed, an area strewn with broken bottles. When her dad moved into elderly housing, he'd been allotted a parking space. Later, following his stroke and the subsequent loss of his driver's license, that space had been taken away. Rose thought this unfair, and urged him to protest to Mrs. Buckle, the housing administrator. He refused, citing the woman's vindictive nature: "The guy at the end of the hall complained about the painters leaving a ladder in the hallway. Now he's waited two years for them to fix a storm window. "

"But, Dad, every tenant is entitled to a parking space," Rose said. "They can't take it from you because you're disabled." But he wouldn't listen nor allow her to complain. She let the matter drop, figuring it was easier to visit on weekdays when parking was plentiful.

She decided to leave her coat in the car. Her cardigan was warm enough; the signs of impending snow had vanished. Indeed, temperatures had climbed to the low forties. After locking the Jetta, she headed for unit three.

The Granite Cove Retirement Center consisted of an administration building and three, three-story residences set in a semicircle. This configuration allowed tenants to keep an eye on each other. Consequently, when Mrs. Scippione fell, on her way to the mailbox, two people dialed 911. Although most residents appreciated this safety factor, Russell McNichols didn't. He claimed his neighbors weren't merely looking out for him, they were looking *at* him. Knowing the nosiness of Granite Cove natives, Rose thought he could be right.

She walked past the administration building, the hub of the center. Amazingly, it was once her dad's elementary school. Seventy years ago, a little boy had raced up the heavy granite steps carrying a lunch pail. Today, that child was a white-haired man carrying a cane.

In her hand she clutched a grease-stained bag from Stella's Sausage Kitchen. Once a week she stopped in to get her dad's favorite sandwich: bacon, onion, and sausage, smothered in Velveeta. It was definitely not on Doc Moss's list of approved foods. On the other hand, man cannot live on turkey breast alone.

Getting off the elevator at the third floor, Rose spotted Jeannette, her dad's attractive, sixtyish neighbor. She was in the hall, hanging a cardboard snowman on her door.

"Hi, Rose," she said, her glance falling on the greasy bag. "Looks like you've brought something for your father."

Rose felt a pang of guilt followed by irritation. It seemed that every time she visited, she encountered Jeannette. "I'm hoping he's still hungry."

"As a matter of fact, he had lunch at my place: roast chicken. Right now he's at the health center. The podiatrist is visiting this afternoon. Your dad thinks he's got bunions."

Rose didn't want to discuss her dad's feet. She held up the bag. "I'll just put this in his fridge. He can have it later." She rummaged inside her pocketbook. "Damn, I think I left his key in my car."

"Since when does Russ lock up?"

Jeannette crossed the hall and swung open the door to number thirty-six. Rose stared at the disarray inside: a pile of bath towels and sheets on the sofa; newspapers stacked on the floor. She wandered into the kitchenette, where dirty dishes were stacked on the counter.

Jeannette stood next to her. "His housekeeper didn't come again this week."

"That's apparent," Rose said.

"I don't like to tell tales out of school, but that's the second time this month that girl hasn't shown up." Jeannette shook her head, her silver curls bouncing. "If my housekeeper did that, she'd be looking for a job."

Rose nodded. "Dad doesn't like to make waves, so people take advantage of him."

Jeannette patted her arm. "He's a big old teddy bear, too nice for his own good. 'Course, that's what I love about him. It's people like Kristal Swekla, his so-called housekeeper, that I'd like to throttle."

Rose felt a pang of alarm at Jeannette's mention of "love," and mentally filed it away. "Kristal Swekla," she said, remembering Florence's niece. "Is she young, kind of chubby, with blond hair?"

Jeannette nodded. "A bottle blond. She's with the Happy Hearth agency, and if she keeps it up, they'll lose their contract with the city. When she does show up to work, she's sloppy. She bangs the vacuum cleaner into the furniture while always talking on the phone."

"Thanks for tipping me off, Jeannette. I'll have to speak to Kristal."

Jeannette chuckled. "I took care of it on Monday. She was outside, smoking on the steps. I told her I was wise to her shenanigans. It's not just your dad she's deceiving. There's Mrs. Bloomburg, on the first floor, who's legally blind. I checked after Kristal left her apartment. The girl had turned on the dishwasher, and that's about it. Hadn't touched the bathroom, from the looks of it. I said I was blowing the whistle on her."

"Good for you. What did she say?"

"She's a snotty little thing. She said, go ahead and report her, because she had a new job that paid big bucks."

"Apparently, she's waitressing nights at Marilyn's Pie Palace," Rose said.

"Marilyn's Pie Palace? The only people who stop there are striper fishermen and the few truckers who use that route. A girl couldn't make ten bucks a night there."

"I understand a new company, a shredding business, has moved in down the street," Rose said. "Business has picked up."

"In that case, I'm happy for Marilyn." Jeannette glanced back at her door. "I'd better finish decorating while it's still light out. Gets dark so early this time of year."

"And I'll tidy up Dad's apartment before I go," Rose said.

"You'd better not leave without seeing him first," Jeannette said. "He'd be awfully disappointed."

As Jeannette headed down the hall, Rose watched her. The woman looked good in stretchy maroon pants. According to her dad, Jeannette taught line dancing classes at the center.

Rose felt a stab of jealousy. Maybe he wasn't so lonely after all…

Auntie Pearl's Helpful Housekeeping Hints!

Auntie Pearl's Helpful Housekeeping Hints

Dear Auntie Pearl:

I'm concerned about my mother, a widow. For the past two years she's been enjoying her senior retirement community. She takes watercolor and line dancing classes and has an active life. However, lately she's been making some troubling remarks.

For instance, she recently mentioned that Gert, a neighbor, had stolen some recipes from her file box.

More disturbing is the fact she believes the maintenance man visits her kitchen while she is sleeping. Apparently Mom found an unfamiliar sponge in her sink. She also suspects he stole her vacuum cleaner and substituted an older model.

I don't want to contact Mother's doctor behind her back, but I must address the situation before it escalates. What do you suggest, Auntie Pearl?

Stumped in Salisbury

Dear Stumped:

Every time I hear about old family recipes carelessly treated, my blood boils. Many cherished keepsakes are lost when seniors move to assisted living facilities, yet it doesn't have to happen. The time to preserve artifacts is before Mom and Dad enter a retirement community.

As you've learned, keeping recipes in a file box will not guarantee their safety. Someone in the family should be delegated to collect and digitize them. If they are put into an electronic file, the recipes can be shared with family members for generations to come. Perhaps at some point you might want to have them made into a cookbook for a lasting memorial.

Signed,

Auntie Pearl

CHAPTER THREE

As Rose had anticipated, Hyacinth called later to approve her attendance at the Thursday night mediums class. "Don't park in the driveway," she instructed. "That's reserved for students."

"Wouldn't think of it," Rose said, although Hyacinth had already hung up.

It was a clear, cold night when Rose drove past St. Rupert's Lutheran Church on her way to Hyacinth's house. On the sloping lawn in front of the church, workmen were setting up the crèche, toiling under bright extension lights. The plywood stable was assembled. Soon the live animals would be added to the setting. Traffic would crawl along as motorists gaped at the trio of life-size plastic Wise Men, assorted shepherds, and—grazing among them—a living donkey, a goat, and three sheep.

Rose took the next left, Spruce Hill Lane. The snowbanked street looked like a Christmas card scene: cozy houses decorated with lights, illuminated Santas, angels, and snowmen.

She cruised to number eighteen, a white Cape-style home with black shutters. Electric candles glowed in the windows flanking the front door. She parked in the street and got out of the car, surveying the narrow road. It wasn't the best place to park, but she had no choice. Shoving her hands into her pockets, she headed up the long driveway past a line of parked cars.

A spotlight illuminated the side door. Rose peeked in the window. A stocky young boy, approximately twelve years old and wearing stretchy green pajamas, stood at a kitchen cupboard, his back to her. He was filling a Red Sox baseball cap with cookies from a jar. When she knocked on the door, he flipped the cap onto his head before turning around. They stared at each other until finally Rose waved. After shoving the cookie jar back, he opened the door.

"You must be Nathaniel," she said. "I'm Rose McNichols. Your mother's expecting me."

When he nodded, a cookie slipped from the cap and fell to the floor. "Mom said to go downstairs." He pointed to a door in a short hallway. "They're in the cellar."

She thanked him and passed through the kitchen. The door was ajar, and a murmur of voices drifted up from the gloom below. Gripping the railing, she descended the stairs.

The Chitwicks' cellar was unfinished, with a concrete floor, cartons stacked high, and a washer and dryer set against the far wall. To the left of the stairs was a wooden drying rack. Underwear—white and no-nonsense—was draped over its rungs. To the right of the stairs, a half dozen people sat in a circle. Rose peered at them, waiting for her eyes to adjust to the dim light.

Hyacinth was the first to speak. "I see our visitor has arrived. Rose, take that chair near the bottom of the stairs. You'll be close enough to observe without being intrusive."

"Thanks."

She was aware of being watched as she hung her jacket on the rickety wooden chair. Once she was seated, Hyacinth got up to pull a light cord hanging in the corner. Although the room was dark, there was sufficient illumination from the appliances and the narrow window behind them. After a few moments, Rose could make out the figures in the circle. She was familiar with everyone but the young woman with dark hair and high black boots—obviously Dionne Dunbar.

"Before we begin, I'd like us to go around and introduce ourselves, first names only. I will start: I'm Hyacinth, the group's guide."

This was followed by

"I'm Chipper, and welcome."

"I'm Florence. Hi, Rose."

"I'm Dionne."

"I'm Milton. Excuse me, are you Rose McNichols, the reporter for the *Granite Cove Gazette*?"

"Yes," Hyacinth said quickly. "She's the visitor I mentioned last week. Rose will be observing tonight."

"Is she writing about us?" he asked, peering at Rose through heavy-black-framed glasses.

Her voice was calm. "Rose is doing a story about my mediums classes, without naming names. I've already been through this with her. She understands the need for secrecy."

"Well, if she intends to take pictures, I'm leaving," he said. "I just want you to know that."

"You have nothing to worry about," Hyacinth said.

"I have to consider my reputation," he continued. "For those in commercial real estate, image is everything."

Florence spoke up: "Milton, it's not like you're at Miss Kitty's, ogling the strippers. You're at Pastor's house."

"That's not the point. We're dealing with the occult here, and people on the outside definitely don't understand."

"I used to think that way," Florence said, turning to Rose, "until I heard my father speak to me. It was the week after he'd passed. I'd gone to his apartment to clean out his things. After an hour, I took a break. I sat in his favorite easy chair, one of them recliners. He was always dozing in it, watching TV, drinking a beer. I got all teary eyed and started bawling my head off. It was then I heard his voice, clear as day. He said, 'Don't cry, Beansie.'"

"Was that a childhood name?" Chipper asked.

"Uh-huh, a family nickname. I was skinny then, even skinnier than I am now. My dad used to say I looked like a string bean. Before long, everyone called me Beansie. Some of my friends still do..."

"I think it's precious," Chipper said. "Matter of fact, hearing Florence talk makes me realize she'd be perfect as Scrooge in our production of *A Christmas Carol.*"

"Scrooge?" Florence yelped. "You mean the old guy that hates everyone?"

"Right. With proper makeup and costume, you'd be perfect. Come to auditions next week."

"Just so long as I don't have to take my clothes off," Florence said.

"Please, can we get started?" Milton said, shifting in his seat. "My wife is ill and I promised to be back early."

"One second, Milton," Chipper said. "I think you'd make a fine Bob Cratchit. The role calls for someone robust and manly."

Milton considered this in silence. Before he could respond, Florence said, "When you get home, fix your wife a glass of warm water with a tablespoon of cider vinegar. I take it every day and haven't had a cold in three years." She added, "It's good for your digestion, too."

Dionne, who'd been examining her nails in the dim light, looked up. "Is that true? How much water?"

"This is all very interesting," Hyacinth said, "but it's time to settle down. Now, as we do every week, let's create a welcoming environment for spirit to enter." She closed her eyes and held out her hands. When the members had joined their hands, she intoned, "We cast aside our worldly cares and invite spirit to enter our circle. It is with a sense of gratitude that we bid spirit entrance." She released her neighbors' hands and sat back in her chair, keeping her eyes closed.

Rose peeked around the circle. Moonlight shining through the basement window reflected on Milton's glasses, his furrowed brow. Next to him, Florence, her chin raised, frowned in concentration. Dionne's dark hair shone; her high-heeled boot jiggled a nervous beat. A serene-looking Chipper had a beatific smile.

In the dark, the furnace emitted a low rumble. The warmth of the cellar, coupled with the silence, made Rose sleepy. Her eyelids grew heavy and she lapsed into a doze until Florence's raspy voice startled her awake:

"There's a little dog here." Florence's eyes were closed. "His fur's brown and tan, kinda scruffy, like one of them terriers. He wants to come into the circle but he's shy, timid. He's whimpering, like, and looking at Milton. His tail's wagging."

The group was silent until Hyacinth said, "Milton, do you want to respond to that?"

"It's not me. I'm allergic to dogs."

After a moment, Hyacinth asked, "Does anyone recognize this dog?"

"You say he's small?" Dionne said. "I had a dog once, a boxer. But his fur was smooth."

"Nope," Florence said, "This dog's knee-high." She chuckled. "Cute as the dickens."

"If you see any cats, they're probably mine," Chipper added.

"Let's leave the dog for a moment," Hyacinth said, raising a hand. "There's a young man who just entered... He's got dark hair, a nice smile. He's in his late twenties, perhaps early thirties. He's impatient. Now he's standing next to me. This man doesn't like to wait." She was silent, her face tilted upward, her eyes closed. "I see aircraft around him... a small plane... Now he's saying a name... Debby... no, he says it's Didi. Does anyone recognize him?"

Dionne, in a shaky voice, said, "Yes, I know who he is. He was a pilot, and he used to call me that... Didi."

Hyacinth paused and said, "He's telling me his name... It's Roger."

Dionne gasped. "Yes, oh, yes. Roger."

"Now he's holding something up. Hmm, how strange," Hyacinth said. "It's a lobster. He's holding a live lobster—"

"The last time we were together, we swam off the rocks at Brace's Cove. Roger dove underwater. He was down there so long I got worried. When he finally surfaced, he held up a lobster," Dionne leaned forward on the edge of her chair.

"He's nodding," Hyacinth said, "saying he's sorry how things turned out. He thought he was doing the right thing. He just repeated it: 'the right thing.'"

With a cry, Dionne leaped to her feet, knocking her chair over. She rushed up the stairs, her high-heeled boots clattering on the wooden steps.

"Whew," Florence said, in the silence that followed. "Touched a nerve."

"Drama queen," Milton muttered.

"Her visitor stirred powerful emotions," Chipper said, a note of envy in his voice.

Hyacinth said, "Let's remember that when we allow spirit to enter, we can't choose who will appear. Sometimes old hurts will be rekindled. However, it's been my experience that spirit wants to make amends, or to leave a message. In any case, it's important to keep an open mind and an open heart." She looked around the circle. "Should we use this time to take a break?"

"I have to get home before the roads freeze," Milton said. "Let's wait for Dionne and finish up."

"She might be too shook up," Florence said, glancing up the stairs. "I hear her crying in the bathroom."

Moments later, the cellar light went on and Dionne descended the stairs, her eyes downcast.

"Don't turn off the light," Hyacinth told her. "We'll finish up here. Some members want to get home before the road freezes."

"I don't mind staying," Dionne said, smoothing her dark hair. "I walked over."

"I'll give you a ride home," Milton said.

She didn't look at him. "No thanks."

"It's a bad night to be out," Hyacinth said. "Let's say our closing prayer, shall we?" She addressed Rose. "It's important to end each session by closing the circle. Otherwise,"—she flashed a rare smile—"we might have a few spirits lingering behind." She held out her hands. Closing her eyes, she intoned, "We close this circle, giving thanks to spirit for providing us wisdom and enlightenment. We encourage spirit to visit again. Amen."

"Amen," the group repeated.

Hyacinth glanced at Rose. "Do you want to take a photo now?"

Seeing the look of alarm on Milton's face, Rose said, "I think I'll just shoot the empty chairs in a circle. With the dim light, it should be effective."

"Suit yourself," Hyacinth said, rising. "I'll see everybody out and meet you upstairs."

As the members filed upstairs, Rose hurriedly arranged the chairs and took a couple of photos. Although skeptical about what she'd witnessed that evening, she didn't want to linger in the dark basement. She grabbed her jacket and headed up the stairs.

She was pulling on her gloves in the kitchen when Hyacinth appeared. "Do you often have such dramatic encounters?" Rose asked.

"It depends upon the relationship between the student and spirit. Sometimes spirit may be a close family member, or a distant relative from childhood, one they scarcely remember." She fixed her pale gray eyes upon Rose. "I think you'd make a fine medium, providing you get rid of your negativity. You give it too much power over you."

Rose felt her cheeks flush. Was she that transparent? "I get it from my mother. The glass wasn't just half empty, it was cracked as well."

Hyacinth didn't smile. "Don't allow negativity to color your experience. The next time you feel yourself giving in to negative thoughts, repeat to yourself, 'My mind is a pool of tranquility. Nothing can mar its surface.'"

"I'll remember that."

Hyacinth opened the side door, letting in a blast of arctic air. "Drive safely now."

As Rose stepped out into the cold night, the door shut firmly behind her. She took a few tentative steps, feeling her leather-soled boots slide. Why hadn't she worn her L.L. Beans, the ones with the inch of rubber traction?

The only remaining car was Hyacinth's Prius. Holding on to it for support, she headed down the sloping driveway. The Chitwicks were not partial to rock salt, she thought, gloomily contemplating the remaining stretch of snow-covered asphalt. As Rose continued her halting descent, the outdoor light suddenly went off, leaving her fumbling in the dark.

"What the—"

She looked around. The Chitwicks' kitchen and entire house was dark. Next door, one light was on inside the neighbor's tall, narrow house. She spotted movement at the window. Otherwise, Rose was on her own, like an explorer in the godforsaken tundra. Holding her arms out at her sides, she slid over the ice-crusted driveway until she reached the Jetta.

During the evening, the city plow had come by, piling up snow in front of her car. Fortunately, a plastic trash barrel behind the Jetta had prevented the plow from pinning her in completely. Inside the car, her breath made white clouds in the air. She put the key in the ignition, turning to look out the back window. There was enough space to back up and maneuver out of her spot.

She shifted into reverse and inched back until she was satisfied. When she shifted the car into drive, she heard the high-pitched whine of tires spinning in the snow. She let out her breath. Double damn. To make matters worse, she didn't have a shovel in the trunk. Unless she wanted to rap on the Chitwicks' door and ask for help, she'd have to blast out of the spot she was in. She imagined Hyacinth's face upon hearing that Rose was stuck in the snow. Not only that but the pastor's car wasn't in the driveway; obviously, he couldn't help.

She pressed her foot on the gas and, at the same time, shifted into reverse. The Jetta roared back, slamming into the barrel with a loud BAM. In the rearview mirror, she saw it topple into the street. Rose swore out loud.

At least her car was freed, she thought, driving a few yards into the road. She got out to check the damage. The barrel was on its side, papers strewn all around it. She felt for the handles and attempted to right it, but the thing was too heavy. What was it filled with—bricks?

Standing back, she glanced at the Chitwicks' house, expecting to see Hyacinth peering out. When a light appeared in the house across the street, Rose sprang into action. She had to at least get the barrel out of the road.

She dropped to her knees and rolled it toward the curb. Not only was the barrel heavy but it was tall. Panting in the cold night air, she gave a final shove. The barrel rolled and at the same time dislodged a large, dark mass.

She struggled to her feet. Had she dumped a pile of clothes on the street, along with all that paper? Worse, what if it was garbage? Peering into the dark, she remembered the LED flashlight in her glove compartment. She stumbled to her car and found it among a jumble of odds and ends.

She returned and pressed the switch, aiming the tiny beam at the barrel. The light reflected off a pair of high-heeled black boots silhouetted against the snow. She moved the beam southward and discovered that the boots were attached to a body.

This time, Rose was not reluctant to wake the Chitwicks. In fact, her screams woke the entire street.

CHAPTER FOUR

Granite Cove cop and Rose's former fiancé Cal Devine was the first to arrive at 18 Spruce Hill Lane. He was followed by a fire truck, an ambulance, and another Granite Cove cruiser as well as one from neighboring Swinden.

Cal pulled into the driveway, turning off the siren. He hopped out of the cruiser and, seeing Rose huddled on the front steps with Hyacinth and Pastor Chitwick, shouted, "Wait right there." He dispersed the neighbors gathered around the body in the street, so the paramedics could do their job.

The Chitwicks wore coats over their pajamas. In his haste, the pastor had grabbed a hat that must have belonged to Nathaniel: a black stocking cap with a big gold bat in flight across the front. Nathaniel, meanwhile, was glued to the window, cramming cookies into his mouth one after another while staring at the scene taking place outside.

From time to time, neighbors wandered over to the Chitwicks, attempting to learn more about the body in the road. Their inquiries were met with the pastor's plea: "Go to bed. There's nothing you can do here."

After conferring with the EMTs, Cal headed up the driveway. He motioned to Rose and the Chitwicks. "Let's go inside. No need to stand in the cold."

As soon as they entered the kitchen, Pastor Chitwick sent Nathaniel up to bed. "He won't get much sleep tonight," he told the others.

"It's been a shock to everyone," Hyacinth said, moving to the stove. "I'll make tea."

Rose, wishing Hyacinth would offer something stronger, asked, "Do you know Cal Devine?"

"As a matter of fact, we met last Christmas," Walter Chitwick said, shaking Cal's hand. "One of the nativity goats broke out and ended up downtown, behind the senior center."

Cal nodded. "It ate a few turkey pies before it was discovered inside the Meals on Wheels van. I hope you fixed that fence."

"The sexton took care of it. I'm told the only way to keep goats in is with an electric fence. Our parishioners wouldn't go for that."

"Let's sit at the kitchen table," Cal said, taking a notepad from his pocket.

Pastor Chitwick pulled out a chair. "This is a terrible situation—a young woman run down." He closed his eyes. "Rest her soul."

"Amen." Cal surveyed the table. "I'll need some information. One of my colleagues is out there interviewing your neighbors to see if they saw anything." He turned to Hyacinth. "Mrs. Chitwick, you made the 911 call?"

She nodded. "I was getting ready for bed when I heard a scream outside. I looked out the window and saw Rose running up the driveway. I went to the kitchen door, and she told me someone was lying in the road. I grabbed a flashlight and accompanied her to the street." She paused and briefly closed her eyes. "We determined it was Dionne Dunbar, one of the members of tonight's class."

Cal glanced at Pastor Chitwick. "Were you asleep during all this?"

"No, ah, I was out, and when I arrived home I saw my wife and Rose standing at the curb. A few neighbors had joined them."

"I understand one of the neighbors attempted CPR," Cal said.

"Marlene Guznik," the pastor said. "She's a retired nurse and a recent widow who's having difficulty coping with her loss."

"How is that?" Cal asked, scribbling on his pad.

Hyacinth got up from the table to pour the tea. From the stove, she said, "Marlene drinks, evenings. I've encouraged her to attend our classes in hopes of reconnecting with Albert, her husband, or at least achieve closure. Tonight when she joined us outside she was unsteady on her feet. Even though she knew Dionne had gone to spirit, she insisted on performing CPR."

Cal looked at her. "Gone to spirit?"

"Yes, she had passed."

"How were you able to determine that, Mrs. Chitwick? Do you have a medical background?"

"My background is in education, but years ago I was in the Peace Corps, stationed in Africa where we frequently dealt with death and disease."

Cal nodded. "For the record, Pastor, where were you tonight?"

"I was counseling a parishioner..."

When he failed to say more, Cal said, "At some point we may have to ask the parishioner's name, for verification…"

"Of course. It's a mother who's worried about her teenage son. She thinks he's involved with a satanic cult." He took a sip of the herbal tea Hyacinth had placed before him. "Are you implying this is more than a hit-and-run accident?"

"It is," Rose said. "When I found the body, it wasn't lying in the road. It was inside that big gray trash barrel."

"That's not a trash barrel," Hyacinth said, spooning honey into her tea. "It's a shredding barrel, for the church's sensitive papers. The company provides a locked receptacle, and once it's filled, they pick it up." She looked at Cal. "It's ironic, now that I think of it, but Dionne was a manager at the shredding company. That's how we happened to have a receptacle. She convinced us of the need for security."

"At first I didn't think it was necessary," the pastor added, "until I started thinking about the old records we sometimes throw out along with personal notes from parishioners. When I learned that the company hires rehabilitated drug addicts and alcoholics, I decided to try it on a monthly basis."

"How long had Dionne Dunbar worked for the company, do you know?" Cal asked.

"Not long," Hyacinth said. "They only moved into their Route 128 location in the fall. Dionne said most of the work is done at night, retrieving the barrels, returning them to the plant for shredding. Dionne was also responsible for bringing in new business."

"I'm familiar with it," Cal said. "It's near Marilyn's Pie Palace."

"Excuse me," Rose said. "I don't mean to sound pushy, but I think you should hear what I have to say about finding the body."

He took a sip of his tea, winced, and said, "I was getting to you, Rose, but go ahead."

The trio listened as she talked about attempting to get her car out of the snowbank and, in the process, slamming into the barrel. "I got out and tried standing it up but it was too heavy—"

"Rose is correct," the pastor interrupted. "Those barrels are heavy. You see, the church office alone didn't have enough material to warrant an account. It was when I invited the parishioners to dispose of their sensitive documents that the barrel began filling up. People fear identity theft."

Waiting to resume, Rose took a sip of her tea. It tasted like burnt black licorice. When the pastor was through, Cal said, "Let's let Rose finish her story."

She gave him a weak smile. "As I was saying, the barrel was heavy, and not only because of the paper inside. That barrel was heavy because there was a body inside. I found out when I got on my knees and rolled it toward the curb. Paper was falling out all over the place and as I pushed, I dislodged a large dark object. When I continued pushing, it rolled out." She looked around the table. "The first thing I noticed was the boots. It was dark, yet I could make out a pair of black boots against the snow. When I got my little flashlight from the car, I realized the boots were attached to legs."

She took a gulp of the bitter tea and turned to Cal. "How come you're not writing this down?"

He ignored the question. "Did you touch the body?"

"Just to determine if it was a person and not a pile of clothes. Remember, it was very dark out there."

"Could the body have been lying *behind* the barrel?"

"I think I'd know the difference," she said, scowling. "The body fell out of the barrel." She shivered, remembering her shock and surprise.

Hyacinth's voice was calm: "It was dark and Dionne was walking home, dressed in black. Perhaps it was a reveler from Mannory Way who drove by. As you know, it's the street where they have the big display of Christmas lights, music, and celebration. Every year it gets noisier and gaudier. As a result, they attract a rowdy, drinking crowd, many from out of town. People sometimes get lost in that maze of roads over there. They end up on our street."

The pastor said, "In November, the neighbors collected signatures and presented a petition to your chief. It didn't change anything." He waggled a finger at Cal. "I told him that one of these days someone's going to get hurt. Now it looks like my words were prophetic."

They solemnly observed the pastor. Rose thought his remarks would have more impact had he removed the Batman cap. At the same time, she needed to make a point. "The pastor is right about the Mannory Way crowd, but why would a hit-and-run driver take the time to put a body into a trash receptacle?"

This question was met with silence until Hyacinth said, "And let's not forget that Dionne was upset tonight. The message she got from a loved one had a profound effect upon her."

"Message?" Cal said.

"A message from spirit. That's the object of our mediums class—students develop their psychic potential.

Those who work at it will often receive word from the other side. Think of it as a fine-tuned radio picking up low-frequency waves."

"I thought it was a Bible class," Cal said.

"That's my domain," Walter Chitwick said with a chuckle. "My wife handles the otherworldly matters."

"I've got a class starting after the New Year," Hyacinth told Cal. "I think it might be useful in your line of work." She placed a hand over his. "You could develop your intuitive skills."

He got to his feet. "Thanks for the tea. I'd better file this report."

The following morning, Rose overslept. The night before, lying in bed, she'd relived the awful moment when Dionne's limp body had rolled from the barrel. *Like a rag doll*, she thought. It was long after midnight when she finally drifted off. Once again she had Chester, her ninety-five-pound black Lab, to thank. His rank dog breath had worked as no alarm clock would.

Fortune smiled upon her when she reached the office. There were no cryptic remarks from Yvonne about being late. Instead, the minute Rose rushed in, Yvonne oozed concern. "I've just gotten off the phone with the chief. He told me all about your ordeal last night, discovering the body. That poor, poor woman... so young and attractive."

"Did you know Dionne?"

"She spoke at a Rotary meeting once, something about the necessity for shredding documents. I was even considering signing us up, but you know how frugal our publisher is."

Rose hung her jacket on the coat rack, keeping her scarf draped around her neck. "Did the chief mention the driver's identity?"

Yvonne shook her head. "The department is contacting body shops. Of course the state police are involved. At this point Chief Alfano says it points to a drunk driver. You know how it is this time of year, the drinking and carousing. He seems to think that whoever hit her may not even be aware of it."

"You mean someone so wasted they just kept driving?"

"It's a possibility. Right before Mother was forced to give up her driver's license, she ran into a huge pumpkin in front of the Gingham Dog."

"The pumpkin was in the road?"

"Not exactly. It was on the sidewalk. Mother got confused, thinking she was applying the brake when it was the accelerator. I had quite a time getting her to surrender her license."

Rose let out a sigh. "Yvonne, this wasn't an ordinary hit-and-run. Whoever killed Dionne got out of the car and stuffed her body into a curbside barrel. Maybe they thought she wouldn't be discovered at first."

Yvonne stared at her. "But how could that be? Victor, I mean Chief Alfano, never mentioned that. He seems to believe it's an impaired driver."

"That's because Cal obviously didn't include it in his report. Apparently he didn't give any credence to my story."

"I don't know what to tell you. When we write up the incident, we can't add extraneous material. I have to quote the police chief."

"There's a world of difference between a random hit-and-run and murder," Rose said. "Looks like I have to speak to the chief myself."

"He's busy this morning with media interviews," Yvonne said. "This afternoon he's giving a talk about holiday home safety at the senior center."

"Is that an efficient way for the police chief to spend his time? Can't they post that information on their website?"

"They do, but many seniors can't afford Internet access. Those that use the library's computer aren't checking out the police website."

"It's ironic," Rose said, "how many seniors have money to go to Foxwoods Casino. The monthly bus from my dad's housing is always full."

"Speaking of bus trips, remind me to make reservations for *The Nutcracker*. It's Mother's Christmas treat."

When Yvonne began humming the Sugar Plum Fairy's theme, Rose swiveled around to face her computer. She felt angry. Why was her report about finding Dionne's body inside the shredding barrel being ignored? She felt like a child being humored. Yvonne had glossed over her remarks. Even Cal and the Chitwicks appeared unconvinced. She'd have to talk to the chief himself—a dismal prospect. No doubt it would go no further than his office.

Once again she wondered why, years ago, she hadn't taken the investigative journalism internship with the Boston news station. As a TV news writer, she'd have commanded respect. Instead, reporting for a small-town weekly that trafficked in bowling scores, she was a step above the supermarket circulars. When it came to news, the mundane was her domain.

Dionne Dunbar's funeral service was held at eleven o'clock on Monday at Frost's Funeral Home. The gathering was small, no doubt because Dionne was a newcomer to town. As in many New England villages, you weren't a native unless your great-grandparents were buried in the town cemetery.

A room off the reception area was set up with three rows of chairs. A middle-aged woman, her blond hair streaked with gray, stood behind the lectern. She smiled as the mourners trickled in. She wore a long stole, patterned with religious symbols, over a tan woolen suit.

Rose found a seat next to Florence in the last row. Jabbing a finger toward the woman, Florence said, "That's Dionne's sister, Dorothy."

"Is she a minister?" Rose asked.

She shook her head. "She's a chaplain. They're like volunteer ministers. They're not ordained or anything."

"Do you know her?"

Florence nodded. "I met her when I was at the hospital visiting my sister-in-law's mother. Dorothy came into the room and introduced herself. She said she'd been living in Granite Cove for a couple of months. She was looking for a place to retire. 'Course she never mentioned that Dionne was her sister. So when I walked into the funeral parlor today, there she was. I said, 'Hello, Reverend,' and she said, 'Call me Dorothy.' Then she told me she's Dionne's sister. I told her how I knew Dionne from the mediums circle. It's a small world." Florence glanced at the door. "Mother of God, will you look who just rolled in?"

Kristal Swekla stood in the doorway, surveying the room. She wore a white faux-fur jacket over a short skirt and tall white patent-leather boots.

"I can't believe she got up in time," Florence murmured.

Kristal took a seat in the middle row, next to Milton Krazner. She shrugged off her jacket. Underneath she wore a lace top, cut low in the back to reveal a stalking-leopard tattoo. Milton glanced at Kristal and twitched his nose at her perfume. He fumbled for a handkerchief and sneezed so violently his chair squealed in protest.

"How does Kristal know Dionne?" Rose whispered to Florence.

"From working at the pie place. Dionne used to come in and they became friendly. Kristal even visited Dionne's condo."

Rose couldn't imagine the fastidious Dionne having anything to do with the slovenly Kristal, but didn't pursue the matter. For one thing, Hyacinth Chitwick, sitting in the row ahead, flashed a look of disapproval.

When the room was full, Dorothy leaned toward a microphone on the lectern.

"Shall we begin?"

She introduced herself, providing a brief background: She was Dionne's sister, Dorothy Dunbar, a former bookkeeper. When her company merged with a leading electronics manufacturer, she'd retired early.

"I wanted to do something different with my life—to serve people in their time of need. One day, while I was visiting someone in the hospital, I met a woman who was in the chaplain's program. It sounded like something I would enjoy. Before long, I was enrolled in their program." She glanced at the ceramic urn sitting on a table near the lectern. "Little did I know that two years later I would be conducting my sister's memorial service."

She continued to gaze at the urn. "As sisters, Dionne and I had little in common, yet we respected each other's differences. She was vivacious where I was quiet and studious. She gravitated toward people and activity while I was content to sit and read. Regardless of our differences, we shared a life history. When she passed, my childhood went with her." She stopped to dab at her eyes with a tissue.

Then she read prayers from a book and concluded with the poem, "Let Evening Come," by Jane Kenyon. After a moment of silence, Dorothy said, "A couple of people have asked to offer eulogies. Could we start with Hyacinth Chitwick?"

She stepped away from the lectern to make room for Hyacinth, who wore a purple beret over her silver hair. Giving the assembled a stern look, she said, "Today we mourn the passing of Dionne Aileen Dunbar, who many feel was taken from us too early. Yet in the book of life and death, there are no guarantees. Thus we must make the most of our time here on Earth.

"Dionne is now free, her physical body cast aside"—here she paused to glance at the urn—"while her immortal body has gone to spirit." She looked around, a faint smile on her face. "I've come to tell you that Dionne has made a successful transition. She is with us *now*." Her look was triumphant as she returned to her seat.

"Thank you, Hyacinth," Dorothy said. "And now we'll hear from Kristal Swekla."

Kristal moved to the front of the room, a wadded tissue pressed to her nose. The light above the lectern glinted on the multiple studs rimming her ear lobe, and on her silver nose ring. She unfolded a sheet of paper with trembling hands and read aloud:

"I didn't know Dionne for very long. I met her when I started working at my new job. She worked for the company next door. We'd talk when she came in for coffee. She was always dressed nice, and though she was ten years older than me, she looked pretty.

"Dionne taught me how to find my self-esteem and feel good about myself. She was an awesome lady, and I'll never forget her. A couple days ago, my boyfriend bought me a kitty at the pet store. I named her Dionne." Blushing, she ducked her head and turned to go.

"Thank you, Kristal." Dorothy said. "Would anyone else care to say something before we close?"

"No time like the present," Florence said, clattering to her feet. Upon reaching the lectern, she crossed her arms and blinked at the mourners. "Like Kristal, I didn't know Dionne for very long. We met at Hyacinth's group. Dionne didn't talk much, unlike me, but you could tell she was interested in the spirit world.

"What stood out about her was how she dressed. While most of us, me included, show up for class in sneakers and sweats, Dionne always wore a skirt and high heels. Her hair was styled nice and her nails were never chipped.

"All I can say is, I hope they catch the person who did this. I hope they go to jail for the rest of their life." She wiped her eyes with the back of her hand. "I guess that's all. Merry Christmas, everyone."

After Florence was seated, Dorothy said, "I'd like to close with the Lord's Prayer, for those who wish to join me."

Pastor Chitwick immediately got to his feet and led the prayer, his voice strong and emphatic.

As the mourners were collecting their coats, Dorothy announced into the microphone, "The Chitwicks have kindly invited everyone back to the church for coffee and refreshments."

"Edith made three sour-cream coffee cakes," Florence told Rose. "I hope you're going back."

"Now I am," she said.

The reception was held in the St. Rupert's Church basement where a long table was set up. A big coffee pot gurgled at one end. Trays of sandwiches and cakes waited.

Florence scurried into the kitchen to help Edith. Rose, also an early bird, glanced at the food table, her stomach growling. She hadn't eaten breakfast, and it was lunchtime. She wondered how long to wait before moving in. While she deliberated, Hyacinth came out of the kitchen and made a beeline for her.

"Rose, if you happen to talk to Dorothy, don't mention your story about finding her sister in the shredding barrel."

"Of course I won't," she said, indignant that Hyacinth would think her capable of such indelicacy. "But it isn't a story, it's a fact."

Hyacinth patted her arm. "I see. On the other hand, it hasn't been substantiated by the police. When the lab tests come back, they'll make their conclusions."

"Lab tests or not, I know what I found."

"Of course you do," she said and moved away to greet the new arrivals coming down the basement stairs.

Minutes later the room was buzzing with talk, albeit subdued. Rose, holding a cardboard cup of coffee, singled out the members of the mediums circle. In an offhand manner, she asked each what he or she had observed the night Dionne was killed.

Milton said he'd rushed home to be with his wife, Marlene. "I only joined Hyacinth's class because Marlene insists I get out more."

Chip had also seen nothing. "It's like what I told the police: I offered Dionne a ride home but she wanted to walk. When I passed her, I gave a little beep." His eyes grew large. "Oh my God, I might have been the last person to see her alive."

Dorothy, meanwhile, was making the rounds of the mourners. She'd removed her suit jacket. She wore a white blouse, her stole hanging from her neck.

She approached Rose and Chipper. "Were you friends of Dionne's?"

Chipper told her about the mediums class. He mentioned Rose's journalistic mission that night.

"Were you and your sister close in age?" Rose asked.

She thought the matronly Dorothy, with her gray-streaked hair and flesh-colored stockings, was a decade older. Thus she was surprised when the woman said, "I was five years older." Dorothy continued, "Because of the age gap, Dionne and I each had our own circle of friends. That's why I want to meet her friends here in Granite Cove."

Florence came out of the kitchen and announced, "We got a pot of real coffee back there for those who want it."

Rose glanced into her cup. "Do you mean all this time I've been drinking decaf?"

"Uh-huh. That's what people ask for, and that's what Edith serves."

"Not me. I need the high octane if I'm to function."

Dorothy peered at Florence's apron. *The Happy Hearth Agency* was printed across the top. "Is that the name of the caterer?" she asked.

"Uh-huh," Florence said. "Edith started the agency a year ago. I been with her almost that long."

"Is Edith hiring?" Dorothy asked. "I'm looking for something else to do here, while I'm selling my sister's condo."

"Aren't you staying in Granite Cove?" Rose said. "I heard you were retiring here."

"I was considering it, but... not now that this has happened. I'll be here until her condo is sold. Given this economy, it could be months. I've been helping Pastor Chitwick at the hospital and the nursing home, but I'd like to find something else to do besides. I'll have time on my hands, and I like to keep busy."

Florence scratched her nose. "As far as catering goes, Edith needs someone for the big parties. My niece left us high and dry. Edith's been talking about getting someone part-time."

"Part-time is all I want," Dorothy said. "It'll help me to get reacquainted with your charming village. Years ago my family had a cottage on the rocks near Brier Neck Beach."

"You might regret it," Florence said. "This town can get to you in the dead of winter."

Dorothy smiled. "That's why I keep busy. Who should I call about the job?"

Florence jerked her thumb toward the kitchen. "Just pop in and introduce yourself to Edith. She's the boss."

The woman excused herself and headed for the kitchen.

Chip watched her go. "I hope we get a message from Dionne at our next class. I think it'd be a great comfort to Dorothy."

"I'm not so sure," Rose said. "She strikes me as a traditionalist."

"By the way," Chip said, "I hope you'll attend rehearsals for the play. Milton, who has a fabulous baritone, is playing Bob Cratchit, and Florence as Scrooge is pure inspiration."

"I'm gonna wear tights under that nightgown," Florence said. "Last week I froze my patootie on that drafty old stage."

"Where are you holding rehearsals?" Rose asked.

"At the middle school," Chipper said. "They've got a marvelous auditorium with excellent acoustics. Plus, it's close to the downtown, so folks can walk over."

"I'm surprised Mayor Froggett is letting you hold it there," Rose said. "He's got a strict policy about using city buildings."

"Pastor Chitwick talked him into it. He promised the mayor two free tickets to the show."

"The pastor's a savvy operator," Rose said.

"You don't want to know what he's talked me into," Chip said, rolling his eyes. "It's a director's nightmare, and I see no way out." Glancing around the crowded room, he said, "Let's not discuss it here."

"Are you talking about Nathaniel Chitwick?" Florence asked.

"*Please*," Chip said. "I've said too much already."

Auntie Pearl's Helpful Housekeeping Hints

Dear Auntie Pearl:

I work on the fourth floor of a large office complex. When I take the elevator, I sometimes encounter a middle-aged man who works in the same building. If I stand near the front, by the elevator door, he will position himself closely behind me. He's practically breathing down my neck! This happens even if we're the only people in the elevator.

I've tried moving to the back, but he will work his way over until he's right next to me. It doesn't matter if other people are sharing the elevator, he will invade my space. I once got up the nerve and said, "Do you mind?" He gave me a startled look and said, "Ma'am?" as if he had no idea what I was referring to. It's gotten so bad, I've been using the stairs. Unfortunately, I suffer from lower back problems, and climbing steps can be difficult.

I've taken this matter to my boss, who says to call 911 if the man touches me. Other than that, she can't do anything. Lately I've considered following this person to his office and speaking to his supervisor. On the other hand, I'm told I could be sued for defamation of character.

Auntie Pearl, do you think I should speak to the man's supervisor?

signed,

Harassed in Hamilton

Dear Harassed:

I had to chuckle while reading your letter. How I remember, as a young woman, taking Boston's MTA trolley to Filene's Basement. On Saturdays, the gropers would be out in full force. Auntie Pearl used her hat pin on more than one occasion!

The days of hat pins are over, although the gropers will always be with us. Nonetheless, I think I can help you, having suffered from lower back issues myself.

One of the best lumbar strengtheners requires you to lie on the floor on your stomach. Clasp your hands in front of you and slowly raise your upper body. Hold the pose for ten seconds and return. After you've done five of these, it's time for the legs. Keeping your upper body on the floor, raise your legs to a comfortable level and hold for ten seconds. Do five sets of these.

When your back gets stronger, you will be able to do more repetitions. And don't forget, stair-climbing is one of the best cardio activities for sedentary people.

Keep up your exercises, and by next year I'll bet you'll be climbing Mount Washington!

Signed,

Auntie Pearl

CHAPTER FIVE

"So, what do you think of my brilliant idea?"

Yvonne's voice cut through Rose's reverie. She'd been staring at a blank computer screen and hadn't heard a word her editor said. Something about a statue? Reluctantly, she turned and saw Yvonne behind her desk, an expectant look on her face.

"I'm sorry," Rose confessed, "I've been mulling over the story I want to write about the hit-and-run."

"Not until all the lab work comes back, and you know how long that can take. Chief Alfano promised he'd let me know the minute they learned anything."

"I just hope they find proof about, you know, the body being in the barrel."

"The people at the state lab can determine anything, even the brand of hair coloring a woman uses. Be patient. Your generation always expects immediate results. No one's willing to wait. When I was starting out in journalism, we didn't have electronic layout. We had to set up each page with scissors and a pot of glue. When we were on deadline, I didn't get home until midnight."

Rather than hear another of Yvonne's lectures on the early newsroom, Rose said, "What were you saying about a statue?"

"It came to me the other day while pushing Mother's wheelchair past the Homer Frost statue. Have you taken a look at it lately? It's eroded and covered in pigeon droppings. Not only that, the horse's rear end seems to be... purple."

"Maroon." Rose smiled. "That's from the days when the graduating senior class painted it the school colors on prank night." She cherished a memory of sitting on the shoulders of Cal Devine, a can of spray paint in her hand.

"It just goes to show the lack of pride and respect in this town," Yvonne said. "The City Council moved heaven and earth to get a drive-through for Mega Mug, yet they allow the city founder's statue to crumble to the ground."

"Why not take it up with the Beautification Society?"

Yvonne shook her head. "Nadine Purrington, the president, is more concerned about decorating the downtown—stringing holly on light poles. If you ask me, it's like putting lipstick on a pig."

"I think everyone agrees the statue needs restoration. Unfortunately, you won't find the funding at city hall."

"Certainly not. On the other hand, if it was Mayor Froggett's ancestor on that horse, it would be top priority."

"What do you propose to do?"

Yvonne clasped her hands in excitement. "I want this newspaper to sponsor an art contest among the Granite Cove Middle School children. After all, they've donated their auditorium for our play. Each child may enter a depiction of the Homer Frost statue, whether a painting, a drawing, or mixed media.

"The art department at the community college will narrow the entries down to five finalists. We at the newspaper will publish those entries and let our readers select the winner." She smiled broadly. "Now isn't that a wonderful community project? We're getting the town's young people involved, and at the same time we're drawing attention to an important issue. Any money raised will go toward the statue's restoration."

"It sounds like you've given this some thought," Rose said.

"Yes, I talked it over with Chipper. He was the one who suggested the college art department get involved. And another thing: our publisher won't allow emailed entries. Mr. Curley said the students have to send them in the postal mail, the old-fashioned way. Chipper said that would make it easier to judge."

"Speaking of Chip, he invited me to attend a rehearsal for your Christmas play. How is it coming along?"

"We're working out a few kinks—what you'd expect with amateurs. Florence, the woman who plays Scrooge, gets carried away at times. I've reminded her that Scrooge was a tough old bird. He may have been apprehensive about confronting the three ghosts, but he didn't dissolve into hysterics." She pressed her temples. "I go home with such headaches."

"Chip hinted at a problem regarding Pastor Chitwick's son. Do you know anything about that?"

Yvonne's face sagged. "Poor Chipper, trying to make everyone happy. It seems the pastor, who got Mayor Froggett's permission to use the middle school auditorium, wants his son to play Tiny Tim." She rolled her eyes. "Have you seen the boy?"

Rose nodded. "Nathaniel's a big kid."

"Poor Milton Krazner. As Bob Cratchit, he's supposed to lift the boy onto his shoulders. It's a travesty. Tiny Tim is intended to be frail and slight. You need two burly men to lift Nathaniel."

"Doesn't Pastor Chitwick realize that?"

"You would think so, wouldn't you?" Yvonne sighed. "Parental love is blind."

After lunch, Betty Ann called to ask if the *Granite Cove Gazette* would run an ad for the nursing home's holiday fair. "They've got a photo of an afghan and the member who crocheted it. They want it in the ad."

"Can't you scan the photo and email it?" Rose asked. "We've got an intern who comes in nights to do the ads."

"I don't have a scanner and I don't know how to use one," Betty Ann said. "I thought you might take a look their table, all hand-knit stuff, and do a little write-up. We'll pay. We've got a fund for that."

"The paper will charge for the ad. The write-up is gratis." She glanced at the clock. "How about if I come over now?" She lowered her voice so Yvonne couldn't hear. "I could use a break."

Five minutes later, Rose left the downtown for the quasi-countryside of Green Pastures Retirement & Rehabilitation Center. Not long ago it was simply called Green Pastures Nursing Home. The name change was made "to better convey our residents' active and diverse lifestyles," according to the new marketing campaign of the corporation that owned the facility and a dozen others like it. Yet despite the campaign, people still referred to it as a nursing home.

Rose parked in the back, next to a dumpster adjacent to the service door. Betty Ann's office was located on this level, in the no-frills service area. With its pea soup-green walls and concrete floors, it contrasted with the public areas. Those rooms boasted flocked wallpaper, chandeliers, and designer furniture that no one sat on.

Rose had first visited Green Pastures five years ago. Her mother was undergoing rehab following a stroke. One day, Rose convinced her to attend a sing-along in the activities center. Rolling her mother's wheelchair into the brightly lit room, she spotted a six-foot-tall woman handing out songbooks. Rose glanced at the ID badge on the woman's broad chest. Could Director Betty Ann Zagrobski be the former Betty Ann Gasaway, her old school chum? She was. The former buddies rekindled their friendship as if the intervening years had never happened.

On another occasion, Rose and her mother attended a scheduled event at the center. Someone called the Irish Fiddler was playing, and the room was packed. Kevin Healey, lanky and boyish, wore a starched white shirt, jeans, and cowboy boots. His was a foot-stomping performance. The Irish Fiddler really knew how to work the crowd with rollicking old favorites that got them on their feet, even those with walkers. Nonetheless, it was his finale, "Danny Boy," that silenced them. His voice transported the audience to their own distant childhoods. Even Rose's stoic mother dabbed at her eyes. Along with the silver-haired ladies, Rose fell in love. Best of all, it appeared that Kevin had noticed her too.

Thus her visits to Green Pastures had borne sweet fruit: a friendship restored and a new romance.

Inside the activities center, two young assistants were setting up tables for afternoon bingo. Rose poked her head in the door. "Is the boss lady around?"

"She's in the break room," one said.

As Rose headed down the hall, two residents scurried past. Although they were using aluminum walkers, the pair moved at a brisk pace. Rose guessed they were the early birds that Betty Ann had complained about. Early birds appeared while the activities staff was still cleaning up from the last program. They demanded entrance in order to select a choice seat for the next program.

"At first I tried locking the door," Betty Ann had told Rose. "But they'd peer in the window and knock. Eventually I have to stop what I'm doing and tell them to come back when the program starts. That's what my predecessor said to do. They drove her crazy.

"When I first started here, I felt sorry for them, hanging outside waiting. I let them in with the understanding they'd sit quietly and wait." She shook her head. "Instead, they'd pester me with questions: 'Are you getting new bingo prizes?' or 'Any coffee left?' My favorite was, 'How come you're not here all day Sunday?'

"Finally, we were forced to lock the door between programs. We needed that time to clean up, write notes, and get the room set up. It's a lot of work, and there's only me and two part-time assistants. Trouble is, the early birds still arrive and continue knocking, forever knocking." She sighed. "When I tell people what I do for a living, they always say, 'That must be so rewarding, bringing joy to the elderly.' They have no idea. You need the patience of Job for this work. It could burn out Mother Theresa."

Rose pushed open the door of the break room to find Betty Ann sitting at a corner table, alone, the *Granite Cove Gazette* spread before her. A cup of coffee and a doughnut were at her elbow. She looked up as Rose entered. "Hey, I was just reading your bogus housekeeping hints column. Did you hear me laughing?"

"Not really."

"Have people caught on that the column is bogus?"

"Nope. They think there's someone in Ohio named Auntie Pearl."

"But don't they comment about the advice? You've gotta admit it's odd."

Rose pulled out a plastic chair opposite Betty Ann. "The only person I have to worry about is Mr. Curley, the publisher. And he's only interested in the politics and sports coverage."

"Maybe you can talk Hyacinth into writing a column: 'Messages from the Dead.'"

"She doesn't use that word, *dead*. She says *in spirit*. And speaking of Hyacinth, I'm invited back to her mediums class. She didn't think I'd gotten a good idea of what goes on, considering it ended with Dionne's death."

Betty Ann nodded. "Which may have been aided by the mediums class. Didn't you say Dionne was upset when she left?"

"She was definitely preoccupied. But I have a theory. Do you know Mannory Way, the street that goes crazy every year with Christmas lights and decorations?"

"Uh-huh. When Tiny was a firefighter, they called it Mammary Way because of the wild parties that went on. I hear that weekends, people come from all over to tailgate. The month of December is one big block party."

Rose nodded. "Those streets are like a maze, the way they connect. I'm thinking that whoever killed Dionne could have been a drunken driver from Mannory who got lost and ended up on Spruce Hill Lane, the Chitwicks' street. It was dark and he was impaired. He didn't see Dionne walking in the road. After hitting her, he panicked, got out of the car, and stuffed her body into the shredding barrel."

Betty Ann looked dubious. "A panicked drunk driver isn't gonna stop and take the time to hide a body. He's gonna hightail it out of there."

"Maybe it wasn't a driver. Maybe someone on foot attacked Dionne in the dark and stuffed her body in the barrel."

"You forget the police confirmed Dionne was hit by a car."

Rose sighed. "That makes me the crazy lady spinning wild stories." She got up from the table. "I think I'll buy a cup of your vending-machine coffee."

"Be my guest. It's only a week old." She glanced at her watch. "I've got ten minutes til Sister Margaret finishes with the Rosary. Then I can show you the holiday table and afghan."

Soon Rose returned carrying a steaming cup to the table.

"So, tell me," Betty Ann said, "are you going back to Hyacinth's mediums group?"

"I think I might. I'd like to find out more from the members: How did they get along with Dionne? After all, they each had a perfect opportunity to run her down."

Betty Ann chewed the last of her doughnut. "Don't you think the police thought of that when they questioned them?"

Rose shrugged. "I'd like to hear their responses."

"When you say members, who are you talking about? Isn't Florence Huke in that group? I can't see Florence mowing anyone down."

"I wasn't thinking about Florence, although I can imagine her absentmindedly running someone off the road."

"Certainly not Chipper Foss, the drama teacher," Betty Ann said.

"Why not? Just because he's gay and wears argyle vests is no reason to disqualify him."

"Okay, so who's left of the murderous mediums?"

"Milton Krazner. He's a commercial real estate broker. As a suspect, he interests me."

"Why is that?"

"He's like a chubby Norman Bates, but instead of an overbearing mother, he's got a domineering invalid wife. I was watching the circle that night, and I noticed things. Like, after holding hands, Milton took a sanitizing wipe from his pocket and scrubbed his palms. I also noticed how his eyes kept straying to Dionne's legs. She crossed them several times. When her skirt rose up, she didn't make an effort to pull it down. Ask yourself whose attention she was trying to attract. It certainly wasn't Florence, Hyacinth, or Chipper. It had to be Milton's."

Betty Ann sipped her coffee. "How do you know his wife's domineering?"

"He mentioned he had to locate a store that was still open so he could buy cough syrup for her. Seriously, B. A., would your Tiny drive around at eleven at night looking for cough syrup?"

"Only if the store sold beer." Betty Ann sat back in her chair. "Do you want to know what I think of your scenario?"

Rose crumpled her cup and tossed it into a nearby barrel. "You think I'm hysterical."

"Not at all. I think you've got an excellent imagination. That's why you're such a good writer. After getting involved in Dr. Klinger's murder last year, you're hungry for another mystery to solve."

"Or maybe I'm not accepting the status quo. The chief wants to keep everything hunky-dory. Let's not ruin the village's good name. Let's not alarm the shoppers during the Christmas season. Just ignore the circus going on at Mannory Way. Those people frequent the bars and restaurants. And if someone gets killed as a result, let's call it a random hit-and-run. We'll wrap it up with a big Yuletide bow."

Betty Ann stared at her. "I understand your frustration, kiddo, but you didn't even know Dionne Dunbar."

Rose stared down at the table. "Maybe because the situation hit close to home, no pun intended. I'm a single woman like Dionne, but I'm also a native."

When Rose's voice trailed off, Betty Ann said, "I sense there's something more eating you."

Rose flashed her a smile. "You should have been a therapist, you know? I guess I've been thinking of my dad. I visited him the other day. I learned that his new *friend* has been cooking for him. B.A., I think they're an item."

"And you're jealous."

"Maybe, but mostly I feel... displaced."

Betty Ann reached out to cover Rose's hand with her own. "Kiddo, I know your dad, and you'll always be number one in his heart."

"I wonder…"

Once again, Rose found herself sitting in the Chitwicks' dimly lit basement, notebook in her lap as she watched the group of four. Earlier, the three members—Florence, Chip, and Milton—had arrived at the same time. They stood in the kitchen saying little as Nathaniel reluctantly took their coats, which he dragged off to another room.

A solemn Hyacinth, wearing a velour caftan, entered the kitchen. She lit a candle inside a hurricane lamp and, holding it aloft, led them down the dark cellar steps. Downstairs, they took their seats, glancing at the empty chair. Its presence silenced them; even Florence failed to comment.

When they were settled, with Rose on the sidelines, Hyacinth spoke: "As you can see, I've left Dionne's chair as it was. I debated whether to remove it and finally decided to let it remain. The chair can act as a conduit for spirit."

Milton leaned forward, elbows on knees. "I've agonized over that night. I should have insisted on giving Dionne a ride home."

"Could have fooled me," Florence said. "You peeled out of here like a bat outta hell."

He jerked around to face her. "How would you know? You were too busy flapping your gums."

"Please," Hyacinth said, closing her eyes. "Your anger will drive spirit away. Discussing the past is a waste of energy. Time moves forward, not backward. Let it go. The universe has its own rules, more complex than we mortals can ever comprehend."

She opened her eyes to gaze at each member. "Have you ever considered that in the Book of Life it was Dionne Dunbar's moment to leave her earthly body?"

Florence and Chipper nodded while Milton looked away.

Now, Hyacinth held out her hands. "Let's make a sacred circle and invite spirit in. First, we'll recite the invocation."

Eyes closed, the group said in unison, "We accept with open hearts those who enter our circle. Spirit, cast your light upon us, we who seek your wisdom."

They fell silent. Once again, the only sound was the humming of the furnace. From the floor above came the sound of canned TV laughter. Rose's eyelids grew heavy, and she struggled to stay awake in the warm and still room.

Just before Rose drifted off, Florence's raspy voice cut through her torpor: "Does anyone know someone named Tillie?"

For a moment, no one spoke. Finally, Milton said, "I assume Tillie is a woman?"

"She is," Florence said, chuckling. "She's a little butterball."

"Are you referring to a frozen turkey?" he asked.

"Milton," Hyacinth admonished, "give Florence a chance."

"Like I said," Florence continued, "she's a short, chubby little thing... with pink cheeks and brown hair. No, wait, that's a hat she's wearing, a close-fitting brown cap. She's got on a tweed coat and those tie shoes that old ladies wear. Altogether she looks like one of those tiny brown birds... sparrows.

"It's funny I said bird, because now she's pecking at something with both hands. Wait a minute, she's typing... she's typing and saying, 'Tell that boy to keep at it.'" After a moment of silence, Florence added, "I think that's it. She's fading away."

"Very good, Florence," Hyacinth said. "Does anyone recognize our visitor?"

Chip cleared his throat. "You know, I think it was my high school English teacher, Miss Bickerton. Her first name was Tillie and she was barely five feet tall. She taught at Granite Cove High School forever.

"Miss Bickerton encouraged me to write, and one day I showed her a couple of plays I'd been working on. I was interested in theater, but back then it wasn't considered cool for guys. Football was cool. Miss Bickerton said I had the makings of a playwright. Because of her, I applied to Emerson and got accepted.

"Living in the big city, I got distracted, partying every night. At the same time, I came out, and that opened a whole new world. My life was exhilarating—and exhausting. My grades suffered. All I cared about was the next party or the latest nightclub.

"When I went home on Christmas break, a bunch of college friends visited. I showed them around Granite Cove. After that, we stopped at the Sacred Cod for a drink. Three hours later, the bartender kicked us out for being rowdy.

"Just as we were leaving, I saw Miss Bickerton arriving with a young woman she introduced as her niece. I must have reeked of booze, so I kept it brief. But as I turned to go, she grabbed my sleeve and looked directly at me. She made that typing motion and said, 'Are you keeping at it?'

"Her words had a profound effect on me. I hadn't been 'keeping at it,' but when I returned to school, I was different. This time I devoted myself to my courses. Instead of partying, weekends, I grabbed a ride to Manhattan. I'd see four or five plays—off Broadway, of course. I soaked it up, the theater. Back in Boston, I worked on new plays, sending them out to producers.

"Before long, I heard that one of my plays had been accepted. It had its premier at a dinner theater in Orlando. When I saw the program and my name as playwright, I felt so proud. On the inside page were the words: 'Dedicated to Tillie Bickerton.'

"Right before graduation, my mother sent me a clipping from the *Granite Cove Gazette*. It was Miss Bickerton's obituary." Chipper's voice trembled. "Not long after that, I was hired as chair of the theater department. I knew I'd pass it on by helping and encouraging my students the way Miss Bickerton helped me."

Florence reached over and patted his hand. "I'll bet Tillie's proud of you."

The room again grew quiet. Milton suddenly sat up. "I see a tall, bald man carrying a suitcase," he said, not attempting to conceal his excitement.

"Is he wearing suspenders?" Florence asked.

"Well, yes. I think he's got suspenders."

"It could be Uncle Neal," Florence said. "He was a Fuller Brush salesman covering northern New England. Aunt Dora used to say he was away from home so long the kids didn't recognize him when he got back. After he passed, she found out he had women on his route, and I don't mean customers."

"He's standing in a doorway, wearing a long overcoat," Milton said. "Outside is a dark-blue car, a heavy car."

"He had a DeSoto," Florence said.

"He's saying, 'Get a move on.'"

"That could be my grandfather," Chipper said. "He was a conductor for the old Boston & Maine Railroad. Grandpa Foss was always telling my grandmother to 'get a move on.' Is he tall? Grandpa was well over six feet."

"Uncle Neal was tall, too, and he had a DeSoto," Florence said.

"It's hard to tell how tall," Milton said, his voice full of wonder. "He's standing in the doorway, but he appears tall... I'm just so elated. Until now I thought you folks were making it up. Wishful thinking, perhaps. Now it's actually happening to me."

"Which is why you must stay with spirit," Hyacinth said calmly. "Don't address members of the group. Focus on spirit or spirit will go away. Tell us what's happening now."

"Let's see, he's still in the doorway. Now he's looking at his watch. It's on a chain... an old fashioned pocket watch. Will you look at that? He's saying he's late and can't wait any longer... Oh, he's gone." Milton held out a hand. "Look, I'm shaking."

"Congratulations," Florence said.

The group sat in contented silence until Hyacinth shifted in her chair. "Dionne's here," she said quietly.

When the members gasped, she held up a hand to silence them. "She says she's at peace... she's been reunited with Roger. She wants her sister to know this. Now she's pointing to the horizon. She's saying something about planes..."

A long pause followed while they waited for Hyacinth to say more. Finally she said, "I've lost contact. I think she's gone."

"I wish she'd stuck around," Florence said, "I wanted to tell her we miss her."

"Earthly sentiments mean little to those in spirit," Hyacinth said. "Of course, there are instances when someone has suffered a violent death. In those cases, they may linger between worlds, unable to make a successful transition."

"Is that like poltergeists?" Florence said.

"No, but it actually happens more than you think. I've been asked to help before. A family here in town called about a troubled spirit in their home. The grandmother reported hearing crying. Furniture in her room would tip over. Her family assumed she had the beginnings of dementia until the teenage daughter had similar reports."

"Wow," Florence said, "did you do an exorcism?"

"I visited the house. On the third occasion, I made contact with spirit. It was a young man, a troubled soul who'd lived there years ago. He'd taken his life, and he finally saw the futility of staying behind. He made a successful transition."

"Awesome," Chipper whispered.

A moment later, Hyacinth rose and pulled the cord to a light hanging above the washing machine. The members blinked and slowly got to their feet. They folded their chairs, stacking them against an ancient Frigidaire. Silently they filed up the stairs.

Before Rose headed up, Hyacinth said to her, "Do you have a minute? I want your opinion about something."

"Sure."

"It's upstairs. Stay here. I'll be right down."

Rose hugged herself and glanced around the shadowy basement. She was glad when Hyacinth returned, closing the cellar door and descending the stairs.

She was clutching an envelope in her hand. "I want to make sure we have privacy," she said, facing Rose. "I'm aware of your investigative work into the death of Dr. Klinger. That's why I thought of you when I received this."

She opened the envelope and removed a slip of folded paper. She handed it to Rose. It was cheap white notepad stationary, the kind found in pharmacies and dollar stores. Typed in the center of the sheet were the words *You are next.*

Rose took the envelope from Hyacinth and compared the two. "Someone used an electric typewriter," she said. "When did it arrive?"

"Two days after Dionne's death. I'm reluctant to go to the authorities, knowing how heavy-handed Chief Alfano can be."

"But you must. This will help the investigation." Rose didn't mention that it would also lend credence to her theory of intentional homicide.

Hyacinth took the note and the envelope from her. "I haven't decided yet. I considered showing it to Cal Devine, but he'd be obligated to turn it in. Chief Alfano would be like a bull in a china shop, disrupting our lives. It wouldn't be fair to my students nor conducive to spirit, having a police presence in this house."

"You're forgetting it could help find whoever killed Dionne. And what about your family? Aren't you putting them at risk?"

"I have a hunch it's got something to do with the anonymous phone calls."

"What phone calls?" Rose asked.

"You know how narrow-minded people in Granite Cove can be. It's as if we're living in seventeenth-century Salem. There's a group of traditional parishioners who don't think it's appropriate for a pastor's wife to be involved in the spirit world. Some have found another church. Some have retaliated. This was an anonymous woman caller."

"What did she say?"

"Always the same thing," Hyacinth said. "Get out." She put the note back into the envelope. "I showed it to you because I trust you'll be discreet, should you decide to investigate. But first you must promise not to tell anyone. No one knows about this, not even my family."

"But I'd be guilty of obstructing justice," Rose said. "I'd be an accomplice in jeopardizing your family's safety."

Hyacinth stared at her. "Either you help me on my terms or you don't. Just be advised that should you go to the police, I'll deny ever showing you anything. After your tale about finding Dionne inside a barrel, they already think you're a bit... shall we say, scattered?"

Rose felt her cheeks flush. She had an urge to call Hyacinth the name she'd labeled her the day they met. She also realized that no amount of arguing would convince Hyacinth to take the letter to the police. She slung the strap of her bag over her shoulder and said, "Let me know if you receive anything else."

Hyacinth blessed her with a rare smile. "I will, and thank you. I'll let you out." Rose followed her up the stairs into the kitchen where Nathaniel was peering into the refrigerator.

Before stepping outside, Rose said, "Would you mind leaving the light on until I get to my car? It's at the bottom of the driveway, and as you know, this street is awfully dark."

"Certainly. We're in the habit of dousing the outdoor lights. We've got a snoopy neighbor, you see." She leaned out and glanced at the house to the left. "Even now, I feel her eyes upon us."

Looking up at the narrow, cedar-shingled house, Rose thought she saw curtains move in an upstairs window. "Goodnight," she said, and headed down the icy driveway, her stance wide to avoid falling. Upon reaching her car, she turned to wave, but it was too late.

The Chitwicks' house was in darkness.

CHAPTER SIX

The next morning, Rose let Chester out the breezeway door and into the backyard. In the kitchen, she heated up yesterday's coffee in the microwave. As she spooned sugar into her mug, Chester began barking, the sound booming in the crisp, cold air. Rose scurried to the door to let him in.

Not too long ago, it wouldn't have mattered how much noise Chester made—Rose had no close neighbors. Now, three new houses stood on a nearby wooded lot, part of an upscale development called Meadowmere Estates. The mini mansions boasted features such as multiple garage stalls, Palladian windows, and turrets. And while Rose had feared the street would be overrun with screaming kids, the houses were eerily silent.

It was Betty Ann who explained the new child-raising practices: "Kids don't go out and play anymore. The days of walking to a friend's house are over. Today's children have playdates; their moms drive them."

"You mean they don't play outdoors?"

She shook her head. "Abduction."

"Oh, for God's sake."

Now Rose called to Chester, who stood with his back to her as he faced down a squirrel. When the barking continued, she grabbed his leash from a hook and skidded across the frozen yard in her fuzzy slippers.

"C'mon." She tugged at the leash and managed to drag him toward the house. But before they reached the door, he stopped and whined, looking beseechingly at her. "Okay," she sighed, and undid the clasp. "Go toity then."

She hugged herself and waited as he ambled to a corner of the yard. She hadn't brought a bag with her, nor did she intend to "pick up" before breakfast. She would wait until she got home from work. Another benefit of winter.

It was fortunate that Frank, her landlord, wasn't occupying his half of the carriage house they shared. In the winter, Frank, a former State Street lawyer, lived in St. Croix, where he tended his waterfront bar. While he was away, Rose watered his plants and made sure the pipes didn't freeze during a cold snap. Her caretaking duties resulted in a rent reduction. All in all, it was a comfortable arrangement.

Back inside the house, Chester clambered up on the mustard-colored sofa and collapsed in a heap, sighing as only a ninety-five-pound dog could. Rose finished her breakfast of granola followed by toast and peanut butter, and then got dressed.

She pulled on her old suede boots with the thick rubber tread. Last year, needing a little glamour in her life, she'd bought a pair of sleek, high-heeled leather boots. It was an end-of-season clearance sale at The Harbour Shoppe. So far, she'd worn them twice. Yes, the boots were sexy and stylish. They were also treacherous on slick surfaces, forcing her to walk stiff legged. In fact, Betty Ann had claimed she walked with "a broomstick down her pants." Now Rose looked at the pricey, neglected boots inside the box. She blamed the grandmotherly sales clerk who'd claimed they made her legs look "like a showgirl's."

She brushed the salt residue from her old boots and vowed to wear the new pair to opening night of *A Christmas Carol*. All of Granite Cove would be there. There was little else to do on winter nights.

She called good-bye to Chester and pulled the side door shut to lock it. After starting the Jetta, she scraped a layer of ice from the windshield. When the car had warmed up, she got in and drove down her rutted street. No doubt it would be paved come spring. Developers were more persuasive with city hall than residents were.

As she navigated the snow-covered potholes she spotted pedestrians ahead in the street. For years—prior to the development—she'd had the road more or less to herself. Now she passed two of the McMansion owners, briefcase-toting men who walked together to the train station. One morning, with the temperature hovering at twenty degrees, she'd stopped to offer the pair a ride. They had exchanged glances and declined. Rose had driven away feeling that her gesture had somehow been misinterpreted.

When she later mentioned it to Betty Ann, her friend had laughed. "Now their wives have you pegged as the local Jezebel."

Rose had scoffed at this until the following week. Walking Chester on Juniper Street, she'd encountered the two wives jogging. They'd silently passed, their cool eyes flickering over her.

Later she'd described their form-fitting running attire to Betty Ann. "Jumpsuits like Spiderman," she said.

"More like Spider*women*," Betty Ann remarked.

Today Rose eased the car to the left, giving the men a wide berth.

She didn't immediately head for the office. Yvonne would not be in early, because she was meeting Chipper to discuss costumes for the play. Rose decided to get a look at Spruce Hill Lane, the Chitwicks' street. The early light might reveal something she'd missed.

She slowed when she spotted a long silver trailer parked outside St. Rupert's Church. Lettering on its side read *Farmer Hobbs Barnyard Animals*. Rose recognized Henry Moffat, the church sexton, standing outside the trailer. A man in overalls and a checkered cap led a pair of sheep down the trailer's ramp. Pastor Chitwick, leaning against the wood rail fence, held a steaming cup of Dunkin' Donuts coffee. He smiled at the scene, his Santa cap incongruous with the clerical collar.

Rose made a left at Spruce Hill Lane. She drove past the neat Cape-style houses, the yards decorated with candy-cane fences, plastic reindeer, and angels. She noted the home of Marlene Guznik, the alcoholic nurse who'd attempted CPR on Dionne. In the woman's front yard, an inflated snowman lay on its back as though inebriated.

A fresh accumulation of snow made the street appear narrower than Rose remembered. Outside the Chitwicks' house, the sidewalk had been cleared. Years ago, the town had religiously kept all walkways shoveled. Now the only snow-free sidewalks were the pastor's, Mayor Froggett's, and Chief Alfano's.

No cars were parked in the Chitwicks' driveway. Rose drove on, slowing to a crawl as she approached the adjacent residence, the tall shingled house that Hyacinth claimed belonged to their "nosy" neighbor. A tan Honda Civic climbed the steep driveway and came to a stop, its brake lights flashing.

The driver's door opened and a short, round, middle-aged woman stepped out. Rose recognized her from Dionne's funeral. She had attended the service, sitting in the back, but hadn't appeared at the church hall reception. The woman hurriedly reached inside the car and pulled out a bag of groceries. As she turned, the bag snagged on the door and ripped. A dozen cans rolled down the sloping driveway to the street.

Rose immediately pulled the Jetta to the curb, hopped out, and began to scoop up the cans of cat food.

"You don't have to do that, miss. I can pick them up," the woman protested.

"It's no trouble," Rose said, stuffing cans into her pockets. "I've got a dog. Happens to me all the time." Her arms laden, she asked, "Do you have another bag for these?"

The woman glanced into her car. "I've got birdseed in the back, double bagged." She leaned inside and picked up the bag. Straightening up, her foot slipped on the ice. She clutched the car door.

"Watch it," Rose said "You need salt on this driveway."

The woman laughed. "I'm a licensed caregiver, helping old folks who've broken their hips and knees. I don't need a warning about winter spills."

Rose deposited the cans into the spare bag. "By the way, how many cats do you have?"

"Just three." The woman glanced back at the house as if expecting to see them at the window. "Would you like to come in? Let me give you a cup of tea."

Rose accepted. She'd been hoping to interview the Chitwicks' neighbor. Now the opportunity had fallen into her lap. "Is my car okay parked on the street?" She didn't want to risk Hyacinth seeing her.

"It's fine. I'm not expecting anyone. By the way, my name's Viola Hampstead."

"I'm Rose McNichols." She held out her hand and Viola shook it.

"Oh my, the reporter for the *Granite Cove Gazette*?" When Rose nodded, Viola said, "I've been reading you for years. I had no idea you were so young...and pretty."

Rose shrugged. "When I was a kid, forty was one step from death's door."

Viola laughed. "It's relative, my dear. Now if you don't mind carrying that bag, we'll go in and you can meet my furry friends."

When the women stepped into the foyer, two cats appeared on the staircase. "The white-and-black one's Pinky," Viola said, "and the tiger is Twinkie. Stinky's probably hiding upstairs under the bed. He's a feral and never took to anyone but me."

"Stinky?" Rose asked, automatically sniffing the pine-scented air.

Viola chuckled. "He often manages to miss his litter box. I think he does it on purpose when I pay too much attention to the girls."

Rose nodded. Although she liked cats, she'd never had one. When she was growing up, her mother hadn't allowed pets in the house, claiming they were unhygienic. Ten years ago her dad found Chester, a young Lab mix, wandering the waterfront. When no one claimed him, Rose adopted the pup. Now she couldn't imagine life without him.

As they moved from the foyer, Rose nodded at the steep staircase. "Do you live upstairs as well?"

"I do. Some of my clients have to move their beds downstairs. I hope I never come to that. I think it's important to have separate areas for living and for sleeping."

Viola led Rose into a small living room. A velvet love seat sat against one wall. Next to it was a brocade wingback chair with a lace headrest. In front of both was an oval mirrored coffee table holding china figurines and a bowl of pink Canada Mints. The room looked like a time capsule circa 1955.

"Sit down and get acquainted with the girls while I put the kettle on," Viola said, and left the room. Rose sat on the love seat and then got up. She went to the window and pulled aside the filmy curtains. The top half of the Chitwicks' house was visible above a tall cedar fence that undoubtedly belonged to them. In order to view their entrance door, you'd have to be upstairs looking out.

She returned to the sofa and looked around the tidy room. The dark flower-patterned rug had not a speck of lint. She wondered how Viola, with a demanding job and three cats, maintained an immaculate house while Rose, twenty-five years younger, was resigned to a life of clutter and disorganization.

Feeling eyes upon her, she spotted the cats. They sat hunched under an end table, staring at her with impassive faces. She leaned forward and held out her hand. "Here kitties." The cats ignored her attempt at sociability and continued staring until she self-consciously looked away.

Soon Viola appeared carrying a tray. "Just move those things aside on the coffee table," she said, lowering the tray. "I made fig bars this morning, so help yourself." She moved to the brocade chair and carefully covered her lap with a napkin before picking up her cup.

Rose watched her out of the corner of her eye. The woman's clothing was neat and prim. She wore a brown cardigan sweater, a tan tweed skirt, and heavy beige walking shoes. Like many older women, Viola had dyed her hair a shade too dark. Hers was the color of chocolate pudding.

Rose bit into a fig square so dry she sprayed crumbs when she spoke. "Do you live here alone?"

Viola nodded. "I have for some time, since my husband left me."

"Oh, I'm sorry to hear that."

She waved away Rose's apology. "It's been years. Today Karl and I are what the lawyers call 'amicable.'"

Rose smiled. "I assume things weren't amicable back then?"

"Karl was a bright man. He worked for the Coast Guard—marine electronics, repairing the ship radios and whatnot. He was a tinkerer. He kept a workshop upstairs and I rarely saw him. He was always in there, repairing some clock or can opener. He's retired now, living in South Carolina."

"Do you have children?"

Viola shook her head. "Karl left when I got pregnant at forty-nine, if you can imagine. For years we tried to start a family, until we learned that Karl wasn't producing enough... whatever they call it, to make a baby." Her face flushed. "When I discovered I was pregnant, he was shocked. Instead of being supportive, he began spending more time in his workshop. One night, after too many drinks, he declared that at fifty-five he was too old to be a father. Not long after that, I came home and found him gone." She gazed out the window. "At least he left me the Buick."

"That's awful, Viola. I hope you got a lawyer."

"I did, Attorney Farley. Karl never balked at paying alimony. He's never missed a month." She sighed. "It was just as well. Things wouldn't have worked out. Karl was too set in his ways. He'd never put up with the mess and noise a child makes." She reached down to stroke the cat at her feet. "Not only that—he'd never have agreed to cats. Today they're my life."

Rose nodded. "Does your former husband have a good relationship with your child?"

"I had a miscarriage my third month. The doctor said it's common for women my age. He said it was probably a blessing." She gazed into her cup. "I'm sure he was right..."

At that moment the clock on the mantle chimed, underscoring the sadness that had fallen over the room. Rose leaned forward to ask the questions she'd been longing to ask. "Viola, I understand the police questioned you about the recent accident involving Dionne Dunbar?"

"Indeed they did," she said. "It was that good-looking policeman, Cal Devine, who visited me. I got a little flustered. He sat right where you're sitting." She smiled primly. "He's awfully attractive."

Rose's smile was forced. After fifteen years she still felt a twinge of remorse coupled with irritation when women praised Cal. On the other hand, she didn't blame them. She and Cal had been high school sweethearts and then engaged for three months when she broke it off. It wasn't that she'd stopped loving Cal; it was the idea of being Mrs. Devine, of playing the role of wife, that seemed so daunting. Marriage, she feared, would destroy their relationship.

Needless to say, Cal hadn't understood. In fact, no one understood. Wounded by her actions, he'd withdrawn. To get away from the gossip, Rose had moved to Portland, Maine. Meanwhile, Marcie Ventamiglia, not wasting any time, rushed in to console Cal. Not surprisingly, she'd gotten pregnant.

Today Cal had what he'd wanted: a family. He and Marcie ("The Barracuda") were proud parents of three sons. Rose, meanwhile, had a steady relationship with Kevin Healey. On the whole, things had turned out for the best. Yet there were times when Rose, spotting Cal looking tanned and fit in his dark-blue uniform, sighed heavily. An involuntary reaction, she reminded herself. She'd done the right thing…

Now she asked Viola, "Did you see anything? I ask because I was the one who found Dionne, and it was… terrible."

Viola leaned forward to pat Rose's knee. "I'm sorry, dear. Such an awful thing to witness." She leaned back in her chair. "I can't tell you how many times I've written the mayor's office or spoken to Chief Alfano about the rowdy crowd on Mannory Way. It gets worse every year, cars racing up and down the streets. Last year I made it a point to copy some license plate numbers on that street. I gave them to the chief, who confirmed they weren't Granite Cove folks." She threw up her hands. "That's all he did. My friends at the senior center say nothing will be done because the Mannory Way hooligans spend money at our bars and restaurants. As long as the merchants are happy, Mayor Froggett is happy."

"You're probably right," Rose said. It seemed as if everybody hated Mannory Way. "I guess you didn't happen to see anything that night?"

She shook her head. "I became aware something was wrong when I heard the neighbors gathering outside." She glanced at Rose. "You must be one of Hyacinth's séance people."

"Not really. I was planning on doing a story on her mediums circle."

Viola shivered. "I'm afraid I'm much too cowardly for such things. I can't even watch the old Alfred Hitchcock TV shows. Gives me nightmares."

Rose felt the conversation was going astray. "You know, Viola, you looked familiar. That's why I slowed down earlier when I saw you outside. Didn't I see you at Dionne's funeral?"

She nodded slowly. "A sad, sad thing. Such a beautiful girl."

"I didn't see you at the reception later," Rose said. "I suppose you had a client waiting."

She set her cup in the saucer. "No. To be honest, I didn't attend the reception because Hyacinth Chitwick and I don't see eye to eye."

"Even though you're next door neighbors?"

"We used to be friendly. Back when we first knew of Karl's problem, Hyacinth got her prayer group to focus on raising his... sperm count." She ducked her head. "A couple of years ago, Hyacinth and I had a falling out over Nathaniel, the son. Mind you, I've nothing but good things to say about Walter Chitwick. A lovely man. The son inherited none of his father's traits.

"One day I caught him throwing rocks at my Twinkie. I used to let the cats go outside until I got wise to that child." She leaned toward Rose. "Did you know that pet abuse is an early indication that someone's a serial killer?"

"I think I read something like that," Rose said.

"When I complained to Hyacinth, she got indignant. She didn't believe me. She seems to think the boy is perfect." She sighed. "My father used to say, 'None so blind as those who will not see.'"

"I can understand how that would drive a wedge between you," Rose said. "Getting back to Dionne, did you know her from the church?"

"Oh, no, my dear. I knew her long before that. You see, I was her father's caregiver when the Dunbars spent their summers in Granite Cove. They had a cottage on the rocks near Brier Neck. Poor Mr. Dunbar had emphysema and Mrs. Dunbar couldn't cope, caring for two teenage girls plus an invalid husband. She was an artist, you see, a very attractive woman. Dionne inherited her looks: the thick, dark hair and dark eyes.

"Mrs. Dunbar used to take her easel out first thing in the morning and set it up on the rocks." She gazed out the window. "I can see her now with that big floppy hat. When she finished for the day, she'd set her paintings on the back porch to dry. I remember she once caught me admiring a lovely seascape. When I complimented her, she wrinkled her nose and said, 'This doesn't capture the fury.' She had a wild look in her eye, as artists sometimes do."

When Viola lapsed into silence, Rose gently asked, "What happened to Mrs. Dunbar?"

"Her name was Suzanne," Viola said. "It's not a common name, and today when I hear it I always think of her, a strong, passionate woman. When summer ended, they'd move back to their winter home in Milton. The week before Christmas, I heard through the grapevine that she'd up and left the family. Apparently a gallery in Florida wanted to show her work, but they wanted local seascapes. Their customers paid top dollar. Mrs. Dunbar went down there on what was supposed to be a temporary visit. I wasn't surprised when she didn't come back. "

"Is she still there?" Rose asked.

Viola's eyes widened. "Oh, no. A month after she arrived, in 1979, Hurricane Frederic struck Pensacola. Mrs. Dunbar was painting on the rocks when a wave washed over her and swept her out to sea." She shook her head. "Can you imagine that?"

"Did you return the next summer?" Rose asked.

"I did. Dionne and Dorothy were young women, late teens and early twenties. Lovely girls, though different as night and day. Dionne was always fussing with her nails and playing the radio too loud, while Dorothy had her nose in a book."

"I understand there was a young man in Dionne's life, a pilot who passed away."

Viola nodded. "His name was Roger. He worked for the fishing captains here in Granite Cove, flying his tiny plane over the ocean to locate schools of fish." She paused. "Roger was a handsome fellow and the cause of the sisters' breakup. After he entered the picture, nothing was the same between them."

Rose leaned forward. "What caused the rift?"

Viola looked down at her folded hands. "I'm afraid that's privileged information, dear. I don't discuss my clients' personal business. I'm sure as a journalist you can understand that."

"Absolutely." She got to her feet. Somehow she'd have to worm the information out of Dionne's sister, Dorothy.

It was four o'clock and already dark when Rose took Chester out for an early walk. She paused outside the new houses clustered in the so-called meadow. Each was aglow with tasteful white lights strung around the three-car garage, the oversized front door, and the turret windows. Despite the display, the houses did not look welcoming. They looked like ads for *Gracious Living* magazine.

She pulled Chester along. She'd decided to visit the middle school that night, to check out the play rehearsals. At the same time, perhaps she'd get a chance to talk to Milton and hear his thoughts on Dionne.

Later, she ate a grilled cheese and tomato sandwich washed down with a glass of chocolate milk. At seven o'clock when she slipped out the door, Chester was asleep on the sofa.

The middle school parking lot lights were not lit, and so Rose parked close to the front door. Inside the building, she glanced around. The old school smelled the same as it had twenty-five years ago when she was a student. In fact, little had changed. The wooden floors showed more warp and wear, but the paneled walls and high ceilings still amplified every sound.

She headed down the stairs to the first floor, her hand gliding over the smooth wooden railing. This rekindled an old memory: it was late winter and she'd stayed after school for detention. Alone, she'd descended the stairs, her footsteps loud in the empty building. On impulse, she'd straddled the wooden railing to ride to the bottom, an act forbidden by Miss LaFlamm, the school principal.

The minute she mounted the railing, she realized her error. She'd failed to remove her fuzzy mittens. They didn't grip the polished wood. Over the side she went, a tall metal radiator breaking her fall. She had no idea how long she lay on the floor in a daze until she looked up at Miss LaFlamm's bulging eyes staring down at her.

Now, as she stepped off the bottom stair, the double doors swung open. Hyacinth and Nathaniel Chitwick appeared, the latter intent on unwrapping a giant candy bar.

"Hello," Rose said. "How are rehearsals going?"

"We're just leaving. I asked Chipper if Nathaniel could do his lines first. This is a school night. "

"How do you like being an actor?" Rose asked, leaning forward to study the boy for latent serial killer tendencies. Nathaniel gazed back at her. He'd inherited his mother's oversized nostrils, Rose noticed. Shrugging, he took a bite of the candy bar.

"Nathaniel," Hyacinth said, "recite one of your lines for Rose."

He dutifully took a step back and threw his arms out. "God bless us every one!" he shouted as melted chocolate ran from a corner of his mouth.

The sound reverberated in the enclosed stairwell. "Very dramatic," Rose said. "I hope Mr. Krazner hoists you high when you say that."

Hyacinth pursed her lips. "We're working on that. I suggested Milton get a personal trainer at the gym. Walter has no trouble lifting Nathaniel, but Walter plays racquetball three times a week." She shook her head. "You know how Milton's set in his ways."

Nathaniel, who'd finished the candy, licked melted chocolate from his fingers. "I'd better go in there," Rose said. "By the way, have you heard anything new from Chief Alfano?"

"They haven't found the car," Hyacinth said. "No clues."

"Did they find any... evidence inside the barrel?"

"Do you mean blood?" Nathaniel asked, wide-eyed.

"Hush," Hyacinth said. "We won't speak of that." She clutched the boy's arm and mounted the stairs. "You'll have to speak to the chief."

Rose heard Florence's shrieking voice even before she pushed open the heavy doors of the auditorium. A cluster of people occupied the first two rows. Chipper and Yvonne, clipboards in hand, were perched on the lip of the stage. The lights were low and the stage itself was empty except for a cot. Florence Huke, wearing a nightgown, lay upon it, kicking her thin legs and keening.

Yvonne waited until the noise was over. "Florence, keep that up and you'll exhaust yourself before the second act. If you're familiar with the play, you know that Scrooge is a reserved man. When the ghosts visit him, he's agitated, not hysterical."

Florence propped herself up on her elbow. "I think it adds excitement when I do it my way. It keeps the audience on the edge of their seats."

"It will send them running for the doors," Yvonne said. Exasperated, she turned to Chipper. "You tell her."

He unfolded his legs and got to his feet, crossing the stage to sit on the edge of the cot. "Yvonne is right, Florence. This isn't a teenage slasher movie. And remember, you're playing a male role. No man could hit those high notes. Scrooge is frightened but at the same time in control. You can show more emotion later when the Ghost of Christmas Future visits. By that time Scrooge is pretty shaken up."

Florence chewed her lip. "Okay, I'll tone it down, but that's not my biggest worry."

"What are you worried about?"

"What if on opening night I get nervous and forget my lines? I'll make a fool of myself in front of the whole town."

"Yvonne will be standing offstage," Chipper said. "She's the prompter. Listen for her cues."

"Jesus, Mary, and Joseph, when I get nervous my mind fizzles out. I get scared just thinking about opening night."

Chipper put a hand on her shoulder. "If you're too nervous to go on, I'm prepared to don the wig and nightgown. I can play Scrooge. I know the lines backward and forward."

Florence sat up and glared at him. "After all my hard work? Never! I'm gonna be the best Ebenezer Scrooge this town has ever seen."

He planted a kiss on her forehead. "That's my girl. By the time dress rehearsal rolls around, you'll be a pro." He rose and motioned to a group of young people leaning against the wall. "Chorus, come on up. I want you rehearsing. Everyone else take a break." He scanned the gathering. "Where's Mrs. Buckle, our pianist?"

"She's in the ladies' room," someone called out.

"When she returns, we'll start with 'We Wish You a Merry Christmas.'"

Rose, standing at the back of the auditorium, removed her notepad from her bag and headed down the main aisle. She spotted Milton to the left, sitting apart from the others. She moved down the row of seats to reach him. "Mind if I sit here? I want to ask you something."

His look was not welcoming. "Be my guest." He was dressed in a navy V-neck sweater and checkered shirt. Spotting her notepad, he groaned. "I hope you don't expect a quote."

She ignored his remark, taking a seat to his left. "You're a good sport to take part in this, Milton. Yvonne claims there's no shortage of women in community theater, while men are scarce."

"Chipper was very persuasive. He seems to think I'll make a good Bob Cratchit."

"Are you comfortable in the role?" she asked.

"Sometimes I even enjoy myself."

"How're things working out with Nathaniel?"

He hesitated. "You mean my son, Tiny Tim? We've had to make adjustments. Chip is working out the technicalities so I won't have to lift the lad. Apparently he'll stand on a chair and throw his arms around me from behind, giving the impression I'm carrying him. The alternative is a herniated disc."

"The audience won't know the difference," she said, patting his arm.

"Maybe not, but Dickens would roll in his grave. I'm sure he never intended for Tiny Tim to weigh a hundred and forty pounds."

"Things'll work out by opening night," she said. "Yvonne claims they always do." At that moment the chorus, accompanied by Mrs. Buckle on piano, began singing. Rose leaned toward Milton and asked, "By the way, I'm doing a story on Dionne Dunbar for *Bay State Living*. Would you mind being interviewed?"

He looked alarmed. "Me? I hardly knew the poor woman."

"You must have formed some impression..."

"Not really. If not for the mediums class, I doubt our paths would have crossed." He abruptly stood. "I'd better take a bathroom break while they practice."

"Sure. Think it over, Milton."

"There's nothing to think over. Miss Dunbar seemed like a nice young woman. It's tragic how she died." With that, he turned away, easing himself along the row of seats to the end. When he reached the aisle, he scurried off.

Rose watched him racing out the double doors. She slipped her glasses on and jotted a note in her pad: Find out Milton Krazner's office address.

Auntie Pearl's Helpful Housekeeping Hints

Dear Auntie Pearl:

I'm a midlife college professor who's finally met the woman of his dreams: Beverly is a school librarian, a devout Christian who sings in her church choir. After a year's courtship, we've decided to get married. And though our future looks promising, I have a family issue that's clouding the horizon.

You see, my sister, Louise, who lives in a neighboring state and has never met Beverly, is planning a celebration dinner at her house. She's sending invitations to all the relatives. And though I love my sister, I'm reluctant to attend because of my brother-in-law, her husband, Frank. The man is a loudmouth alcoholic who makes vulgar, chauvinistic remarks. He's ruined more holidays than I care to remember.

Beverly is not accustomed to such behavior and is certain to be offended. Do I risk alienating my sister by refusing to go, or do I risk exposing my fiancée to what could be an unpleasant evening?

Torn in Taunton

Dear Torn:

Right now my biggest concern is Louise, your sister. It appears the burden of entertaining has fallen on her shoulders, and I assume she's no spring chicken.

Today's hosts no longer knock themselves out. The new style of dining is casual and collaborative. I'm talking about the potluck dinner. The fun lies in never knowing what will appear at the table. Whether manicotti or marinated Brussels sprouts, surprise creates excitement.

Potluck would allow your sister to get acquainted with Beverly and enjoy her guests without being *chained to the oven. By the way, for a nice hostess gift, consider my book: Auntie Pearl's One-Pot Wonders.*

Order from my website: auntiepearlcooks.com.

Signed,

Auntie Pearl

CHAPTER SEVEN

The following day, Rose dropped in at the Granite Cove Library to speak to head librarian Ruth Bushmill. The woman was lining up candidates for the spring Adult Enrichment Lecture Series. Once again, she'd asked Rose to participate and talk about the *Granite Cove Gazette* and her position there.

When Rose last spoke, the men in the audience of retirees had focused on the paper's sports coverage. One had angrily declared, "You folks don't give the Bruins the credit they deserve." Rose had advised the critic to get in touch with Stewart, their sports editor. The man answered, "That guy's a sorehead." Against this, Rose had no defense.

She didn't particularly like speaking in front of people unless it was the stand-up comedy routine she performed on St. Paddy's Day at Green Pastures Nursing Home. The members of that audience, having been served beer at lunch, were in a receptive, albeit groggy, mood. She didn't take it personally when a few fell asleep.

After promising she'd once again be a speaker, Rose headed for the parking lot. As she unlocked the Jetta, a police cruiser slid into a nearby parking space. Cal Devine got out from behind the wheel. Despite the cold, he wore no jacket. He smiled, leaned against her car, and said, "You're a busy gal about town."

"What do you mean?"

"I mean, yesterday you're visiting Pastor Chitwick's neighbor. Last night you're at the middle school, and today you're at the library." His mirrored sunglasses prevented her from reading his eyes.

"Excuse me," she said, "those are all respectable places. What's your complaint? Are you stalking me, Officer Devine?"

He laughed and removed his glasses. "You're cute when you're feisty. I was merely making a point. You can't be anonymous in this town when you drive a lime-green Jetta."

"I get your point. Maybe I'll get the car painted so you'll never know my whereabouts."

His look was direct. "I'll always know where you are."

His stare was so unnerving, she dropped her keys and knelt to pick them up. "Speaking of cars," she said, "have you make any headway on the Dunbar hit-and-run?"

"We've got the paint chip number, but it doesn't match any work done in body shops up and down the Northeast coast."

"What about the tests? Didn't they find blood in the shredding barrel?"

"Yes, among other things."

She gave him a triumphant look. "So that proves the body was put inside the barrel like I told them. Why isn't Chief Alfano questioning me?"

"Because by the time we arrived on the scene, the area had been contaminated by five or six people. You've got the neighbors picking up the bloodstained paper scattered everywhere and shoving it back into the barrel. You've got another neighbor performing CPR on the body. You've got a dark street and no witnesses."

"Something tells me that if Dionne hadn't been a single woman with no ties in this town, more would be done. "

"Trust me, we're doing everything possible for a hit-and-run fatality. Unfortunately, the trail is as cold as the tip of your nose." With that he surprised her by leaning forward to kiss the very spot.

"Cal!" She glanced around, half expecting to see Cal's wife drive by. Marcie Ventamiglia Devine, from an old Italian family, was not one to mess with. "That's not very professional." Her prim tone sounded like Ruth Bushmill, the librarian.

He smiled and pushed himself away from the car. "Blame it on the Christmas season. It messes with my head." While heading to his cruiser, he stopped and turned. "By the way, what do you know about Marilyn's Pie Palace?"

She shrugged. "Their butterscotch pecan pie is excellent."

"Have you heard about any funny business going on there?"

"What do you mean by *funny*?"

"Keep your ears open and keep this quiet. We've heard rumors they're selling more than apple pies."

"Meaning what? Marilyn's a member of Yvonne's church."

"It's probably an employee making a little money on the side. Let me know if you hear anything and get back to me, okay, honey?"

Honey. She nodded, hoping he didn't notice her flaming cheeks.

Back at the office, she put in a call to Granite Cove Document Destruction Services, the shredding company where Dionne Dunbar had worked. She asked to be put her through to Dionne's replacement and was placed on hold. Immediately, she was treated to a recorded pitch extolling the company's services: *"Did you know that paper shredding is the best solution for the safe destruction of sensitive documents? Our document destruction services reduce cost and increase protection for your confidential client and business records—"*

A nasal voice interrupted the spiel. "This is Emma Ubbink, Director of Outreach Shredding Services. How may I help you?"

Rose identified herself and went on to explain that she was writing a piece about local efforts to be environmentally cautious. "I'd like to include your company in the article." When Ms. Ubbink didn't express any enthusiasm, Rose played her trump card: "While I'm at it, I'd like some figures from you. The *Granite Cove Gazette* may be needing your services. You wouldn't believe the stacks of newspaper in our basement."

The woman's voice got warmer. She arranged a meeting for the end of the week.

Yvonne, overhearing the conversation, looked alarmed. When Rose hung up, she said, "I hope you're aware that Mr. Curley won't approve such a thing. Given the cuts he's made in our budget, I'd be afraid to ask."

"I know," Rose said. "But if I present as a potential customer, I'll be treated a lot better."

"Why do you want an appointment with that outfit?"

Rose gave her a look of surprise. "Because they're a new company and they provide a valuable service. Our readers want to know about paper shredding. What do *you* know about it?"

Yvonne frowned. "Now that you mention it, very little outside of the fact it's something we citizens should be doing."

"Exactly. It's an important topic to cover." Rose didn't mention that the shredding plant had been Dionne Dunbar's last place of employment. While Yvonne had approved Rose's request to do a story on the dead woman, she didn't want her laboring over it.

"After all," she'd said, "it's gruesome, and people need cheering up this time of year. Why don't you talk to Farmer Hobbs about his animals on the church lawn? Mother and I love to stop and watch them. They're adorable."

Later that afternoon, Rose met Betty Ann at Mega Mug.

"Just coffee for me," Betty Ann said. "If you hear me order pastry, I want you to take it from me and fling it against the wall. I'm serious, kiddo."

"You've never ordered coffee only," Rose said, leaning back in the booth to unbutton her wool jacket. "Are you watching your cholesterol?"

"No, it's an emergency; I can't fit into my black velvet pants. They're the basis of my entire holiday wardrobe. Without those pants, I'll have to refuse every party invitation."

"What happened? Did you wash them?"

"Don't be daft. I'd never wash velvet pants. They're snug because I've been attending too many holiday parties. Yesterday morning the director of nursing hosted a coffee for the staff. It was held in the activities center because we've got the tables. They served eggnog, cheesecake, and sticky buns. What was I supposed to do, lock myself in my office?"

"I'm glad I don't face temptation like that at work," Rose said. "As for your pants, can you move the buttons over?"

Betty Ann shook her head. "Only a skinny person would say that. I haven't had a buttoned waistband since my baptism. All my pants have elastic waistbands. And now my favorite pair makes my butt looks like the Hood blimp painted black."

They were interrupted by Muriel, who'd worked at Mega Mug for so long she'd served Rose and Betty Ann when they were in high school. She stood over them silently, holding her order pad.

"Just coffee for me," Betty Ann announced, "with sugar substitute."

"Five dollar minimum per person during the holiday season," Muriel said tonelessly. "That don't apply to the counter, if you wanna sit there." She turned and squinted in that direction. "Oops, too late. They're all filled up."

"In that case," Betty Ann said, her face brightening, "I'll have the grilled chicken patty with cheese on whole wheat."

"Comes with fries or onion rings."

"Can I substitute fresh fruit?" she asked halfheartedly.

"No substitutes at lunch."

She sighed. "Alright, if you insist. I'll have the fries."

Rose ordered a BLT. "Can you bring a piece of foil to wrap half the sandwich to take home?"

After Muriel left, Betty Ann said, "There are two kinds of people in this world: those who take half a sandwich home and those who finish both halves." She gave Rose a baleful stare. "You know which one I am."

"Don't be so hard on yourself," Rose said. "Buy another pair of black velvet pants. There's no law against having two pairs."

"That's not the point. They're not just *any* pants, they're miracle pants. They're the Holy Grail of pants. Not only are they comfortable, they minimize my butt."

"You're a big, beautiful woman," Rose said. "Appreciate your curves."

"Knock it off, McNichols. I don't wanna hear that kind of crap from someone who's a size eight."

"Ten."

"Whatever. Do you know what it reminds me of?" When Rose shrugged, Betty Ann said, "It reminds me of a woman named Gloria. She used to be a volunteer at Green Pastures. Gloria visited with the reclusive residents, or those who had no visitors. She encouraged them to attend programs. When they declined, she'd remind them how much fun it was to sing along or play bingo with the other residents. She wouldn't accept the fact they might be tired or in pain. Gloria was relentlessly cheerful.

"Finally, I had to speak to her. I said, 'Gloria, you are in midlife, while these people are at the end of their lives. They don't want to sing World War Two songs or make a wreath for their door. They want to be left alone."

"Um, I don't get the connection," Rose said. "Gloria sounds beastly. How can you say I'm like her?"

"It's the inability to put yourself in another's shoes, or in this case, pants. In other words, don't tell a big woman to embrace her curves if you have none."

Rose glanced down at her flat chest. "Gee, thanks."

"Look, let's just forget it. I'm just stressed this time of year. It's busy at work. Residents' family members show up during the holidays. They hang around in the corridors getting in the staff's way. The nurses send them down to the activities center to 'see what's going on.' The interruptions are endless."

Muriel arrived with their coffee. "Here's the cream," she said, setting a small metal pitcher on the table.

"I meant to ask for skim milk." Having said that, Betty Ann poured a river of cream into her cup. "This will have to do."

As they ate, Rose talked about her visit with Viola Hampstead and the woman's connection to the Dunbar sisters. "Apparently Dionne and Dorothy had a falling out over a man named Roger, a pilot. I get the impression he dumped Dorothy for the younger sister."

"With men, it always boils down to one thing," Betty Ann said, "who's the cutest. What'd Roger do, fly off into the sunset with the kid sister?"

"I don't know. Viola clammed up on me at that point, claiming it's confidential. What I'd like to do is talk to Dorothy. "

"In that case, she's at Green Pastures on Fridays at two. She helps Father Gladioli give out Communion."

Rose smiled. "And I just happen to be visiting you when I bump into her?"

"You didn't hear it from me, kid. You know, I feel bad for Dorothy. She's frustrated by the department's handling of her sister's hit-and-run. Alfano never calls or keeps her up to date on the investigation. Unfortunately, she's not the type to squawk."

"I'm no fan of the chief, but in this case there's little to report. I talked to Cal, who claims they have no clues." Rose wiped her mouth on a napkin. "And by the way, it wasn't a hit-and-run. It was murder. Would a hit-and-run driver get out of the car and stuff the body into a barrel?"

Betty Ann frowned. "Could it be that during the impact her body somehow ended up in the barrel?"

"Betty Ann," Rose said, her voice raised, "the barrel was standing straight up when I knocked it over with my car. I got out to investigate and found the body *inside* the barrel. I am not delusional. I do not have dementia or psychosis. I'm a reporter. I trust what I see." She balled up her napkin and threw it at the table. "Why for God's sake won't anyone listen to me?"

Betty Ann glanced nervously at the nearby diners who stared. "Shh, honey, I believe you. If you say she was stuffed into a barrel, she was stuffed into a barrel." She flipped open the menu. "You got me so nervous I'm ordering the lemon crunch cake for dessert."

The Granite Cove shredding company's plant was a bland two-story building made of cinder blocks with narrow slit windows. It was on an unpaved road a short distance from Marilyn's Pie Palace. The shredding plant had been the first company to lease space in what the town fathers called Harvest Hollow Industrial Park. One year after its arrival, the plant stood alone in the clearing. Although city hall had offered tax breaks and other inducements, no businesses wanted to locate on that lonely stretch of land.

The old timers claimed it was because the area had once been an Indian ceremonial site. Not only that—the vast woods surrounding the park were said to be haunted. Town archives dating back to the seventeenth century indicated that those accused of witchcraft in nearby Salem had hidden in the dense woods. Later, a group of outcasts had formed a settlement therein. Now all that remained was a grave site with names etched into the boulders scattered about. All in all, Harvest Hollow was said to be jinxed.

Now Rose drove into the parking lot where there were a half dozen cars and two green trucks with Granite Cove Document Destruction Services printed on the doors. The building itself was like a concrete fortress. A single door looked as if it had been carved out of the stone; coupled with the narrow windows, it gave the impression that the company wasn't out to win any prizes in aesthetics.

Rose stepped into an office bright with fluorescent lights. A gray-haired man in a vest and bow tie sat behind a tall counter, typing on a desktop computer. He looked up when she entered.

"I've got an appointment with Emma Ubbink," Rose said.

"Have a seat. I'll call her."

She looked around the room and spotted a straight wooden chair sitting alongside cartons stacked to the ceiling. When the man resumed typing, she said, "I'm sorry to hear about Dionne Dunbar. What a terrible loss for you."

Without glancing at her, he said, "Thank you."

One minute later, Emma Ubbink, small and trim in a gray suit, appeared in the doorway. Her streaked brown hair was worn in stiff waves fanning her narrow face.

"Ms. McNichols?" she asked, peering through cat's-eye glasses. Rose got to her feet. "Let's talk in my office," Ms. Ubbink said. "I'll point out some general aspects of our operation on the way."

With that, Rose followed her to a tiled corridor that hummed with sound coming from behind the closed doors that lined it. Midway up the corridor, Emma stopped before a metal door. "This is a secure area where the shredding takes place," she said, turning the knob. Inside, four men wearing safety goggles sat before four waist-high shredding machines. Lining the walls were heavy gray bins like the one Rose had backed into.

Talking loudly over the noise, Ms. Ubbink said, "The end product will be baled and taken to Shoreline Recycling. They'll process it into pulp."

Rose nodded. "Interesting."

Leaving the shredding room, they proceeded down the corridor and came to a halt before another unmarked door. When Emma Ubbink opened it, they were hit by a blast of cold air. She motioned Rose inside. They stepped into a cavernous space with a concrete floor and an open garage door at the back. Here men in quilted nylon jumpsuits stacked blocks of shredded paper into a truck bed.

"If more businesses used shredding services, the cost of pulp wouldn't be so high." Ms. Ubbink peered at Rose. "Working at the *Gazette*, you must be aware of that."

"Absolutely," Rose said. She'd often heard Mr. Curley citing the high cost of pulp, along with online news content, as the biggest threat to his chain of suburban newspapers.

"Let's go," Ms. Ubbink said, her thin shoulders quivering in the cold.

Rose hoped they would go directly to the woman's office. She had questions regarding Dionne Dunbar. At the same time, she had to use caution when dealing with Emma Ubbink. The woman was a company wonk, not given to loose talk.

Back in the corridor, they stopped before another door. The room inside held a collection of tagged gray receptacles sitting under fluorescent lights. "The company delivers secured bins to your site and collects them when they're full," Ms. Ubbink droned. "We have a special coding system for each client."

"Secured, you say?" Rose said. "On the night of Dionne Dunbar's hit-and-run, the Chitwicks' shredding receptacle was open."

Emma pursed her lips. "We don't encourage our clients to leave receptacles open. Pastor Chitwick, however, allows parishioners to stop by and add material prior to our picking it up."

"I see," Rose said. "But doesn't that negate the purpose of shredding? Anybody can get their hands on what's inside if it isn't locked."

Ms. Ubbink smiled patiently. "Some of our clients are more concerned with being environmentally friendly than with protecting their identity." When Rose merely nodded, she said, "Would you like to go to my office now? I can create a cost-effective proposal customized to your specific needs."

"Sounds good," Rose said, stifling a yawn. Under the fluorescent lights she felt her soul shriveling. The thought of hearing a cost-effective proposal from the efficient Ms.

Ubbink was excruciating. Resigned, she followed the woman down the hallway to a sparsely furnished office.

Ms. Ubbink sat behind a desk devoid of anything but a computer and an office phone. Rose sat opposite and gazed up at a framed diploma, the only wall adornment. It was a degree from Coastal Atlantic University.

"Is that a New England college?" she asked as Ms. Ubbink pulled a calculator from a desk drawer.

"I took online classes for a degree in management and graduated last year."

"Congratulations," Rose said, picturing Emma Ubbink in cap and gown, sitting before a laptop while "Pomp and Circumstance" played. "Was Dionne Dunbar also in management?"

Ms. Ubbink was quick to respond. "Dionne was hired to do outreach—contacting community and business leaders to secure contracts. She had no experience in management."

"I see. I imagine she got many new contracts."

"When she put her mind to it," she said, glancing at Rose. "Dionne needed to work more at professional presentation."

"What do you mean?"

Ms. Ubbink pursed her pale lips. "I give workshops on professional presentation. Dionne never attended. I teach our salespeople how to act when dealing with potential clients. A professional presentation inspires confidence."

Rose wondered if Ms. Ubbink realized that her current presentation was giving her audience an urge to flee. Apparently not, as she warmed to her subject: "Now, my goal is in making the operation more professional in its interactions with the public. I don't know if you noticed the new uniforms on the shredding techs. Productivity increases when you follow a professional business model."

"They look very… professional," Rose said, stifling another yawn. The room was stuffy. She'd ask the woman to open one of the windows, but a glance told her they were sealed shut. Ms. Ubbink sat up straight. "Now let's talk about your newspaper. How many people are employed at the *Granite Cove Gazette*?"

"Ah, before I forget, I'll be seeing Ms. Dunbar's sister Dorothy at the end of the week. Is there anything you'd like the family to have, any personal items left behind?"

"As a matter of fact, I've collected some odds and ends from her desk and put them in a box. There's nothing of value: lipstick, a notepad, one or two photos. I didn't want to throw it out, yet I had no family names."

"I'd be happy to give it to Dorothy."

"Fine." She cleared her throat. "I'll give it to you before you go. Let's finish collecting data so I can formulate an estimate." She set a clipboard before her. "Now, how many copies of the newspaper are printed weekly?"

Rose sighed. She wasn't going to get off that easily.

After bidding Ms. Ubbink good-bye, Rose headed to the parking lot. She carried a folder containing the estimate along with brochures extolling the joys of shredding. She also carried a small cardboard box.

Once in the Jetta, she tossed the folder onto the back seat and turned her attention to the box. It gave her chills to imagine that Dionne had probably opened it every day. Inside were practical items, such as a tin of Advil, a small notepad, two red lipsticks, and a bottle of nail polish. Wrapped in plastic was a small framed photo. She slipped on her glasses and studied the picture. Three tanned, smiling men— two middle-aged and one younger—held a fish. It was big, the kind associated with Ernest Hemingway. The younger man, dark-haired and strikingly handsome, stood to the side, his smile restrained. The picture had been taken at the wharf; in the background was a sport fishing boat. Rose didn't need psychic powers to know the younger man was Roger, Dionne's lover.

She placed the photo back in the box and removed the notepad. Scribbled notes covered the pages, stopping midway through the notepad. She flipped to the end. The last notation was *Milton Krazner, Commercial Realtor*, with a phone number and an asterisk next to his name.

As she drove past Marilyn's Pie Palace, Rose decided to stop and get something special for her dad. She could talk to Marilyn about Dionne at the same time. After all, according to Kristal Swekla, the woman had been a regular at the restaurant.

The pie restaurant was the building's latest incarnation. Originally a Howard Johnson's, it had later been a bait and tackle shop. Following that, it was a tourist trap selling clamshells with badly painted seascapes, and bikinis woven from fishing twine. Marilyn had occupied the building for two years. Rose felt guilty for not patronizing the place more. She was glad the shredding plant provided a new source of business.

She pushed open the door and was enveloped in a wonderful aroma of fresh pastry and coffee. An older couple in bulky quilted coats sat at one of the five booths.

"Good to see you, Rose." Marilyn, in a frilly apron, smiled from behind the counter. "How about a warm slice of squash pie? If you'd come earlier, I could have given you our Christmas special, the Holy Night Pie."

"What's that?"

She indicated the couple in the booth. "Chet and Audrey have ordered it three times this week. Matter of fact, I spoke to Yvonne at church about putting a coupon in the paper—fifty cents off. What do you think?"

"Advertising's always a good idea. What's in the Holy Night Pie?"

"I'm out right now, otherwise I'd show you. The pie resembles a winter landscape: crushed Oreo cookies for the earth, and for the green, pistachio pudding. On top of that is a layer of whipped cream with coconut for snow. On the very top, there's holly berries—red M&M's—and silver sprinkles. Talking about the Holy Night Pie doesn't do it justice. You've got to see it."

"And taste it," Audrey called out. She had a dollop of whipped cream on her chin.

Marilyn nodded to her. "Those two are my best customers. They buy half a pie to share. When Kristal comes in at five, I'm going in the back to make more. "

"Oh, that's right," Rose said. "Florence Huke said Kristal was working here. How's she doing?"

Marilyn shrugged. "She's not the neatest employee, but she's friendly to the customers. The shredding plant's got half a dozen guys working the graveyard shift who come here on break. Kristal's a natural born flirt, though she wears too much makeup for my liking. I'm old-fashioned. My granddaughter, who's twelve, had her ears pierced. Can you imagine? My mother wouldn't let me wear lipstick until I was a senior in high school."

"Did Dionne Dunbar come in here?"

"She did, rest her soul. She didn't eat pie because she was always watching her figure, but she'd come in for coffee. She'd talk to Kristal and once gave the girl some earrings. I don't come in nights much. I leave it to my daughter Cheryl and Kristal to handle the evening shift. My husband's got diabetes and I gotta help him."

Rose nodded sympathetically. "I'd like to come in some night and talk to Kristal about Dionne. I'm doing a story about her for *Bay State Living*."

"I hope they catch whoever did it. If they find out it was that crowd over on Mannory Way, I hope to God Mayor Froggett closes that circus down. It's sacrilegious." She glanced at the couple in the booth, now winding on their scarves. "I've gotta get their check. You want a nice slice of prune whip for your daddy?"

"Do you have apple pie?"

"No apple today, but the prune's good. Got a touch of molasses."

It never failed to amaze her that Marilyn was often out of the most common varieties of pie yet always had a supply of prune or rhubarb.

"I'll come in soon to talk to Kristal," Rose said. "Maybe I'll try some Holy Night Pie."

"Call ahead to be sure it's available," Marilyn said over her shoulder. "I got a feeling this'll be our season's big seller."

CHAPTER EIGHT

Rose felt the tension in the newsroom the minute she arrived. At the door she encountered Coral, the Home & Garden columnist, who was just leaving. With a roll of her eyes, Coral brushed past Rose. Inside, Yvonne paced while talking on the phone. Stewart was barely visible, burrowed behind his desktop monitor. As Rose descended the stairs, he glanced up at her and rolled his eyes as well.

"Why don't I walk over now and show you?" Yvonne said into the phone. A moment later she continued, "I don't feel comfortable sending it over the Internet. We don't know what we're dealing with." With a furrowed brow she listened to her caller and in a quieter voice ended with, "Fine, Victor. Whatever you think is best."

Victor. Yvonne had to be awfully upset to use the chief's first name in front of them. Rose hung her navy peacoat on the coat rack and headed for the coffee pot as Yvonne hung up the phone.

"Oh, Rose, come here please. What a morning I've had." Yvonne clamped a hand to her forehead. "This arrived in the mail." She thrust a sheaf of papers at Rose. "I just talked to Chief Alfano. Originally I thought of calling the FBI, but Stewart convinced me to work with the local police." She sank into her chair. "Oh, Lord, the publicity. This could become a media scandal. What if they descend on our town?" She sank into her chair and scratched her forearm. Stress always aggravated Yvonne's eczema. "And tomorrow night is our annual holiday party. Maybe we should cancel. What will Mr. Curley have to say? I could lose my job over this. After all, the poster contest was my idea."

Rose glanced at Stew, who was tapping his head. "Yvonne, what's this all about?"

Yvonne pointed to the papers in Rose's hand. "It's the Homer Frost poster contest results. I've been saving them for the judges. The response hasn't exactly been overwhelming. I told Mr. Curley that young people today don't know how to use the postal mail. Anyway, this morning I was delighted to find three entries in the mailbox. That is, until I opened them. Look at the one on the bottom."

"Let me look at all of them," Rose said, taking the sheets from the folder. The first had a title written in heavy black marker: "Homer is My Hero." Below that was a rendition of the famed (in Granite Cove) horse and rider statue. The youthful artist had given the horse what looked like a unicorn's horn. Instead of the Civil War era military hat, the rider wore a Red Sox cap.

The second entry was even less skillful. A dwarfed Homer Frost perched on his horse like a circus monkey. His legs were so short they didn't reach the stirrups. The title was "Save Our Stattue."

"Hmm, I guess dictionaries are obsolete in the digital age," Rose commented. She turned to the last entry and was immediately struck by the sheer energy emanating from the computer-generated work. The setting was a photograph of the park. Superimposed upon it were sections of the statue that the artist had digitally "exploded" and spread across the park's trees, grass, and benches. The horse's legs protruded from the foliage and from a trash barrel. The torso of Homer Frost perched upon the granite fountain, while his head floated in the Frog Pond.

"I can't believe a middle school child did this." Rose said. "I can't even do basic Photoshop." She turned the poster over. The name "Diablo" was scrawled in pen. "Doesn't *diablo* mean devil in Spanish?"

Yvonne nodded, looking grim. "Now you see what we're up against. Chief Alfano and I are taking the poster to Ms. Fedderbush, the middle school principal. If this is some sort of threat, the school should be notified immediately." She stared at the poster. "Any child that created this is seriously disturbed."

"How many entries have you received?"

"Nine."

"My friend Betty Ann's stepson is a middle school student. He's into animation—superhero stuff—and hangs out in the graphics lab. Since this was probably done on a school computer, Jonah might know who did it." At the same time, Rose hoped Jonah wasn't behind the disturbing poster.

"I can't let you take it out of this office. I'm going to the station now to see the chief."

"Can you make a copy? I'll only show it to Betty Ann and Jonah. Whoever did this isn't going to voluntarily own up, especially if the police are involved."

"You may be right. Jonah might tell her what he wouldn't tell a teacher or police officer." Yvonne nodded. "I'll make one copy, but you are to hold this in strict confidence." Holding the poster by its edge, she headed for the copy machine

Rose thought the timing was propitious. Now she had a legitimate excuse to visit Betty Ann and "accidentally" bump into Dorothy Dunbar on the chaplain's rounds. When Yvonne handed her the sheet, Rose said, "Don't worry, we'll get to the bottom of this."

"Free booze always tastes better." Kevin Healey gazed appreciatively at his glass of scotch. He and Rose stood, drinks in hand, surrounded by guests at the annual *Granite Cove Gazette* holiday party, which was being held at the Gingham Dog.

"Yvonne didn't want to serve hard liquor," Rose told him. "She wanted wine and beer only. Stewart convinced her otherwise. Coral talked her into holding it in this function room."

The room was a new addition to the Gingham Dog. Owners Brad and Scott had realized the community needed an upscale venue for receptions and parties. Prior to that, villagers were reduced to renting the upstairs room at the Sacred Cod or the old standby, the function room at the Cove Motel. The latter was basically a beige carpeted box with all the appeal of a plastic storage pod.

Likewise it took some convincing to persuade Mr. Curley, the newspaper's publisher, to hire the Happy Hearth to cater the event. "Can you believe he wanted to serve supermarket cold cuts?" Yvonne confided to Rose. "I told him I would not host a party that served cold cuts." She shuddered. "When he hesitated, I said he could reduce our Christmas bonuses to cover the catering cost."

"What did he say to that?" Rose asked, frowning.

"He didn't get a chance. Stewart piped up and said he wouldn't be able to buy presents if he didn't get his Christmas bonus."

That's a good one, Rose thought. Stew would never spend his trust fund on something as trivial as family presents. Nonetheless, it bothered her that Yvonne would make such a magnanimous gesture at the expense of her poorly paid staff. On the other hand, Rose wasn't surprised. The annual holiday party was Yvonne's moment to shine— especially in the eyes of Chief Victor Alfano.

The money matter was resolved when the staff of the *Barnacle,* their sister paper in Harborvale, opted for a modest celebration of beer and pizza. This allowed the *Gazette* to splurge.

Now Rose gazed at the bar where their publisher stood with an arm around Mayor Froggett as if the pair had never exchanged a harsh word. "One hand washes the other," she said to Kevin. "City hall buys space in our paper, and we in turn endorse Ken Froggett every time he runs for office."

Kevin took a swallow of scotch. "It's not as if the mayor had any opposition. Any credible opposition, I mean. Remember that guy from the wharf, the union organizer who ran against him? He looked like a pirate. Talked like one too."

"Nobody has the guts to run against Ken Froggett," she said. "Yet everyone knows he's as crooked as our roads."

Kevin studied the tall, rangy man. As always, the mayor wore his signature outfit: a maroon sports jacket and gray tie. "He gets a healthy salary. So why does he wear the same old wig? That thing looks like a crow's nest hit by lighting."

Rose burst out laughing, spilling red wine down the front of her silk blouse. "I can't get through a night without making a mess," she said, dabbing the stain with a tissue.

"Your shirt's red. Don't worry about it." Kevin straightened his bow tie and stood up straight. "You didn't mention how I look, babe."

She looked him up and down, taking in the red jacket, polka-dot bow tie, and bright green pants. "I think you ought to let people know you're entertaining later tonight."

"Why don't you come down? My brother Terry's doing a couple sets. Did I tell you? He's got a regular stand-up gig Wednesdays at Remington's in Boston."

"I thought Terry was a science teacher."

"He is, during the day." He put an arm around her. "Come join us. Nobody puts on a Christmas party like the Sacred Cod. Besides, a bunch of my Boston College buddies are dropping by. They want to meet you."

Before she could respond, Florence appeared, carrying a tray. Spread on a paper doily were golden puff pastries. "Fresh from the oven. I thought I'd serve you kids first. This crowd's like seagulls at a clambake." She held the tray aloft. "I know Edith's shrimp puffs are your favorite, Rose."

"Florence, I dream of Edith's shrimp puffs. By the way, do you know Kevin Healey?"

"The Irish Fiddler," Florence said, smiling up at him. "The fish cutter's union had a retirement party at the Sacred Cod last spring. My sister took me as her guest. You had me shaking my bootie to an Irish jig, and I'm not even Irish."

"You could have fooled me, lassie," he said, kissing Florence's hand.

"Oh, he's wicked, darlin'," she said to Rose. "Take a couple napkins. Eat up."

After scooping up shrimp puffs, Rose turned to Kevin. "I need to speak to Florence for a minute. Do you mind?"

He rattled the ice in his glass. "I'm down a quart. I'll be at the bar."

When he left, Florence said, "Mother of God, that boy makes me wish I was twenty years younger." She sighed. "I wish Kristal could meet someone nice like that."

"Speaking of Kristal," Rose said, "I stopped by Marilyn's Pie Palace the other day. Marilyn seems pretty happy with your niece."

"God willing she keeps her. Kristal don't like working six p.m. to midnight, but she likes the money. Like I told you, she put a down payment on a Miata. Then she bought one of them little Apple computers." Florence shook her head. "Money burns a hole in that girl's pocket."

"Business is picking up at Marilyn's," Rose said.

"Thanks to the shredding plant down the street. The guys come in and leave big tips. I heard some of them are kinda simple, you know, in the head. I suppose Kristal leads them on. She always was a flirt, like her mom. Not that it ever got 'em anything but trouble."

"Where is Kristal's mother now?"

"Last I heard she was bartending up in the Canadian Rockies. Let her stay there, is what I say."

"I wanted to ask if Dorothy Dunbar is working for Edith."

Florence nodded. "Nice gal. She's got her religious duties as a chaplain, but her nights are free. She's perfect as hostess when we cater a party at Hemlock Point. Dorothy knows how to talk to the swells. I'm no good at that. You know me, Rose. I grew up on the wharf."

"Sounds like it's worked out for both Dorothy and the agency," Rose said.

"Yeah, but I don't think she'll be with us long. Soon's Mr. Farley clears the title on Dionne's condominium, Dorothy's putting it up for sale."

Before Rose could respond, Yvonne appeared. She wore a wrap dress the color of the cabernet in her glass and a shade of blue eye shadow not seen since 1968. "Rose, dear, don't stay in one spot all night. Circulate. Greet our guests. And by the way, Harriet Moffat, the Garden Club president, wants to discuss plans for a window box contest this spring. Doesn't that sound like fun?"

When Rose nodded glumly, Yvonne turned to Florence, grabbing a napkin from her tray and heaping shrimp puffs upon it. "These are getting cold, Florence. Time to circulate, both of you."

After Yvonne floated away in a cloud of White Diamonds perfume, Florence motioned for Rose to move closer. "This is between you, me, and the bar stool. Some nights after rehearsal, the chief's car is in the back parking lot. Yvonne always lags behind so she's the last to leave the building."

"He parks his cruiser there?" Rose asked, her eyebrows raised.

"Nah, he ain't that dumb. It's a black Town & Country SUV." She elbowed Rose. "Plenty roomy, if you get my drift."

Rose nodded slowly and looked across the room. Yvonne had delivered the shrimp puffs to the chief and was twirling the end of a filmy scarf draped around her neck. He wore his navy dress uniform with enough medals to sink the *Queen Mary.*

Rose turned to Florence. "Yvonne's right. We'd better circulate."

She headed toward the makeshift bar where Stewart served as paid bartender. "It's a win-win deal," he'd admitted. "I drink for free and collect the tips. Not only that—people tell the bartender their innermost secrets."

As Rose waited for her wine, Hyacinth Chitwick appeared at her side. "Happy holidays, Rose. You look lovely in that blouse. Blood is your color."

"Why, thank you, Hyacinth," Rose said, casting a glance at the woman's outfit. Hyacinth wore a skirt and sash that appeared to be made of burlap. A large copper pin anchored the sash to the jersey underneath. "That's a unique pin."

"It's an ancient Druid symbol for Christmas. I took a metalworking class a couple of years ago. By the way, I want to thank you for the story you did on our mediums class. We've had inquiries since then."

"I'm glad to hear it. And how's Nathaniel? Has he learned his lines for the play?"

"As you know, he doesn't have many. It's his physical presence that brings so much to the role. No one can do a soulful gaze like my son."

Before Hyacinth moved away, Rose asked, "You haven't been getting any more letters, have you?"

Hyacinth stared at her for a moment and finally said, "Yes. Two days ago. I knew you'd be here tonight, so I brought it with me. Nonetheless, if you hadn't asked, I wouldn't have mentioned it." She tapped her forehead. "I choose what thoughts will occupy my mind." With that, she opened a brocade purse the size of a cigarette pack. It hung on a long silk cord that crisscrossed her chest. She removed an envelope and slowly unfolded it. The outside address was, again, typed by a manual typewriter. Rose withdrew the folded sheet of paper. In the center of the page were the words *This is no joke. You are next.*

The following day, Rose visited Green Pastures. Her objective was to show Betty Ann the Homer Frost poster entry and later "accidentally" meet up with Dorothy Dunbar.

It was after lunch, a slow period for the activities department as residents rested in their rooms. Rose, sitting in Betty Ann's glassed-in office, stifled a yawn. As always, the nursing home was uncomfortably warm. She wondered how her friend could function in an environment where the thermostat was set at eighty. Once, when visiting her mother, Rose had attempted to open a window in the shared TV room. Her action was met with fierce opposition. The residents, dozing in their chairs, had awakened and shrieked in alarm, "There's a draft!"

Now Betty Ann examined the poster carefully. Finally she said, "I don't think Jonah's screwy enough to have created this." She held the sheet at arm's length. "On the other hand, maybe the kid's a budding genius."

"Unfortunately, Yvonne doesn't see it that way. Neither does Chief Alfano. Yesterday they visited Ms. Fedderbush, the principal."

"Frettin' Fedderbush," Betty Ann said. "She's been after Tiny and me to make an appointment to discuss 'family dynamics.' As if we haven't been through enough therapy with Jonah. You watch, she'll escalate this situation, probably call in the SWAT team."

"She can't do anything without the approval of the superintendent," Rose said, "and he listens to the chief." She reached for the poster. "In the meantime, can you show this to Jonah in confidence and see if he knows anything?"

"I'll do that," Betty Ann said. "Jonah hangs out in the school graphics lab. He and a buddy are into animation. We're encouraging that. The teacher's an older guy who used to work at an animation studio. Although Jonah's in danger of flunking most of his subjects, he's passing Graphic Communications with flying colors."

"He'll find his niche," Rose said. "Every pot has a lid." She got to her feet. "Now I'm going in search of Chaplain Dunbar."

Betty Ann glanced at the wall clock. "She should be on Hollyhocks at this time. Do you know where it is—to the left of the lobby?"

"I'll find it. And by the way, don't forget December twenty. Save the date. *A Christmas Carol* is playing that night. Why don't you ask Tiny to come?"

"If he doesn't have to bartend. If he goes, he'll probably fall asleep. He always does at the theater—unless there's nudity."

"The only thing close to nudity will be Florence Huke in a nightgown."

"I don't think that'll keep him awake."

Rose left the activities center and soon approached the nurses' station, a white molded plastic desk that resembled a giant marshmallow. Recessed ceiling lights shone down on the two nurses behind the desk. Heads down, they scribbled patients' notes, the endless documentation required by the nursing home, the state, and the federal government. The patients' files, thick loose-leaf binders, sat on a rolling cart.

Rose waited until one of the nurses turned weary eyes upon her, then asked if they knew the whereabouts of Chaplain Dunbar.

The nurse pointed her pen toward the hallway. "She should be down that corridor."

Rose thanked her and set off to roam the hall. As she passed open doorways, she glanced in. Many residents were in bed or propped up in wheelchairs, their thin frames leaning forward as if ready to topple. Seeing them reminded her of a line from Yeats: *An aged man is but a paltry thing.*

She was dismayed by the difference between the residents' rooms and the public areas. While the lobby, dining room, and sitting rooms were spacious and nicely furnished, the residents' rooms were crowded and poorly lit. To make matters worse, each was occupied by two or more people, similar to a hospital room. Rose discovered this fact when her mother was a temporary resident at Green Pastures. The day Lucille McNichols moved into her cramped, soulless room, she also learned that Phyllis Klodzik was her roommate.

"You reach your golden years and life plays tricks on you," Rose complained to Betty Ann. "Your roommate is your nemesis, someone you've loathed since high school."

Betty Ann sympathized. "Only Donald Trump can afford a private room. For the rest, insurance won't pay."

"My mother and Mrs. Klodzik are stuck in that tiny room pretending the other isn't there," Rose said. "I hope Phyllis doesn't snore, because my mother will throw something at her. Mom's never had much patience anyway. Since her stroke, she has none."

"If it's any consolation to your mother, Phyllis has dementia and probably has no idea who your mother is. Who can remember something way back in high school?"

"My mother can," Rose said. "Phyllis beat her to the English department's essay prize. Mom was editor of the school newspaper. Phyllis was a C student. Later Mom found out that Phyllis had a relative who worked at Little, Brown, the publisher. Apparently she got help with her essay."

Betty Ann shrugged. "Sure, it's tough to accept. But that happened sixty years ago. Your mother was still nursing a grudge?"

"B.A., don't tell me you don't have any long-term grudges."

Betty Ann frowned, lost in thought. "Yeah," she said. "It goes back to high school as well—the breeding ground for grudges." She glanced at Rose. "Do you remember Norma Demaso? Kinda bad complexion but big boobs?" When Rose nodded, Betty Ann said, "I was going out with Vinnie Ackerley, the basketball captain, and she was on the pep squad. The way she hung around his locker, I had a hunch she was after him.

"One day I heard about an incident at a game played at Medford High. Apparently Norma was outside the bus, holding a cigarette, wearing the little red skirt the pep squad members wore. When Vinnie showed up to board the bus, she asked him for a light. He didn't have one, of course, but went searching for one.

"When he came back with a BIC lighter, she got up on her tippy toes and kissed him. One of my friends saw them. It was no peck on the cheek, either. It was a full frontal body press. Anyway, I confronted Vinnie and he laughed.

Then I got mad. I said that tramp Norma knew exactly what she was doing. Vinnie defended her. Guys are such pushovers. He said Norma lived down by the wharf, she had a tough life. I should have let it go, but I was furious at him and Norma. I called him an idiot and more.

"That weekend we had a date to go to Boston to see the Christmas trees on the Common. Vinnie canceled at the last minute. He claimed his dad needed him to move furniture." Betty Ann sighed. "Monday, I was in Sociology class when someone mentioned they saw Vinnie and Norma at the movies in Revere. He'd driven all the way to Revere, hoping I wouldn't find out."

"So tell me," Rose said. "What if, forty years from now, you found yourself in a nursing home sharing a room with Norma Demaso? What would you do?"

"That's easy," Betty Ann said. "I'd put ground glass in her Pepto-Bismol. That's exactly what I'd do."

Auntie Pearl's Helpful Housekeeping Hints

Dear Auntie Pearl:

Recently our church held a silent auction to raise money for a new roof. The town merchants donated goods and gift certificates. Among the offerings was "Dinner for Two" at the Yellow Dinghy, a delightful local café. While I was writing my bid for this item, my neighbor Doris appeared and noted what I was doing. She took me aside and told me that the restaurant had a terrible black ant problem. An inside source had claimed the kitchen was infested with these ants. That was enough for me. I thanked Doris for the warning and moved on.

Not long after that, I spotted Doris and her husband coming out of the Yellow Dinghy carrying doggie bags. When I got home, I phoned my cousin Shirley, who'd helped organize the church's fundraiser. I asked if she would find out who won the gift certificate to the Yellow Dinghy. Shirley called me later to say it was Doris.

Auntie Pearl, we've been good neighbors to Doris and her husband. Now I'm tempted to speak to our pastor about her deception. My husband said to let it go. What do you think I should do?

Tricked in Topsfield

Dear Tricked:

Auntie Pearl may be a modern woman, but she prizes old-fashioned solutions to household problems. Borax not only freshens the laundry, it eliminates ants. Here's what you do: On a dry, sunny day, simply sprinkle the powder around the foundation of your home. Borax is safe for humans and animals, but deadly to ants.

It works as an antiseptic, too!

Signed,

Auntie Pearl

CHAPTER NINE

Rose stood in the center of the corridor, uncertain which way to proceed, when a door opened and Dorothy Dunbar stepped out. A rust-colored stole with embroidered gold crosses hung from her neck. Her hair was pulled back with a scarf.

"Why, Rose, how nice to see you. Are you visiting?"

"I was hoping to interview one of the residents, Mabel Coughlin, but I'm told she's asleep."

This was no lie; Mabel was soon turning 101. Rose planned at some point to interview her as she'd done on Mabel's hundredth birthday. Becoming a centenarian wasn't so unusual today. It was Mabel's "lifestyle" that was inspiring. She wore high heels and played the piano at the weekly sing-alongs. The woman attributed her remarkable health to growing up in a Dorchester triple decker and climbing four flights of stairs.

"When I see young people waiting for the elevator, I shake my head. You watch, they'll be using a cane by the time they're seventy," Mabel predicted.

Now, Dorothy said, "I see Mabel on Tuesdays when I assist Father Gladioli with Communion. Today I'm helping Pastor Chitwick."

"How do you keep everyone straight?" Rose asked.

Dorothy laughed. "It helps that I'm a retired bookkeeper and thus organized. Actually, my days end later than I plan.

I also deliver Communion to homebound members of the parish. Many are elderly and lonely. You can't rush in and out. Often I'll sit and talk. It makes for a long day, but I have a feeling of satisfaction when I leave."

"I'm glad I bumped into you," Rose said. "Maybe you're aware that I'm writing a story about your sister for *Back Bay Living*. Her death was a terrible tragedy for Granite Cove—and right before Christmas. If you feel up to it, I'd like to schedule an interview. "

Dorothy glanced at the wall clock at the end of the corridor. "I don't have to be at hospice for another hour. Would you like to go to the visitors' parlor and talk? This time of the week there's usually no one in there."

The visitors' parlor, named Sunnyfield despite its northern exposure, was empty. They seated themselves on a striped love seat that faced a fake fireplace. Rose took a steno pad from her bag and again thanked Dorothy for seeing her.

"It's no trouble," the chaplain said. "It also gives me a chance to learn more about you. I've been enjoying your articles in the *Granite Cove Gazette*. You have a gift for making each citizen appear unique. But then I've discovered the town is full of colorful people. When we summered here years ago, we weren't a part of village life. People were polite but kept their distance. It's only after living at my sister's and interacting with the townspeople that I've come to feel accepted."

"I'm told we're a clannish lot," Rose agreed, "but it doesn't mean we don't approve. By the way, I've met someone who was your father's caregiver when your family summered here: Viola Hampstead."

Dorothy nodded. "I've been meaning to call on Viola when my schedule lightens. Between my chaplaincy duties and helping Edith, I've had little time for catching up." She tugged her gray wool skirt over her knees. "Yes, Viola was devoted to my father. When Mother left us, he was inconsolable. Dionne and I were young. We couldn't adequately care for him. He had emphysema, you see, and needed skilled nursing care.

"The best medicine, he felt, was the sea air. Dad loved our cottage. He spent hours on the porch with his binoculars, observing the gulls. He was an amateur ornithologist. Apparently the rocks around Brier Neck, where we lived, are a stopping ground for a variety of gull species."

"That's what I'm told," Rose said. "They stop and move on."

Rose didn't blame the birds; she herself had spent the first half of her life devising plans to escape Granite Cove. She'd yearned to live someplace where people discussed topics other than the high school football team and the fishing industry. Later, she got her wish. However, after living in an upscale Boston suburb whose downtown was lined with designer stores but no coffee shop, and whose residents dressed all in black, she changed her mind. Rose had missed the cry of seagulls and the smell of fish sticks in the air.

"I always thought Viola was sweet on Dad," Dorothy continued. "He was a distinguished-looking man with old-fashioned manners. Viola's marriage, I understand, had provided little comfort."

"That's what she tells me," Rose said. "I don't mean to pry into personal matters, but Viola mentioned a young man, a pilot who worked here in Granite Cove. She said he came between you and your sister." She added, "Viola wouldn't elaborate."

Dorothy turned to gaze out the window. "I guess it's safe to say that Roger did come between us."

"Yet," Rose said, "it's apparent you made up with Dionne. At the memorial service, you spoke so highly of her."

Dorothy turned to Rose, a hint of a smile on her lips. "You're assuming it was Dionne, the younger, pretty sister, who stole Roger's heart."

"Well... I mean..." Rose felt heat rising on her neck. "Isn't that what—?"Dorothy placed a warm hand over hers. "I don't mean to make you uncomfortable. Of course you assumed a man might choose the younger, prettier sister. I'm sure everyone thought likewise. Why would a handsome young pilot want to spend time with Dorothy, the bookworm, when he could be with vivacious Dionne?"

She straightened the stole around her neck. "Here is what happened that summer long ago: One morning Dionne visited the harbor front to see about renting a rowboat. It was while making inquiries that she met Roger. He worked as a pilot for sea captains, helping them locate schools of fish. Before long, Roger became a regular visitor to our cottage on the rocks. While Dionne was upstairs getting ready, he'd join Dad on the porch. My father was curious about Roger's work and enjoyed talking to him."

She closed her eyes and leaned back against the cushions. "I can see them now, late afternoon on the porch, sitting in wicker chairs. I would be curled up with a book on a rattan lounger in the corner, listening to their conversation.

"Roger was from Caribou, Maine, far from home. He was mature for twenty-five. Sometimes, on the porch, he'd turn around and ask me what I was reading. At that time I was absorbed in the lives of the saints. I read everything I could get my hands on."

When her voice trailed off, Rose quietly asked, "When did Roger's interest turn from Dionne to you?"

Dorothy stared straight ahead as if watching events unfold. "He had a life-changing experience. One afternoon he was at sea in his little plane when heavy clouds rolled in. His instrument panel suddenly stopped working. Roger would have to navigate by sight alone. At the same time, he saw nothing but gray—gray ocean, gray sky. No landmarks. He didn't know if he was heading toward shore or farther out into the Atlantic.

"Roger had never been a religious person, but now he asked for help. He realized his life had been purposeless and empty, and he vowed if he got out alive he'd change. At that moment, he said, his head cleared. He immediately knew his course. He was no longer lost over the ocean.

"That night he arrived to pick up Dionne. They'd made plans to go to Canobie Lake Park in New Hampshire. Dionne loved roller coasters, and they had a new one, more thrilling than the last.

"However, after what had transpired that afternoon, Roger was still shaken and in no mood for amusement parks. From my corner of the porch, I heard him haltingly tell Dionne about his near brush with death. When he finished, she said, 'Does this mean we're not going out?'" Dorothy smiled. "For my sister, staying home on a Saturday night in the summer was a near-death experience.

"Dionne marched into the house, slamming the screen door behind her. Roger waited a moment on the porch, uncertain what to do. As he headed down the steps to leave, I called to him. I'd heard his account and wanted to hear more. I believed he'd had a divine intervention, similar to those experienced by the saints.

"To escape Dionne's wrath, we left the porch and climbed out onto the rocks. We sat for a while, watching the boats, their lights bobbing in the darkness. Roger told me what had happened that afternoon. As he described his confusion and growing panic, I felt his fear. He wanted to know what it meant. There was no reason for his instrument panel to quit. He had it checked later at Beverly Airport, and they could find nothing wrong.

"He wondered, had he been singled out? When he finished, I told him a little of what I'd read. In the lives of the saints, such 'miracles' were not uncommon. Before Roger left that night, I loaned him a couple of my books.

"He still continued to see Dionne. But while she was upstairs getting ready—my sister was never on time—he talked to me about what he'd read. I loaned him more books. Dionne noticed our private conversations and didn't like it. She began calling me 'Saint Dorothy.' Finally she instructed Roger to wait in his Jeep instead of coming to the house. She wanted all of Roger's attention." Dorothy shook her head.

"Time is a great balm, but it's important to set the record straight. Roger's experience on the ocean was what led him to become a Christian. As he got deeper into his faith, he had less in common with my sister."

She smiled. "All early converts are alike in their need to share with others who understand. And because Dionne didn't understand Roger's obsession, or his wanting to share it with me, we began meeting at the library in town. I'd pick out books I thought would be useful, and we'd discuss them. To be honest with you, I never expected Roger to develop romantic feelings for me. Although I was aware of his good looks, I saw him as a fellow pilgrim and felt obligated to help him along his road."

She gazed out the window with a serene expression. "Village libraries are so peaceful in the summer. We'd take our books and retire to an alcove overlooking the gardens, a gentle breeze wafting in through the window." She sighed. "Those were idyllic afternoons. I felt close to Roger, as if I'd always known him."

Dorothy closed her eyes. "One day we were in the stacks trying to locate a biography about a German theologian from the late nineteenth century. It was warm in the stacks, and quite dark. We were on our knees, searching the dusty lower shelves, when I became aware of Roger's scent. It was a clean smell, like the ocean in May. I must have been staring, because he turned to me. We clutched each other. The books I held tumbled to the floor..."

After a moment she resumed: "He had to tell Dionne. Fortunately it was the end of summer and Roger was returning to Maine. In November, he planned to fly down to Fort Lauderdale to work for a charter fishing company. Dionne was starting college in Connecticut, a freshman, while I was in my last year at Bryant. It was decided that I would join Roger during my Christmas break.

"I don't know how my sister took Roger's news. I was at school when she went off to college. I didn't hear from her. If my father suspected something, he wisely didn't mention it.

"That semester I scrimped and saved to visit Roger in Florida. The upcoming trip was like a beacon during the dark days of autumn. One morning in late November, I made a reservation with Greyhound. I pictured myself during the long bus ride to Fort Lauderdale, happily dreaming of Roger and me, finally together. That afternoon, while Roger flew south en route to Florida, his little plane was hit by lightning. They never located the spot where it went down. A section of the wing washed ashore in Hilton Head, South Carolina." She attempted a smile. "Ironic, wasn't it?"

At seven thirty that night, Rose drove to the middle school parking lot. She'd decided to drop in on the play rehearsal, ostensibly to take notes but actually to talk to Hyacinth and Milton. She'd been feeling increasingly nervous about the anonymous letters. By maintaining a silence, was Rose an accessory and thus liable? The situation was worrisome; it was time to confront Hyacinth. At the same time, she needed to talk to Milton about Dionne's notebook.

She parked in the second row and glanced around. Although lights glowed from inside the brick school building, the lot was only dimly lit. She quickly locked her car and scurried to the front door.

Inside the lobby, the walls were lined with posters and flyers. *This is a Nut-free Zone,* one proclaimed. Another illustrated the appropriate way to sneeze. When had that trend taken over? she wondered. It seemed that overnight the population had begun blowing their noses into their sleeves. Appalled, Rose continued to use tissues.

She swung open the double doors of the auditorium. The first few rows of seats near the stage were occupied. She crept down the sloping aisle and slipped into the row behind Hyacinth Chitwick.

After removing her jacket, she turned her attention to the brightly lit stage where a small group was clustered. Yvonne, clipboard in hand, sat near the lip of the stage next to Chipper. Florence, wearing a flannel nightgown and sneakers, lay on a cot. Milton stood in the center of the stage with Nathaniel crouching behind him. Furniture had been strategically placed: the narrow cot, a fireplace with mantle, a side table, and a battered leather recliner.

Chipper took Nathaniel's arm and moved him back. "Let's do this gently," he told the boy. "Don't leap onto Milton. Instead, can you drape yourself across his back, right before he attempts to stand?" When Nathaniel nodded, Chipper glanced around. "Wait a minute. Let's give Milton a little support." He grabbed the edge of the table and pulled it closer.

As the cast members watched, Florence said, "Tiny Tim's supposed to be crippled, so if this doesn't work, maybe he could sit in a wheelchair and Milton could push him."

"For God's sake, Florence," Milton said, "they didn't have wheelchairs in Dickens's time."

"They didn't have La-Z-Boys, neither," she said, nodding at the recliner.

"No bickering," Chipper said, dragging the table to Milton's side. "The wardrobe department has a lovely old quilt to cover the chair. Keep in mind this furniture is only here to suggest Scrooge's bedroom. By the dress rehearsal, we'll be properly fitted out." He turned his attention to

Milton, who was on his hands and knees staring at the floor. "Let's try it now, Milton, using the table for support."

Chipper turned to Nathaniel. "Okay, Tiny Tim, remember to go easy. Don't fling yourself onto his back. Drape yourself instead. Are you ready?" When the boy indicated he was, Chipper stepped back, joining the others. "Let's do it."

Nathaniel took a few steps backward, frowning in concentration. After a moment he approached the crouching Milton, throwing his arms around the big man's shoulders while straddling his back. All was silent as Milton, one hand clutching the table's edge, grunted and slowly came to a standing position, his face beaded with sweat.

Nathaniel waved and shouted, "God bless us, every one!"

With that, the observers broke into applause.

"Great job, Cratchits," Chipper said, helping Nathaniel down. He glanced at his watch. "Let's take a ten-minute break. The chorus has to rehearse, so don't be late getting back."

As Milton wearily descended the side access stairs, Rose waited at the bottom. Seeing her, he said, "Ms. McNichols, if you don't mind, I have to visit the men's room."

"I'll wait. You haven't returned my phone calls, so I thought I'd speak to you in person."

"I've been busy. There's a new retail complex going in at the wharf, in case you don't know. I'm handling the leases." He turned away. "Now if you'll excuse me—"

"I've been busy too, writing a profile on Dionne Dunbar. I thought you might shed some light on her."

"Didn't you hear Hyacinth explain how some members of the group wish to remain anonymous? Perhaps anonymity means nothing to you, not that I'm surprised."

"I wasn't referring to the mediums group, Mr. Krazner. I'm referring to Dionne's personal relationships, the ones she wrote about in her notebook. Needless to say, you're in it."

He moved closer and glanced around. "What is it you want? I've got a sick wife at home."

"I just want to talk to you about Dionne—off the record."

He took a handkerchief from his vest pocket and mopped his broad forehead. "How about Wednesday morning?"

She withdrew her notepad and scanned a page. "Wednesday morning at eleven?"

He nodded. "At my office. If you know so much about me, I don't have to tell you where that is."

She put the notepad away. "That's right, you don't."

When Milton vanished up the aisle, Rose looked around the auditorium. She spotted Hyacinth on the other side, moving down a long row of seats to reach the aisle. Rose rushed to intercept her.

The pastor's wife wore a long-sleeve purple T-shirt with the letters S.O.U.R. across the front. Seeing Rose's curious glance, she said, "It stands for Spirit of Universal Resonance, the acronym for my business."

"Yes," Rose said, "you mention it in your recorded phone message."

"I try to educate people that we are all spirit, and spirit is universal. Communication between the spirit world and the earthly plane will resonate freely if one uses the appropriate frequency."

"And what is that frequency?" Rose asked, stalling for time until she could discuss the more important issue.

"Just as you fine tune a radio's frequency, you also prepare your mind to intercept messages from spirit. This is what we do in class. We train the mind to be an open channel. But first"—she stared intently at Rose—"we must get rid of negativity. Spirit is loath to enter when there is negativity."

Rose had the uncanny feeling that Hyacinth was peering into her mind's warehouse of negativity. Before the woman could suggest an antidote, Rose said, "Say, wasn't that wonderful the way Milton lifted Nathaniel? I think the play will be a big success."

Hyacinth shrugged. "I suppose Milton will get better with practice." She slid her arms into a fleece vest.

"I'll let you go," Rose said, "but first I need to ask if you've gotten any more threatening letters."

Hyacinth pulled on the zipper. "None."

"Because I'm not comfortable with the way things are. My knowing about your letters and not doing anything could incriminate me. I believe that whoever ran Dionne down is threatening you, Hyacinth. Maybe you wish to keep it secret, but think of your family."

Hyacinth's expression was stony. "I'm sure that whoever hit Dionne was another drunken Mannory Way partygoer. As for as for my letters, no doubt they're from a jealous parishioner. It's common for men of the cloth to attract needy women. Call it forbidden fruit." She shrugged. "Walter's had to deal with such situations in the past. It's an occupational hazard."

Rose tried vainly to picture the pastor, with his chipmunk cheeks, as a sex symbol. "Maybe you wish to see it that way, Hyacinth, but I believe it was no accident that killed Dionne. I think it was deliberate, and I think they've got their sights on you. Meanwhile, I'm suppressing evidence by not coming forth."

Hyacinth's smile was maddening. "You've got a writer's fertile imagination, Rose. You're making the incident more than it was—a tragic hit-and-run accident." She slung her pocketbook over her shoulder. "Now, if you'll excuse me, I've got to take my son home. Tomorrow's a school day."

The sun broke through, the following morning. Although the temperature hovered at thirty-five degrees, the sun's rays reflecting off the snow made it feel warmer. After lunch, Rose went out to her car in the municipal parking lot to make a private phone call. The Jetta was toasty inside. In fact, the warmth was so inviting she fought an urge to take a midday snooze. Instead she took a big gulp of coffee from her insulated mug. Then she punched in Cal's number on her phone.

"Rosie, you caught me on the way out. Where are you?"

"Right now I'm in my car in the parking lot behind the office."

"Parking? Wish I could join you."

She ignored the banter. "I need to talk to you in private. It's about something that was revealed to me in confidence, and"—she sighed into the phone—"something tells me I shouldn't keep it a secret."

"You've come to the right place, honey. Tell you what, I'm going to St. Rupert's Church in an hour to check out a situation there. How about meeting me in the parking lot? There shouldn't be many people this time of day."

"Thanks, Cal. I'll see you there."

She put her phone away, feeling a sense of relief as well as trepidation. She'd been flattered when Hyacinth confided in her about the letters. Yet, before long, the knowledge had created a burden, which grew heavier with each passing day. Although Hyacinth thought the letters were the work of an obsessed parishioner, Rose—certain that Dionne's death was no accident—felt otherwise. In any event, she would be relieved to discuss the situation with Cal.

As she reached for the car door handle, she spotted Viola Hampstead, two rows away, unlocking her little tan Honda. The sun's glare prevented the woman from noticing Rose. A thick scarf covered Viola's lower face while a brown fitted hat concealed her hair. Viola's face was so covered up, Rose wouldn't have recognized her had she not been parked nearby.

After a quick look around, Viola tossed something into the car and hopped into the driver's seat with an agility that belied her age. She backed out of the parking space and raced out of the lot.

Minutes later, when Rose returned to the office, Yvonne called out, "Have you drawn a name for our Secret Santa?"

"I didn't think we were doing it this year," Rose said, descending the stairs.

"Of course we're doing Secret Santa. We do it every year."

"For the past two years," Rose reminded her.

"For a young woman, you're awfully glum. Where's your holiday spirit?"

The editor's giddy mood led Rose to believe that something had happened between Yvonne and the chief at the office holiday party. The day after the party, Stewart had sidled up to Rose at the copier. Talking from the side of his mouth like a film noir character, he'd informed her that Yvonne had hired a caregiver for the night of the party with instructions that she might be "late."

"What of it?" Rose said. "She had to play hostess for Mr. Curley."

Stew got to the point. "Did you see how she and the chief were cozying up?"

Rose hadn't missed a thing. At one point she'd spotted Yvonne feeding shrimp to the police chief. She hoped Yvonne had remembered to remove the toothpicks.

Nonetheless, she didn't want to admit her curiosity to Stew. It made her feel embarrassed and guilty. Spying on Yvonne and the chief was a secret vice, like her subscription to the *Enquirer*. Thus she neither encouraged nor discouraged Stewart's talk. The latter would result in him keeping his stories to himself, and Rose would miss the juicy tidbits. How Stewart unearthed his information, she never knew. Yet she didn't doubt him, no matter how wild the tale.

For instance, he once told Rose about Coral, the Home & Garden columnist. According to Stewart, she'd been stopped by the Granite Cove Police last summer for driving intoxicated on a back road in Hemlock Point. At the time, Coral had been wearing nothing but a bra and panties. Because Coral's father-in-law was a retired state police captain, the incident never made it to the police blotter.

Now Rose told Yvonne, "I've got plenty of holiday spirit. But from last year's Secret Santa I got an old snow scraper when I'd bought a twenty-five-dollar gift card to Mega Mug."

Keeping his eyes on the computer monitor, Stewart piped up, "I'll have you know that was a new scraper."

"Oh, sure. It was all beat up."

"That's 'cause it was in the remainder bin."

"We were instructed to spend at least twenty dollars on a gift, Stewart," Rose said.

He looked up. "That kind of materialistic attitude takes the joy out of the season."

Rose glared at him. "It's cheapskates like you who—"

"Now, now, let's have no bickering," Yvonne said. "Rose, I want you to draw a name." She reached into her desk and withdrew a coffee can covered in red felt. "And Stewart, if you don't spend at least twenty dollars for a gift, I'll see that it's deducted from your paycheck."

"And I'll call the ACLU for forcing employees to embrace your religious beliefs."

Yvonne nodded at her desk phone. "Fine, be my guest."

"Okay," he relented. "I'll buy a present, but I want you to know it means I won't be able to get my sister anything this year."

"I'm sure the pleasure of having you as a brother is more than enough." Yvonne winked at Rose, who grinned in return. After picking a name—Coral's—Rose remembered whom she'd seen in the parking lot.

"Yvonne, are you familiar with Viola Hampstead?"

"Why, yes, the little woman who used to do caregiving for Mother."

"You say 'used to.' Why did she stop?"

Yvonne replaced the can in her drawer. "Let's see. I believe Viola was something of a disappointment..."

"Do you mind saying why, or is it personal?"

"Nothing like that. Viola was very nice, but I'm afraid she wasn't creative enough for Mother. She was a mediocre Scrabble player, while Mother's played in tournaments at the county level. Not only that, Viola balked at doing toileting—"

"I see," Rose said, and decided to let the matter drop.

CHAPTER TEN

Before meeting Cal at St. Rupert's, Rose took a detour to Mannory Way. Like the city of Salem during Halloween, Mannory Way had become a Christmas destination for revelers. The houses that dotted the meandering street had been built five years earlier, when the much-anticipated extension to Route 95 opened. Developers marketed the area to those working in Boston, commuters who'd previously considered the North Shore too far away.

Mannory Way was presented as an alternative to condo or apartment living, to those who wanted the security of home ownership. But the population was young and mobile. When the Granite Cove Chamber of Commerce commissioned a study, it discovered that Mannory Way residents viewed Granite Cove as a place to sleep, Boston being their preferred choice for entertainment. Consequently, the chamber launched a new program: *Just Say Hi, Neighbor!* Friendliness, they figured, was all it took to lure the newcomers to Granite Cove's downtown "and all it has to offer."

Mega Mug was one of the first to reach out; the restaurant offered a free doughnut to anyone who could prove, via a real estate tax bill, that he or she was a new resident. Despite similar lures by various downtown establishments, the only local hangout that won the newcomers' loyalty was the Sacred Cod. Mannory Way residents adopted the ancient waterfront bar and restaurant as their own.

Tiny Zagrobski, a bartender at the Cod, had no problem with the newcomers even though he frequently had to quiet them. They tipped big, and often. "Mannory Way?" he said. "God love the little devils."

"They're not a nice crowd," Yvonne had declared not long after the sidewalks were poured. "We were led to believe by Spencer Farley, the developer's attorney, that the area would attract young professionals. I had second thoughts when I saw the gigantic satellite dishes sprouting from rooftops and the oversized garages housing heavy trucks. Why would anyone commuting to Boston want a truck?"

Rose shrugged. "Protection against Boston drivers?"

"Furthermore," Yvonne said, warming to her topic, "Phyllis at the chamber tells me two-thirds of Mannory Way residents are divorced or separated. Folks call it Heartbreak Hill. She claims that on summer weekends they gather at a designated backyard, preferably one with a pool. They charge twenty dollars per person to party all night, drinking and running around half naked."

"How does Phyllis know that?"

"Her son Timothy is friendly with a young man who lives there. Timothy says the friend's home is like a fraternity house with people coming and going. Phyllis is afraid Timothy will meet the wrong sort of girl."

"I suspect that's why Timothy hangs out there," Rose said. "It's not called Mammary Way for nothing."

"I feel sorry for the families who were duped into buying. I'm told the police often go out in response to noise complaints. In the meantime, Mayor Froggett is reluctant to take action, even after the tragic hit-and-run."

"Just say hi, neighbor," Rose said, "and then kick butt."

Yvonne sighed. "I'm glad Mother and I live downtown. Our condominium is quiet at night. We love to bundle up and sit on our little lanai."

"If the chamber program succeeds, it won't be quiet for long," Rose said. "They want the rowdies to go downtown and spread the wealth."

"Somehow I can't see that bunch at Mega Mug, unless they start serving beer." She slapped a hand on her desk. "And that will never happen as long as I have breath."

"Amen."

Now Rose navigated the U-shaped street that was Mannory Way, dodging the trash barrels that lay in the road. The city trucks had come and gone, but no one was at home to bring in the barrels. The street looked abandoned under the bleak winter sun, the gaudy decorations devoid of gaiety. The towering inflated Santas and snowmen of the evening now lay bunched in the dirty snow. Like an aging burlesque queen, Mannory Way needed a cloak of darkness to get into a party mood.

· At the end of the road, Rose swung onto the main street and headed toward St. Rupert's. She pulled into the driveway of the church, passing between a pair of blue spruce flanking the entrance, and continued to the parking lot. A half dozen cars were there, including Cal's cruiser. Instinctively she parked as far away from his car as possible.

When she stepped out of the Jetta, she saw him standing at the split-rail fence watching the nativity animals grazing on the slope below. He turned, as if sensing her, and watched her approach.

"You look like one of Santa's elves in those tights," he said.

She yanked her skirt down over her red leggings. "I'm five-ten. Too tall for an elf."

"I wasn't talking about height. I was talking about cute."

"You want to see cute, come to *A Christmas Carol.* Florence Huke plays Scrooge in a cap and nightgown."

"I'm taking my two oldest boys. Marcie's working the ER that night."

Any mention of Cal's wife made Rose feel awkward. To cover up, she said, "I heard that some guy recently pulled a knife on a nurse in the ER. I hope Marcie wasn't on duty at the time."

He shook his head. "That was a meth addict en route to Bridgewater. No, she wasn't on duty. If she had been, there'd be nothing to report. No one tries that stuff on Marcie."

She heard the faint undercurrent of pride in his voice. "I guess your wife's a dynamo."

He grinned. "Why, Rosie McNichols, I believe you're jealous."

Angry and embarrassed, she whacked him with her pocketbook. "Don't flatter yourself, Cal."

"Then how come you're blushing? You can't lie to me. I know you too well."

She turned away to face the animals. "I've got to get back to the office. Can we get down to business?"

"Okay, okay, but first give me your opinion." He gestured at the fenced-in tableau before them: the wooden stable, the donkey peering over the fence, two sheep and a goat at the food bin. Then he inhaled and asked, "Do you smell manure?"

"Manure?" She leaned over the fence and sniffed the air. "The only thing I smell is diesel exhaust from the passing cars."

"Right. We got complaints from a couple of women who rent on Mannory. They're busting our balls with their threats. The smell is the latest. They're threatening to file a complaint with the health department."

"You mean to shut this down?" Rose asked, incredulous. When he nodded, she said, "But everyone loves St. Rupert's pageant. People come from all over to see it. You can't have a Christmas pageant without donkeys and sheep."

"I told them it's an old tradition."

"I assume they're not locals," she said.

"Nope, and neither is their landlord, the guy who owns the house. By the way, he hasn't paid his real estate taxes in three years."

"So basically they're calling the cops and using town services for free."

"They're not the first," Cal said. "Many of the original Mannory Way buyers can't make mortgage payments, so they're renting out. Some houses have four or five guys under one roof. The other night they had a keg party in the snow, a dozen guys running around with their shirts off." He turned to rest his back against the fence. "That's the life of a Granite Cove cop. Now, you wanted to talk about something?"

Haltingly at first, she told him about the threatening letters and Hyacinth's response. "At first she was upset by it. Now she appears to be brushing them off, claiming it's a parishioner with a crush on the pastor. Hyacinth said it's not unusual for women to become attracted to 'men of the cloth.' She called it forbidden fruit."

He nodded. "Happens with cops, too."

"Well, I can understand in your case. But Pastor Chitwick is... well, he's nerdy."

"That's a fair assessment. But what makes you think it's not a lustful parishioner?"

"It was the second letter, the one that said 'You're next.' Obviously the writer was referring to the hit-and-run. Don't you see? Whoever killed Dionne is threatening Hyacinth. Now I'm wondering if she might have been the target all along—a case of mistaken identity." She paused. "Maybe they're targeting all the members of the mediums class."

He scratched his chin. "The message could be interpreted several ways—"

"Cal Devine, you don't believe me, do you? You still think Dionne's hit-and-run was a random accident. You're disregarding my version of the story about finding the body inside the recycling barrel."

"It was dark that night, Rosie. You were shook up."

She crossed her arms over her chest. "I'm a seasoned journalist, not some shrinking violet who falls apart in a crisis."

He grinned. "You're a prickly rose who's cute as hell." When she bridled at this, he placed a restraining hand on her arm. "Don't hit me again with your bag. Just listen to me." He faced her. "When I was a criminal justice major in college, I took a lot of psychology courses. We learned the effects of shock on the nervous system. Under extreme circumstances your perception becomes distorted. Adrenaline causes the brain to record events incorrectly. Over the years I've found that to be true."

She stepped away from him. "Thanks for the lecture on psychology, Officer Devine. Your opinion of me isn't flattering. Because my story doesn't jibe with your theory, I must be addle-brained."

"No, you were confused." He sighed. "Okay, let's agree to disagree. In the meantime, I want to talk to Hyacinth. Do you think she'll show me the letters?"

"Probably not. One thing I know: she'll be furious with me for telling you. She said if I did, she'd deny them and you'll think I'm making up another wild tale."

He smiled. "If it's any consolation, honey, I believe you."

Her eyes widened. "You do?"

"I mean, I believe that you saw the anonymous letters." He shrugged. "If she won't show them to me, there's little I can do."

"Just lay on the old charm," Rose said, "and you'll have no trouble."

"That's what I'm afraid of. I'll make sure to visit when Pastor Chitwick is at home."

"Don't count on it," she said.

When Rose got back to the office, Yvonne called out, "Just the person I was looking for, our incomparable, intrepid reporter."

Rose paused on the stairs, her eyes narrowed. "What's this all about?"

"Can't I give a compliment without arousing your suspicion?"

"Sorry," Rose said, continuing down the stairs. "It's just that you sprang it on me the minute I walked in the door." Besides that, Rose was still irritated by her meeting with Cal. She unbuttoned her coat and approached Yvonne's desk. "So, what's up?"

Yvonne waved a pink Post-it. "You're going to like this one. Your admirer Myrna Phipps is having a party to introduce Manuel del Toro, a visiting artist from Spain. Apparently, he's up-and-coming in the art world. "Not only that—the party's being catered by the Happy Hearth."

"I guess I can do that," Rose said. She'd get a chance to hear Florence's take on the members of the mediums class. The woman had a natural curiosity coupled with a lack of discretion when it came to other people's business.

Additionally, there was the lure of Myrna and Lester Phipps's Hemlock Point waterfront mansion. The older couple looked upon Rose as a savior ever since she'd solved the mystery of their beloved dog Raul's neurosis.

"Give me the details," she told Yvonne.

Yvonne stuck the note to her desk with a sigh. "How I envy your footloose and fancy-free lifestyle."

"I'm not footloose," Rose grumbled. "Kevin and I have been dating steadily for quite a while."

"Ah, Kevin, a sweet lad. You're not taking him to the Phippses' party, are you?"

"No, he's got a Christmas gig at the Sacred Cod that night. And if you recall, Kevin was a huge hit with the Phippses at their party last year. Myrna adored him."

Indeed she did. The older woman had lured Kevin into a dark pantry on the pretense of installing a lightbulb. She'd thrown herself at him until Kevin managed to escape and hide in a vacant bedroom upstairs.

"He's charming," Yvonne said. "Nonetheless, I keep picturing you with someone more mature and urbane."

"You talk like Kevin's in high school. I'll remind you he's only four years younger."

But Yvonne had wandered to the coat rack, from which she removed her lavender poncho and matching hat. "I'm going to Mega Mug to pick up a sandwich," she said. "I've instructed their counter girl on how to make a wrap without using bread. You simply layer the ingredients within two large leaves of romaine lettuce." She looked in the hall mirror and adjusted her hat's floppy brim. "Dieting is so hard this time of year," she said, pursing her lips.

When she finally swept out the door, the room was quiet until Stewart spoke up. "Nothing like a love affair to help lose weight. The pounds drop along with the knickers."

"Are you speaking from experience, Stewart?" Rose asked without turning around.

"Don't get self-righteous with me, McNichols. By the way, I saw you in the parking lot with Cal Devine the other day. You two looked cozy. "

"That was business, I'll have you know. You're such a weasel, spying on everyone." She had a sudden revelation. "Know what? Too bad Yvonne didn't ask you to play Scrooge in *A Christmas Carol.* You've got all the man's qualities."

"I wouldn't be caught dead with that pack of losers. And by the way, regarding the Phippses' party, Yvonne first asked Coral to cover it and she refused. Her husband's having gallbladder surgery. You were second choice." He snickered.

Rose hunched her shoulders, staring at her computer screen yet seeing nothing. What had Hyacinth said about avoiding negativity? Something about imagining her mind as a clear lake and not allowing anything to mar its surface. Stewart's nasty remarks had churned the waters of her mind into a tsunami.

At the same time she recognized something behind his bitterness: jealousy. Despite his family name, Stewart was rarely invited to parties. The guy was a black cloud, socially. Unable to change the situation, he retaliated by belittling others. When Rose won the prestigious Woman of the Year award, he claimed it was because the Women's Professional League had felt sorry for her. After all, Martha Farley *had* attempted to drown Rose one summer night. "Mad Martha" would have succeeded if Cal Devine had not come to the rescue.

Stewart's attack had the spitefulness of a schoolyard bully, yet it felt familiar. Hadn't Rose responded in similar fashion when Cal accused her of being jealous of his wife? Though not as vicious as Stewart, Rose had retaliated with bite. No doubt what lay behind Stewart's bluster was a lifetime of hurt.

The silence in the room was deafening. She cleared her throat and half turned in her chair to ask him, "You really think Yvonne's lost weight?"

Before leaving the office for the day, Rose called Betty Ann at home. Her friend had had a short workday at the nursing home. The first Thursday of each month, Green Pastures held Family Night, similar to a school's open house, when loved ones visited. The chef prepared special French dishes such as *boeuf au jus,* otherwise known as pot roast.

"They used to use real tablecloths instead of place mats," Betty Ann said. "But that didn't last long. The tablecloths sometimes got caught in the spokes of the wheelchairs. When residents backed away from the table, they ended up taking everything with them." She shook her head, remembering one such incident. "It was a disaster."

Rose told her about the Phippses' party in honor of artist Manuel del Toro. "I can bring someone, so I immediately thought of you."

"I dunno," Betty Ann said. "You know how I feel about those Hemlock Point phonies. Why is this Manuel guy being introduced to Granite Cove? No one that I know buys art."

"Mrs. Phipps is targeting her Hemlock Point friends and neighbors—potential benefactors."

"I hope they don't expect me to shell out," Betty Ann said. "The last time I bought art was at the Dollar Store 'cause I liked the frame."

"The only thing Myrna Phipps expects from her guests is envy. Honestly, you've never see such a house. They've got their own private beach and dock."

When Betty Ann sighed into the phone, Rose added, "Did I mention the Happy Hearth is catering? You haven't lived til you've tried Edith's parmesan crab cakes."

"Oh, what the hell, I'll go. It won't kill me to rub elbows with the Hemlock Point swells. Besides, I could use a night out."

"Will Tiny be home to babysit?"

"Are you kidding? Jonah's thirteen. Some of his friends are now babysitting, though I hope to God the parents lock up the liquor cabinet. And by the way, can you stop by the house on your way home? I'd like you to ask Jonah about that drawing of the Homer Frost statue. When I showed it to him, he just nodded. I think he knows something, but he's committed to telling me—the stepmother—nothing."

"I know Yvonne is very interested in what Jonah has to say, but"—she glanced at her watch—"Chester eats at five o'clock. You know how dogs are."

"No, I don't, but I know how teenage boys are. They graze all day. Chester won't perish if you're a half hour late. I'm putting the chardonnay on ice. Come on over."

Two hours later, Rose pulled up outside the Zagrobskis' olive-green ranch house. A large satellite dish jutted from the snow-encrusted roof. She parked the Jetta on the gravel shoulder and headed up the walkway flanked by tall plastic candy canes. As she raised her gloved hand to knock on the front door, it opened.

Betty Ann, wearing a floor-length red-and-green striped dress, appeared. "Get in here, kiddo. It's freezing."

Rose stepped inside, unbuttoning her coat. "I like your caftan. Very appropriate for the season. Are those candy canes?"

Betty Ann plucked at the voluminous material. "I bought it from a catalog. Vertical stripes are slimming, or so I'm told." She sighed. "It seems I don't wear clothes for fashion anymore. I wear them for camouflage." She headed into the kitchen, saying, "Go into the living room."

"I'm sure it's great for entertaining at home," Rose said, "but maybe not for a party." She placed her coat on the arm of an overstuffed chair.

Betty Ann emerged from the kitchen with two glasses of wine and handed one to Rose. "Entertaining at home? The last time I did that was a farewell dinner for Tiny's mom when she left for Florida. And don't worry, I don't plan on wearing this to your Hemlock Point party." She motioned Rose to join her on the sagging sofa. "Did I tell you? I found another pair of miracle pants."

"Miracle pants?" Rose sank into the cushions.

"Remember how I had only one pair of black pants that didn't make my butt look like a washtub? Well, I took a chance and ordered a pair from a new catalog. Mother of God, they're a feat of engineering."

"I'm glad you found a substitute." Rose took a sip of wine. "And I apologize for the caftan remark." She glanced at the vivid green-and-red stripes. "You wear whatever you want to the party, candy cane caftan or polyester pajamas. Friendship is more important than fashion."

"Don't worry, kid, I won't embarrass you. This thing's basically a housedress, an upgrade on the kind my mother used to wear with pastel fuzzy slippers. Remember those? When she went downtown, she'd take off the housedress and put on a daytime dress." Betty Ann sighed. "Such was a woman's lot back then."

Rose nodded. "Today we're free to wear sweatpants and cut-offs downtown, which I don't consider much of an improvement." She glanced around the room. "By the way, where's your tree?"

"Don't get me going on that. We're waging a battle under this roof. Tiny and Jonah want a real tree and I want artificial. I just learned that Sears is having a sale on them."

Rose wrinkled her nose. "I classify artificial trees in the same category as fake flowers. Why bother?"

"That's because you're thinking of the fake trees from years past. Today they're so lifelike you can't tell the difference, even up close." She sat up straight. "As a matter of fact, I had a conversation with Janet Loopstock today. She came in to decorate her mom's room for the holidays. I commented on her little tree, it looked so real. She said she's got one at home that looks so natural it fools everyone. Her son came to visit and his Irish setter lifted his leg on the tree." She gave Rose a triumphant look.

"So, you want a tree that dogs pee on?"

"That's not the point. If I can get an artificial tree that looks so realistic no one can tell the difference, why bother with the mess of a real tree?"

"I don't know. A fresh balsam has that wonderful smell that welcomes you when you walk in the door."

"Janet sprays hers with bathroom pine freshener."

Rose shook her head. "There's a big difference. To me, a fake tree is like... like having a fake black Lab. Just prop it up in front of the fireplace. It won't shed or need to go toity in the middle of the night. Why bother with the mess of a real dog?"

Betty Ann glanced at the ceiling and stood up. "I hear Jonah moving around up there. Before he takes one of his marathon showers, let me get him." She swept out of the room.

Rose waited, sipping wine and examining Betty Ann's collection of Santa candles arranged on the coffee table. The new additions were brightly colored, while those she'd bought in high school in the '80s looked dull and faded.

Minutes later, Rose heard heavy footsteps on the stairs. Jonah appeared in the arched doorway, followed by Betty Ann. As always, Rose marveled at the contrast between Jonah and his father Tiny. The latter was beefy, with powerful shoulders. The son, on the other hand, was a wraith, his skimpy T-shirt loose on his bony frame. Yet according to Betty Ann, the boy had a ravenous appetite. Jonah, nonetheless, had inherited Tiny's curly black hair. Although the elder Zagrobski maintained a military buzz cut, Jonah's hair was an unruly mass.

Rose got up from the sofa and hugged the boy, feeling him tense up. "Merry Christmas, Jonah."

"Yeah," he muttered, stuffing his hands into the pockets of his cargo pants.

Betty Ann poked his back. "Can you say 'thank you' to Rose?"

"Yeah. Thanks." Below furrowed brows his eyes flitted around the room.

"Don't worry about it," Rose said. "Believe it or not, your stepmother and I were once your age." When he glanced at her in disbelief, she continued, "Now, I hear you're a tech wiz in the computer lab." She took the folder Betty Ann produced, and removed the sheet inside. "I wonder if you know anything about this picture." She handed it to him. "Your answer will be kept in strict confidence."

He stared at it for a moment, his lips curling into a smirk. "Yeah, I saw Tanker working on this. It's not that great, ya know. The kid's lame."

"Uh-huh. Do you know Tanker very well?"

He gave her a scornful glance. "Kid's a dork. Mr. Chambers, our graphics teacher, lets him use the computers any time he wants because Tank's an honors student. He helps out, checking for viruses, stuff like that." He shrugged. "No one likes him, 'cept a couple of the teachers." He handed back the sheet.

"Thank you, Jonah." Rose tried to sound casual despite the fact her heart was beating fast. "Do you happen to know Tanker's real name?"

"Yeah. It's Nathaniel Chitwick."

Auntie Pearl's Helpful Housekeeping Hints

Dear Auntie Pearl:

My roommate and I, professional women, recently acquired a third roommate, Sasha. It's obvious that she hasn't had the same upbringing as we have. Sasha has some unpleasant habits that are difficult to overlook.

For instance, while watching TV in the living room, she'll clip her toenails. Also, she uses her netti pot (a nasal irrigation device) at the kitchen sink. Last week I had my book club over and was mortified to find Sasha's dripping underwear draped over the bathroom towel rack!

Talking to the woman does no good. How best to resolve this situation?

Sickened in Somerville

Dear Sickened:

I agree that underwear dripping from a towel rack is unsightly, and I have the perfect solution: Unclip one or two rings from your shower curtain (don't worry, you can re-clip them later.) Hang one pair of underpants on each clip. If they drip, the water ends up in the tub.

This trick is also marvelous for when you're staying in a hotel. It is an efficient way to launder your personal undergarments when on the road.

Hope I've helped!

Signed,

Auntie Pearl

CHAPTER ELEVEN

Milton Krazner's office was located downtown in the old Purdy Building, also known as the "seagull building." The latter was due to the nesting habits of the town's gull population. The semi-enclosed roof of the five-story office building offered protection from the elements, and thus it was a good spot for raising young birds.

No one minded their presence; in fact, many tenants weren't even aware of it. The situation went unnoticed until the rooftop became a popular breeding ground. Before long, sightings of rare Arctic gulls were reported. Soon birders from all over the Boston area arrived. Their cars clogging the parking lot, they stood outside, their binoculars trained on the rooftop.

Eventually the building's tenants squawked. Not only did they have to fight the safari-jacketed intruders for parking spaces, but their cars were covered in bird droppings, and the noise was deafening.

Following a barrage of complaints to City Hall and the Public Health Department, Jake Jedrey, the building inspector, was ordered to clean up the roof. The birds had to go. Jedrey announced his intention of ridding the Purdy Building of seagulls, and the feathers started to fly. Wildlife supporters, bird watchers, and animal rights groups were outraged. A battle ensued, often playing out in the pages of the *Granite Cove Gazette.*

Eventually all parties reached an agreement: when the nesting season was over and the young gulls had flown, Jake Jedrey and a crew from the DPW would clean up the roof. "Eviction Day for Gulls" ran the headline in the *Gazette* when that time arrived. Due to the well-publicized controversy, the event drew wildlife enthusiasts, activists, and retirees from the next-door senior center.

Before the cleanup crew began its work, Rose interviewed Jedrey in the parking lot. As they spoke, an earnest young man from the Audubon Society interrupted. "I hope you know what you're doing," he said. "Seagulls can get pretty temperamental this time of year."

Jedrey chuckled and patted the fellow's shoulder. "Listen, son, when you were in diapers I was working the wharves. Been around seagulls my entire life."

With the TV cameras whirring, Jedrey turned to the trio of DPW men lounging against the truck having a final smoke. "Okay, boys," he shouted. "Let's move up."

After the crew disappeared inside the building, the crowd fanned out across the parking lot in search of a spot to observe the action. Moments later the crew appeared on the roof, Jedrey giving the spectators a thumbs-up. The senior citizens and curious townspeople cheered. The wildlife supporters booed.

All attention was focused on the rooftop as the crew dragged hoses and buckets. Jedrey barked orders like a drill sergeant. Amidst the activity, a flurry of seagulls took to the air with shrill cries. The activists responded, waving their signs and chanting slogans such as "SOS: Save Our Seagulls." When the last gull had flown away, the crowd below began to break up. Mothers stuffed babies back into strollers and retirees headed back to the senior center while the activists loaded their signs into car trunks. Rose was putting her camera into its case when someone shouted, "Look!"

A dense mass moved rapidly across the sky. People stopped in their tracks and gazed at the strange sight.

"It's a UFO!" a woman gasped.

"It's El Niño!"

"No, it's... birds."

Soon the aerial oddity was identified: a flock of seagulls flying in tight formation toward the Purdy Building. In the parking lot, the stragglers stared, frozen to the spot. Five stories above them the crew, busy power washing the roof, didn't notice or hear the approaching gulls.

"It was like a scene from that movie, *The Birds*," Doris Zack was later quoted in Rose's story. "I've lived here all my life and never seen seagulls act like that."

When the gulls swooped down, the men, caught unawares, swung their brooms and rakes at the avengers. When the men realized they were outnumbered and no match for their attackers, they tossed their makeshift weapons and raced for the door. Jake Jedrey was the first to reach it.

"Revenge of the Seagulls" read the caption below Rose's photo. The picture was picked up by the Associated Press and subsequently appeared in hundreds of newspapers, on TV, and on the Web.

Now Rose rode the elevator to Milton Krazner's office on the third floor. The Purdy Building had undergone recent renovations. Its window trim had been replaced and the exterior bricks painted. To prevent a recurrence of the seagull debacle, the building superintendent had adopted a border collie specially trained in discouraging pigeons, Canada geese, and gulls.

Harborside Commercial Realty read the sign on the door of number 314, and below that, *Milton V. Krazner, President.* Rose entered a reception area devoid of personality. The walls, carpeting, upholstered chairs, and desks were tan. She glanced around. An empty reception desk sat to the left of the entrance. Framed photos of Milton shaking hands with Granite Cove officials adorned the walls, along with plaques from the Rotary club and the Chamber of Commerce. The only remarkable aspect of the room was a picture window that offered a dazzling view of the frozen harbor.

Rose was gazing down at the ice-encrusted fishing trawlers when a side door opened and Milton appeared. "I thought I heard someone," he said. "My secretary's taking an early lunch."

"I was enjoying the view," Rose said. "I don't know why people rent space in the Harbour Tower when they could be here."

"Not only that—this building is far sturdier. I was one of the first brokers approached when Harbour Tower opened. Just between you and me, they're not worth the money. You wouldn't want to see their windows after a major hurricane." He stood back and held his door open. "Come in, Ms. McNichols."

"It's Rose," she said, stepping into his office. More photos of Milton with what passed for luminaries in Granite Cove decorated the walls.

He gestured to a straight-back chair and seated himself behind a glass-covered desk. It held a phone and computer.

Rose wondered how people managed such pristine surroundings, though in Milton's case she wasn't surprised. The man was an incurable neatnik. She glanced at his manicured hands, which looked far better than hers. The only telltale sign marring his impeccable surface were two half moons of sweat staining the armpits of his blue Oxford shirt.

He glanced at his watch. "I'm meeting with the environmental people in an hour. I've been trying to sell a gas station outside town for three years. If they don't approve it, I don't know what to tell my client. It's always new rules and regulations. Meanwhile, my client has sunk thousands into cleaning the property." He shook his head. "There's no pleasing those people."

"You've got a point," she said, realizing two things: Milton was stalling, and he was nervous. This gave her an advantage. "I know you're busy, so I won't keep you. I'd like to talk about your relationship with Dionne Dunbar."

Abruptly he sat back in his swivel chair. It rolled away from his desk. Rose had the impression he'd like to keep rolling.

He cleared his throat. "First I'd like to state that I knew the woman only through the mediums class. As you've attended the gatherings, you know there's little socializing. Hyacinth gets down to business, as she should. We arrive on time and are soon seated. Sometimes Hyacinth leads us in a guided meditation. The rest of the time we're quiet unless we're commenting on our perceptions or responding to another's message.

"Members have a shared goal, but they don't become buddies. Once or twice I've given Ms. Dunbar a ride home, but we weren't friends by any means." He peered at Rose over his black-framed glasses. "Unless I'm mistaken, the police have ruled Ms. Dunbar's death an accident." He smirked. "Perhaps our local reporter has inside information?"

Rose didn't have to be a medium to see how the interview would go. Milton's lips were sealed tighter than a clam at high tide. She decided to play her trump card. Leaning forward, she placed a notepad on his desktop.

"Milton, I recently visited the shredding center, Dionne's former place of employment. They gave me the contents of her desk. Among them was a notebook she kept to record certain... information." As he stared at the notepad, a twitch appeared in the pouchy skin under his left eye. She pushed the notepad closer. "I discovered that you were paying Dionne. Was she blackmailing you?"

He was quick. His hand came down hard over hers.

"Ouch!" She pulled her hand away. "That hurt!"

He opened a desk drawer, tossed the notepad inside, and slammed the drawer shut. Sweat beaded his forehead. He stared at her with narrowed eyes. "I want you to leave now or I'll call security."

"I'm not leaving until I get my notebook."

He shook his head and reached for the phone.

She sighed. "Go ahead and take a look. Do you really think I'd bring real evidence with me?"

He slowly opened the drawer and removed the notepad. After turning a few blank pages, he tossed it onto the desk. "You tricked me."

"It's the oldest trick in the book." She couldn't help smiling. "Now do you want to tell me? This is not for publication. What you have to say will remain with me."

"If my wife found out..." He mopped his forehead with a handkerchief. "You probably won't believe me, but I never had sex with that woman."

"Your wife?"

"No... Dionne."

"Then why was she blackmailing you?"

He rose and moved to the window. "It wasn't exactly blackmail, it was for... special favors."

"What do you mean by that?"

He let out a long sigh. "Dionne liked attention. She also liked to be in control. She was that kind of woman. One night in the fall, I gave her a ride home after class. She invited me in for a drink. I only stayed twenty minutes because my wife gets anxious when I'm away too long.

"Dionne was an excellent judge of character. In that short time, she picked up on clues from me. You could say she read me, spotting my weaknesses. Personally, I thought she was taking the wrong class. She should have been studying witchcraft, not spiritualism." He turned to look at Rose. "I'll be honest; Dionne Dunbar excited me. That long dark hair, those red nails and high-heeled boots... shiny black leather." He shuddered.

"Did you have an affair with her?"

"I wouldn't call it an affair, certainly not a love affair. She spotted my weaknesses and played to them. She knew what I craved."

"Are you saying she was a, what's the word, dominatrix?"

He nodded, his back to her. "There was no actual sex exchanged. In this case, Dionne cleverly determined my predilections, if you please, and proceeded to act them out. Together we engaged in a... drama unlike anything Dickens could have crafted. Dionne provided the dialogue and the wardrobe."

"Did you meet at her condominium?"

He shook his head. "Too risky. No, we met in offices in buildings I was listing, places I knew would be vacant. We once met at a former convent." A note of amusement crept into his voice. "Dionne left her riding crop behind. I went back the next day and found it."

"When did she start demanding money?"

"After our second interaction. She'd taken secret photos of me and threatened to send them to my wife and Mayor Froggett. When you took out the notepad, I thought it was the photos." He turned to stare. "You didn't find any, did you?"

She shook her head.

"It's what keeps me up at night, wondering who has them."

"Did you think of asking her sister, Dorothy?"

He turned to face her. "The chaplain? I should ask if she found photos of me wearing a baby diaper?"

"I see your point," Rose said. "So when Dionne started demanding money, did that put an end to your... theatricals?"

"Not really. I could afford it. Even when she demanded more money I didn't mind." He gazed out the window and said quietly, "Those were the most exciting moments of my life."

When Rose reached the entrance to the newspaper office, the door opened and Stewart slipped out. Normally an encounter with the sportswriter would cause her spirits to sink. Lately, however, she and Stew had been getting along; she wished to maintain that status.

"Going for the day?" she asked.

He stopped and carefully wrapped his long scarf around his neck until it covered his lower face, his reddened nose poking out. In a muffled voice he said, "I'm going to the high school to interview the basketball coach." He jerked his head in the direction of the door. "You might not want to go in there."

"Why's that?"

"All hell's broken loose over the Homer Frost poster. The superintendent of the school's talking about a lockdown. Yvonne's having a meltdown." He pressed the bridge of his nose. "Can't handle it today. My sinuses are killing me. She cranks the heat up too high in there."

What Rose could see of Stewart's face was as pale as a cod belly. She felt a pang of sympathy. "Why don't you go home after the interview? I've got some information about the poster that I think will calm Yvonne down."

He muttered something and turned. She watched him shuffle away, his rubber boots slogging through the slush. For a minute she was tempted to join him; the prospect of Yvonne's histrionics was depressing. Then she reminded herself she had good news and so she yanked open the door.

Yvonne stopped pacing to address Rose. "It's all over for me, dear. When this gets out I'll lose my job." She resumed pacing. "All I wanted to do was promote a little community spirit, and it's backfired." She gave Rose a beseeching look. "Who'll hire me after this?"

Rose removed her jacket and scarf, hanging them on the coat rack. She turned to her desk. "Do you want to sit and tell me the latest, because I have something to tell you."

Yvonne glanced at the wall clock. "I put a call in to Chief Alfano. He's at a meeting now. Lord knows what will happen when he finds out."

Rose regarded her calmly. "Stew said it had something to do with the poster."

Hugging herself, Yvonne lurched from one end of the room to the other. "Don't mention that word, *poster*. I wish I'd never thought of it. This will reflect badly upon our newspaper, mark my words. I've tried hard to build our reputation and win the readers' trust. You know how I've always put the newspaper first, before my needs?" She stared at Rose.

Rose didn't know that, but she nodded anyway. "I can't help you, Yvonne, unless you tell me what happened."

Yvonne finally lowered herself into her chair. "You know how the chief and I visited Ms. Fedderbush, the middle school principal?" When Rose nodded, she continued. "She showed the poster to the school psychologist, who apparently showed it to an art therapist. That woman said whoever created the poster needed an intervention.

"At some point, the superintendent saw the drawing. Now he wants to alert the state police and send a letter to parents, apprising them of the situation." She sighed. "They may close the school until they find the responsible party." She gazed dolefully at Rose. "If I lose my condo, Mother could end up in a home."

"Yvonne, I think I can help. I wanted to say something at rehearsals, but you were busy. I should have told you right away. I didn't realize this poster business would get so out of hand." She told Yvonne about her visit to Betty Ann and her conversation with Jonah, who had claimed to know the identity of the poster's creator.

"Nathaniel Chitwick?" Yvonne looked at her blankly. "That roly-poly boy with the chubby cheeks?" She shook her head as if to clear it.

"We don't know for certain, but Jonah seemed pretty sure. In any event, speak to the chief and see how he wants to proceed."

Yvonne pulled a tissue from her sleeve and blew her nose. "I must look a fright." She attempted a smile. "If what you're saying is true, perhaps it's possible to handle this quietly." When Rose nodded, Yvonne got to her feet and smoothed her hair. "I feel relieved. Somehow I think you're right. The Chitwick boy looks angelic, yet he doesn't fool me."

She sat down again and leaned toward Rose. "This is just between the two of us. Chipper brought in an antique pewter candleholder for our set. One night the stage was empty, the footlights out. I was sitting in the wings making notes when Nathaniel appeared and quietly crossed the stage. He stopped at the table that held the candleholder and knelt to tie his sneaker. At the same time, he slipped it into the pocket of his parka. I saw him glance around, his expression much like a weasel's."

"Did you say something?" Rose asked.

"I told Chipper. He'll deal with it when the play's over." She glanced at the wall clock. "I won't wait for the chief's call. I'm going over there now."

Rose watched Yvonne slip into her poncho, her demeanor now confident. Yvonne was so single-minded in her mission, she forgot to put on her boots. Out she went into the slushy streets in linen espadrilles, blissfully oblivious.

CHAPTER TWELVE

On the night of the Phippses' party, Rose pulled into Betty Ann's driveway at quarter of seven. She parked behind Tiny's truck, an '80s survivor of the Massachusetts roadways. When Betty Ann complained about the fuel the battered relic burned or its noxious emissions, Tiny merely shrugged. The old blue truck with 210,000 miles had been his dad's; for Tiny, maintaining it was a labor of love.

"Besides," he had asked her, "what am I supposed to do, drive a Prius?"

Rose turned off the ignition and got out of the Jetta. The night was clear and cold. The moon, a thin silver crescent, was high above. According to the *Farmer's Almanac*, the Christmas moon was as far from Earth as it would ever be. In defiance of this seasonal darkness, the Zagrobskis' side deck was outlined in colorful lights.

Rose rapped on the storm door.

Tiny, in a white T-shirt, welcomed her into the kitchen. "Wow, you look hot. I don't know if I trust you two gals tonight. Maybe I should go with you."

Rose stood under the fluorescent light and unbuttoned her coat. "I'm sure you'll be more fun than the folks we're meeting tonight." She sniffed the air. "Something smells good."

"Cheeseburgers," Tiny said, turning to the stove. He scraped a black skillet with a spatula. "Three for me and one for Jonah. Do you know what I like on mine?" When Rose shrugged, he continued. "Sautéed onions, ketchup, mayo, mustard, and relish. Do you know what my son likes?"

Although she had no idea what young boys liked, she remembered Stewart's preference. "Soy sauce?"

"Soy sauce?" Tiny scratched his nose. "No, Jonah likes hummus on his burger. Do you know what hummus is? Chickpeas, mashed up. This generation is weird." He placed the patties in the skillet. "Imagine what would have happened when we were in school, if the cafeteria had tried putting hummus on our burgers."

"It would have been grounds for a sit-in. Speaking of Jonah, I wonder if I can speak to him before we leave?"

Tiny waved the spatula in the direction of the stairs. "Go on up. He's in his cave."

As Rose climbed the stairs, Betty Ann was coming down. "What's wrong, you gotta pee?" she said. Rose explained about speaking to Jonah.

"Just bang your fist on his door. Eventually he'll hear you."

Rose did as instructed. The music abruptly stopped and Jonah swore. Seconds later, the door swung open. He stared dully at her.

"Yeah?"

"Jonah, I want you to know that I spoke to my editor today. I confided the name of the artist who did the poster. She's very grateful for the information and won't mention how she obtained it."

He shrugged. "It's no secret. I mean, Tank worked on it during class. Mr. Chambers helped him with the layers and stuff."

"Oh. Then why didn't he sign his name? He called himself 'Diablo.'"

Jonah ran a hand through his unruly curls. "Because he's sick, man. Tanker's an idiot."

She nodded, having nothing more to say. "Did you think of entering the contest?"

"You kidding me? That's so lame."

"Okay," she said, turning away. "I just wanted to let you know."

The door shut firmly behind her. Seconds later the music resumed. As she headed down the stairs, Rose uttered a prayer of gratitude, thanking St. Theresa for giving her an aging black Lab to share her home and not a teenage boy.

When she and Betty Ann were buckled in, Rose switched the car heater to high. After a minute, Betty Ann fanned her face. "Turn it down, will you? I'm getting what feels like preliminary hot flashes."

"Sorry." Rose adjusted the controls. "This is the only heat I can afford. At home the thermostat's so low I wear a wool sweater and scarf at all times. You look nice, by the way. Are those the new black pants?"

"Yes, I'm all in black, the fat person's uniform. I've got Santa earrings for a little color. The Hemlock Point dowagers might think it's tacky. I'm sure they'll be decked out in their ancestors' jewels."

"Some of the older ones go over the top with vintage ball gowns and tiaras. Don't worry, you look quite stylish."

"I don't mine a few creaky old fossils," Betty Ann said. "Just as long as the bartender knows how to make a good margarita."

"Don't count on it. This crowd tends to serve sherry at their soirees."

Betty Ann thought for a moment. "I'm willing to bet this Manuel del Toro is probably a big phony."

"Who cares," Rose said. "At least there's Edith's seafood puffs. Have you had dinner?"

Betty Ann glanced at her. "What kind of question is that? Of course I've had dinner. I never leave the house on an empty stomach." She removed a lipstick from her clutch purse. "By the way, I hope Jonah wasn't rude to you. I'm trying to pound some manners into the kid, but it's like the missionaries preaching to the savages. I can't even enlist Tiny's help. He always blames Judy's influence on the boy, and says I must be patient."

"He wasn't rude. He was your average thirteen-year-old. In any case, Yvonne was so relieved to learn about the poster. Jonah was a lifesaver as far as she's concerned."

"What will she do now?"

"Because it's Pastor Chitwick's son, they'll handle it with kid gloves. After all, Nathaniel hasn't done anything wrong except submit an anonymous entry that people find disturbing. Yvonne said the chief may ask Cal to call on the Chitwicks to discuss the issue."

"That's an excellent idea," Betty Ann said. "Alfano would end up offending Hyacinth for sure. Cal, on the other hand, would be diplomatic."

"So long as he's not his usual cocky self," Rose said, gripping the steering wheel.

Betty Ann glanced at her profile. "Odd choice of words... cocky."

"Very funny."

"Sorry. I forget Cal's a sensitive subject."

"He is not a sensitive subject. The past is past."

Betty Ann sighed. "Still, he could make it easier by getting fat and wearing designer jeans. Maybe he was cocky back in high school, but at the same time he was gorgeous and a star football player. He wasn't stuck on himself like most of those jocks. He had a sense of humor about everything."

Rose glanced at her friend. "Are you trying to make me feel worse? If so, it's working."

Betty Ann patted her shoulder. "We all have to live with our choices. Tiny carries a load of guilt for divorcing Judy. After her third rehab, he couldn't take any more, mentally or physically. His doctor said his stomach looked like raw meat."

"I didn't mean to be short with you," Rose said. "Even though Cal and I broke up fifteen years ago, I still have moments of doubt. After all, we were high school sweethearts. I was definitely in love, but I wasn't ready to get hitched." She paused, reflective. "That's an appropriate word, hitched. Like two oxen, joined forever."

"You were too young," Betty Ann said.

"I wanted to keep things as they were. Cal wanted to settle down and start a family. That's why I left town: the pressure. My mother referred to it as 'running away.' But if I'd stayed, a June wedding was inevitable as bluefish in August."

Betty Ann chuckled. "When you hit Interstate 95, Marcie was knocking on his door. She probably got pregnant their first date."

"I knew women would waste no time circling Cal's wagon."

Betty Ann sighed. "We have to go with our gut feelings. When Tiny proposed, I said to myself, 'Do you want a guy who's loud, sexist, and saddled with an obnoxious, messed up kid?'"

"Obviously you did," Rose said.

"He was good in bed. That tipped the balance."

Rose laughed. "Unfortunately, as an only child I have the burden of carrying on the family genes. The family tree ends with me."

"Is your dad worried about it? Has he mentioned it to you?"

"Of course not."

"Then let it go. Whether you know it or not, the universe is unfolding according to plan. Have faith in the process."

"You sound just like Hyacinth," Rose said.

"Geez, thanks."

As the Jetta rumbled over the unmarked dirt roads that passed for streets in Hemlock Point, Rose spotted the sign in front of the Phippses' house. She turned into the narrow, winding driveway.

"Marbella," Betty Ann said, reading the wooden sign. "Imagine living in a house that has a name."

"What's the big deal? Anyone can name their home."

"Yeah," she snorted. "I'll call mine *Chez Spuds*."

They came to the end of the driveway. The Phippses' house was a sprawling stucco affair nestled among wild beach roses and scrub pine and overlooking an expanse of sea and sky. Bright cherry-red tiles on the roof bespoke the home of a tile mogul. Tiny lights glittered in the surrounding pine trees.

A man in a reflective vest waved his flashlight in an arc, directing them to a parking spot. Rose slid the Jetta between a classic Mercedes sedan and a Jaguar.

'Wow," Betty Ann said. "If I didn't know this was Granite Cove, I'd swear we were in Beverly Hills. Speaking of which, did you know the actress Betty Davis rented this house one summer back in the fifties?"

"How'd you know that?"

Betty Ann gave Rose a scornful look. "I researched it. As a journalist, you ought to be aware of that."

Rose slipped the key from the ignition. "No, maybe because our readers are more interested in the whiting count than in dead Hollywood actresses."

Betty Ann shrugged. "Be that as it may, this is Betty Davis we're talking about. What bigger claim to fame can Granite Cove boast?"

When it came to celebrity minutiae, it was hard to top Betty Ann's knowledge. Ever since high school, when she was president of the New England branch of the Joan Collins Fan Club, she'd kept abreast of Hollywood stars' lives.

"You're right. I'm filing that away for a future summer column." Rose grabbed her purse from the back seat. "Let's go meet the artist. Maybe he'll become Granite Cove's second biggest claim to fame."

"I doubt it," Betty Ann said, climbing from the car. "I did a search on Manuel del Toro and came up with nothing, other than an October appearance at a Worcester community center."

"Myrna says he's been in the US for two months."

"I don't care if his medium is finger paints," Betty Ann said. "I'm only here for the food and booze. "

"That's the holiday spirit," Rose said.

Together they walked up a winding flagstone path toward the entrance. The polished mahogany door gleamed beneath an overhead light. High on a nearby terrace, a Christmas tree twinkled in the darkness.

Betty Ann clutched Rose's sleeve. "Look at that," she said, indicating a long leaded window beyond the terrace. Inside, a chandelier cast a mellow glow upon the silver-haired guests assembled beneath it. The men were in tuxes and the women wore long gowns and jewels that glittered in the reflecting light.

"It's like a scene from *Masterpiece Theatre*," Betty Ann said in a hushed voice. "An English country manor." She looked down at her high-heeled boots. "I'm gonna stick out like a nun at a beach party."

"Betty Ann, where's that famous chutzpah of yours?"

"It's an act, kiddo," she said, staring at the scene within. "Sorry to break it to you."

Rose tugged her arm. "Come on, it's freezing out here."

"Wait." Betty Ann leaned forward, peering intently. "You see that man standing by the window, the one that looks like an ambassador?" When Rose nodded, she said, "See the wistful look on his face? I'll bet he's a widower with tons of money yet no one to share his life." She turned to Rose. "Do me a favor, will you? Introduce me as Bettina, not Betty Ann, just for tonight. Can you remember that?"

"What's gotten into you? Of course everyone looks glamorous from out here, but approach and listen to their conversations. When I took Kevin to one of Myrna's parties, he called it the 'night of the living dead.'" She beckoned for Betty Ann to follow as she turned toward the entrance.

Betty Ann trailed after her. "You may be right, but no way can I go back to serving Hamburger Helper after tonight."

"I didn't know they still made that," Rose said, over her shoulder.

"It's Jonah's favorite." Betty Ann let out a long sigh. "How can I return to that kid after a night at Marbella?"

Rose raised a gloved hand to knock. "You think these people don't have kids?"

"They ship them off to boarding school. Meanwhile, the parents travel. Some don't see the kids for years."

"How do you know?" Rose asked.

"I happen to read up on the lives of the British aristocracy."

Rose rapped on the polished door. "Then remember that Lester Phipps is a self-made man who made his fortune in tiles. He's neither British nor an aristocrat. He loves *The Three Stooges*."

The door swung open to reveal a tuxedoed Lester Phipps. He wore a red sequined Santa hat and matching cummerbund. From his height of five feet seven, he gazed up at the newcomers. "Rosie!" He wrapped his arms around her in a bear hug. Then he turned to Betty Ann, his eyes sweeping over her. "Who's this gorgeous Amazon?"

"Bettina Archibald," she said before Rose could speak.

He raised himself up to kiss her, saying, "Don't tell Myrna."

"I'm no kiss-and-tell gal," she said, letting her coat fall open to reveal a low-cut black sequined top.

"Myrna will be disappointed you didn't bring Kevin," he said to Rose. "But Ms. Archibald's a lot easier on the eyes." His arms around them, Lester Phipps guided the women down a hall lined with marble busts set on pedestals.

"Make sure you meet this Manuel character," he said. "We got him set up in the library. Myrna's already bought a couple of his paintings." He rolled his eyes. "Maybe you kids understand modern art, but I'm from another era. When I was a kid, we had a Norman Rockwell print hanging in the parlor. It was the one of the old country doctor and the little girl with her doll. You familiar with that?" When the women assured him that they were, he continued, "That's the kind of art I like—something with feeling. 'Course, I wouldn't say that to this crowd."

They came to the chandeliered room where the well-dressed guests mingled, speaking in muted tones. "After all," Phipps continued, "I'm from Akron, Ohio. My country club friends here think we eat peas with a spoon." He chuckled. "And you know what?"

"What?" they said in unison.

"They're right!" He gave them a final squeeze. "Now I'm heading to the bar for a real drink."

They watched him make his way through the guests, stopping to slap a shoulder or whisper in an ear.

"I like him," Betty Ann said. "He's real."

"He's not your average Hemlock Pointer," Rose agreed.

She scanned the room and spotted Myrna in conversation with a trio of women in long shimmery dresses. Mrs. Phipps's gray hair was worn in an upsweep secured with jeweled combs. She looked like central casting's idea of a 1940s society matron. Her floor-length emerald satin dress was cut low, revealing puffy white breasts like unrisen dough.

They went and introduced themselves to her, Betty Ann slipping in her newly adopted name. "Rose, I'm delighted to meet your friend," Myrna Phipps said, "but tell me, where's your young man?"

"Kevin's playing at the Sacred Cod tonight. He sends his love."

When Rose had told Kevin where she was going that evening, he'd shivered, remembering how Myrna had lured him into a dark pantry. After banging into pots and pans, he'd escaped her clutches, hiding in a maid's room upstairs until Rose rescued him.

Now Rose asked Myrna Phipps, "Where's Raul tonight?"

"The little peaches is upstairs, asleep," Myrna said. "The groomer visited this afternoon. It was a long session. We're getting ready to leave for Palm Beach, you know." She patted Betty Ann's arm. "Make sure Rose shows you Raul's bed. It's quite special." She waved them on. "Go get some champagne and introduce yourselves to Manuel del Toro. And Rose, take plenty of photos." With that she glided away to join another group.

"What's so special about Raul's bed?" Betty Ann asked.

"It's a replica of Marie Antoinette's bridal bed."

"Mother of God," Betty Ann muttered, surveying the room. "I've never seen so many well-dressed old people.

Check out the lady with the fancy cane. She's looking at me like I buy my underwear at Goodwill."

"That's probably her normal expression. I'll bet she can't see two feet ahead of her. And if she could, she'd be jealous. Look how Lester's ogling you."

They grabbed glasses of champagne from a passing tray and Rose said, "Why don't we meet the artist and get it over with? For a moment I forgot this is a working night."

"I notice how Myrna reminded you."

Rose nodded in agreement. "I'm just a pauper on the Point, one who must sing for her supper. Nonetheless, taking photos gives me something to do. Otherwise I'd have to make conversation."

They moved down the hall to the library and immediately spotted the artist. Wearing a black beret and a vintage dinner jacket, Manuel del Toro stood in the center of an admiring group of silver-haired ladies. Easels set up around the room's perimeter held oversized paintings. Rose and Betty Ann stood back, waiting for a chance to introduce themselves.

"He's short," Betty Ann muttered. "Can't be much over five feet four. Do you know the word *toro* means bull in Spanish? This guy looks like a pint-size llama in a beret."

"I didn't realize artists still wore berets," Rose said, her voice low. "I thought that was a cliché."

"I wonder if that's his real name," Betty Ann said. Maybe he's a shoe salesman from New Jersey."

Rose removed her camera from her bag. "Why don't you stay here and save our place. I'll photograph some of the paintings."

"Don't be long," Betty Ann said. "I'll need more champagne shortly."

Rose joined the people clustered before the easels. In ornate gold frames, the paintings were a bold mélange of geometric shapes amid slashes and swaths of primary colors. On the whole, there was nothing restful about Manuel del Toro's work. She peered at a *sold* sticker affixed to a frame, squinting in an attempt to read the price. Finally, she slipped on her glasses.

"Wow," she gasped.

A couple standing nearby nodded. "Marvelous, isn't it?"

"At eight thousand dollars it had better be," Rose was tempted to reply. Instead she raised an eyebrow and said, "Not one of his better works," and moved on.

After photographing the paintings along the back wall, she spotted Florence Huke in the adjoining room. In a white blouse and black skirt, Florence carried a tray and moved energetically among the guests.

Rose put her camera away, deciding to speak to Florence. Before leaving the room, she glanced back at Betty Ann. Her friend was not alone. Lester Phipps, smiling broadly, handed her a glass of champagne. Taking her elbow, he led her to a corner of the room. Rose knew Betty Ann would be happily occupied grilling Lester about the habits of Hemlock Point habitués.

Rose worked her way through a maze of silk and chiffon until she reached Florence. "What have you got?" Rose asked. "Anything with crab or lobster?"

Florence grinned. "When I saw you earlier, I says to Edith, 'I'm putting aside some shrimp puffs for Rose McNichols.'" Now she held out a silver tray laden with an array of seafood delicacies. "Better grab 'em while they're hot."

Rose took a napkin and studied the assortment. "Busy tonight?"

"Uh-huh. I got my orders: no chitchatting with the guests." With her free hand, Florence adjusted her lopsided black bow tie.

"Whose orders? Edith's?"

"Yup. She's a real bossy britches tonight. When I showed up at her house, she snapped at me for wearing tie shoes. She knows I can't wear high heels with my bunions."

"Tell Edith I think you look very professional," Rose said, selecting four salmon-colored puffs.

"Tell you the truth, I'd rather cater Mayor Froggett's parties," Florence said. "After a couple hours, the councilors kick off their shoes. God knows what else after we're gone. But they tip big. Say what you will about our mayor, he takes care of his people."

"That's what I've heard—on the public's dime."

Florence shrugged. "He likes to blow off steam, like everyone else. Matter of fact, that's how we got this job tonight. Mrs. Phipps was at a city hall party we catered and fell in love with Edith's crab mousse." Florence leaned close and said, "She donated big to the mayor's campaign. In return, he gave her some arty farty title."

Rose nodded. "Director of Cultural Resources." She glanced around the room. "I think the mayor's here tonight." She'd spotted the man's salt-and-pepper toupee among the crowd. Now she popped her last puff into her mouth and grabbed another from the tray. "Before you move on, I want to mention that I had a talk with Milton the other day. I'm doing a story on Dionne for *Back Bay Living*."

"I heard that." Florence said, "God rest her soul, but that dame was after him."

"After Milton?" Rose asked.

Florence nodded. "A couple weeks before she passed, I was leaving the Chitwicks' house one night after class. I'd walked over because we'd had an early frost and my car didn't have its winter tires. Anyway, I was the last to leave, and Hyacinth saw me to the side door. Soon as I stepped onto the stoop, the outdoor lights turned off. Most people leave a light on to be hospitable, but not Hyacinth. Once you're out the door, you're on your own.

"So there I was, heading down the driveway. There's enough light from the moon so's I could make out Milton and Dionne walking ahead to their cars at the end of the drive. Milton reaches his first. He's unlocking his door when Dionne suddenly slips and falls. He goes, 'Are you okay?' and she goes, 'Ohh, it's slippery.' Those high-heeled boots she wore, anyone would fall on their keester.

"Milton wasted no time rushing over to where she's lying, looking like Tiny Tim without the crutches. He helps her to her feet an' she's clutching him like a Titanic survivor. For a few seconds they're in a clinch. They didn't notice me behind them. Then I took another step and slipped. Before I knew it, I was flat on my butt." She rolled her eyes. "You can bet Sir Galahad didn't rush over to help me up. No, he races to his car and takes off. They both do, leaving me there like a turtle on my back." She glanced around the room nervously. "I gotta move on before Edith sees me."

"Thank you, Florence," Rose said, grabbing another puff. "By the way, do you know what's wrong with Milton's wife?"

"Someone said it's her heart. It mutters or something."

"Mutters? Do you mean murmurs? She has a heart murmur?"

"Something like that." She nudged Rose with her elbow. "You better rescue Betty Ann. Mr. Phipps is on her like barnacles on a buoy."

"She loves the attention," Rose said, taking a note pad from her purse. "Now I must interview the artist."

"He likes the ladies, too," Florence said and scurried away.

Before approaching Manuel del Toro, Rose grabbed a glass of champagne from a passing tray. She was enjoying herself, free to partake of the food and drink. Her journalist's salary might be dismal, but there were the occasional perks.

She wormed her way into the group of aged socialites clustered around the artist who held court in the center. Rose heard one lavender-haired woman ask, "Tell us, Manuel, do you have a muse?"

The little man fished the olive from his martini and chomped on it. In a heavily accented voice he said, "My last painting, *Into the Vortex*, was done soon after meeting Myrna. That woman has fired my soul and set free my spirit." He drained his glass.

She's also padded your bank account, Rose thought. Holding her notepad in front of her, she asked, "Is Mrs. Phipps one of your patrons, Mr. del Toro?"

He blanched and looked down his broad nose at her, not an easy feat when she towered over him. "That word, *patron*, is repugnant to me, young lady. Patrons are for those whose work cannot stand by itself. Manuel del Toro stands alone."

"I guess the word I meant was admirer," she said. No sense in annoying the guest of honor.

He rewarded her with a smile. "Ah, I see you are writing a story. Some day you must visit and I will show you clippings. I have a scrapbook that my mother started years ago. The world will delight in the story of Manuel del Toro."

She scribbled on her pad. "Where are you from, Mr. del Toro?"

"I am from a little town called Ronda, high in the mountains of Spain. My father and his father before him had a tavern, very popular with artists and writers. Everyone gathered there, even your Hemingway. In fact," he raised a finger, "Pablo Picasso, as a penniless young man, did a mural on the tavern wall."

"That must be a national treasure," she murmured.

He shrugged. "My mother made my uncle paint over it. She did not want naked women on her walls. My mother was very religious."

"How did you find your way to Granite Cove?"

"It is a long story. I would like you to first read my scrapbook. Then you will understand the journey of Manuel del Toro. First, tell me your name." He leaned forward, his breath smelling strongly of gin. When she told him, he whispered hoarsely in her ear, "Tonight you are a rose among thorns."

She laughed as if she hadn't heard the remark before.

After a few more questions and a promise to look at his scrapbook, Rose thanked the artist. "Hola," she said, and wandered off in search of Betty Ann. She found her friend alone in a room off the corridor, standing at a window looking out at the rocks and the dark sea beyond.

"What a view," Betty Ann said. "I'm studying it to remember every detail." She turned to Rose. "So, what do you think of Manuel?"

"I'm withholding judgment until further research. And by the way, it's pronounced man-well, the 'man' as in Thomas Mann."

"Excuse me, Professor McNichols. I'm not familiar with the cultural scene."

"I'm not sure the artist is a member of that scene."

"Whatever the little fellow is, he's smitten," Betty Ann said. "He was looking up at you like you were a totem pole he wanted to climb."

Rose shrugged. "I always attract little guys."

"Me too. Lester Phipps wants to give me a tour of his mother's assisted living facility, Sea Ledges, in Rockport. The place is so fancy, when you get up in the middle of the night to take a pee, someone makes your bed. Tell you the truth, I'm tempted. You can't normally tour Sea Ledges unless you're with a family member." She turned back to the window. "Mr. Phipps knows I'm an activities director. Of course it'd be strictly professional."

"Of course," Rose said. "In any case, Bettina, I wouldn't bring it up in front of Mrs. Phipps."

Betty Ann stared into her empty champagne glass. "This stuff has gone to my head. If Tiny found out, he'd toss Lester off the rocks into Ipswich Bay."

Rose grinned. "Tiny? Jealous of a little guy like that?"

"He seems to think I'm irresistible to men. I do nothing to dissuade him."

Auntie Pearl's Helpful Housekeeping Hints

Dear Auntie Pearl:

I never thought I'd be writing you. My situation concerns my husband, Arnold. For over thirty years he was an accountant for a company that made flagpoles. Three months ago, Arnold retired and found himself at loose ends. He doesn't like to garden, play golf, or bowl. Consequently, he began spending more time at home and was often in the way.

Upon my suggestion, Arnold agreed to visit the local senior center and check out the activities. When he arrived home, he said he'd signed up for a walking group that meets three times a week. Auntie Pearl, I was relieved. It's not that I don't love my husband; it's just that I'm not accustomed to having him around so much. One day he was a professional in suit and tie, the next he's in pajamas, snoozing in the recliner.

Arnold enjoyed the walking group and never missed a day. Before long he noticed the benefits; he'd lost weight and felt healthier. At home he was easier to live with. I thought his new hobby was a godsend— until I made a startling discovery.

One morning, Arnold got a call from a woman named "Ginger," who left a message on the answering machine. Calling my husband "Arnie," she said she wouldn't be walking that morning. The next time my husband was scheduled to walk, I followed in my car. I learned that his walking "group" consisted of Ginger, a middle-aged woman with dyed blond hair and pink leggings. I discovered that after their walk they have coffee at Starbucks. Knowing that our neighbors might have seen them is humiliating.

When Arnold got home, I read him the riot act. He swore Ginger is nothing more than a walking partner. He even offered to quit if it made me so upset. While I know my husband is an honest man, it's Ginger that I worry about. On the other hand, if Arnold stays home he'll be underfoot again, and I can't handle that.

Auntie Pearl, I don't want to endanger my marriage, but what should I do?

Distraught in Dracut

Dear Distraught:

How many good walks are ruined by the "rewards" people think they've earned? Whether it's walking, running, or cycling, it often ends with a "treat" at Starbucks or Dunkin' Donuts. Furthermore, folks overestimate how many calories they've burned when they help themselves to coffee and pastry.

Additionally, the carbohydrates cause a spike in blood sugar. This sets the body up for a crash when the levels inevitably fall. What is the quick fix? More carbs! This vicious circle wreaks havoc with the adrenals.

A healthy scenario would involve your husband and Ginger bringing water with them. They could still have a refreshing break that wouldn't disrupt their glycemic levels. For those who find carrying a water bottle cumbersome, I've seen nifty harnesses that allow you to strap the bottle around your waist.

Not only that—with the money your husband saves, you could take a mini vacation and get your marriage back on track!

Signed,

Auntie Pearl

CHAPTER THIRTEEN

Cal rapped on the Chitwicks' aluminum storm door. He bounced on the soles of his feet to increase his circulation. It was a frigid afternoon, the kind when you fear your nose will snap off in the cold. He glanced behind him at the street, hoping to see the pastor arriving. Apart from the police cruiser, only Hyacinth's Prius with its bumper sticker, Honor the Light Within, was in the driveway.

Now she appeared at the door, her smooth silver hair tucked behind her ears. She wore no makeup except a shimmer of lip gloss. "Cal, come in," she said, swinging open the door. "Unseasonably cold, isn't it?"

"We usually get a couple days like this before Christmas. It won't last." He glanced around. "Is Pastor here?"

She shook her head, frowning. "He knows you're coming. Maybe I should have reminded him before he left this morning. This is a busy time of year for the parish."

"Does he have a cell phone?"

"He does, but he rarely turns it on. I'm sure Walter got tied up counseling someone. He'll be along. Why don't we get started, rather than waiting around?" She crossed the kitchen and opened the cellar door. "We'll go down here where we won't be interrupted."

She headed down the cellar stairs, leaving Cal no choice but to follow. When he reached the bottom step, she was already seated within the circle of chairs. She patted the adjacent seat. "Sit here. You'll find whatever you need to say will flow within this sacred space."

He looked around the dim basement. "Do you have a lamp?"

"We've got a light over the washer, but it's harsh. I only put it on when I'm doing laundry." She patted the neighboring chair again. "Before we begin, would you like some herbal tea?"

Cal, who had a suspicion of all things herbal, said, "How about coffee?" He lowered himself into the seat next to her.

"You policemen and your coffee. Herbal tea, such as skullcap, is a healthy remedy for job stress." She touched his knee. "And it won't leave you with coffee jitters."

"Coffee jitters is what keeps me going."

He removed a notepad from his pocket, turned a few pages, and cleared his throat. "I'll just go ahead. We can fill Pastor in when he arrives." He scanned his notes, although it wasn't necessary. He knew how he would approach the issue.

"You're maybe not aware of a situation that's been brewing at the middle school. It concerns Nathaniel's poster entry in a contest the *Granite Cove Gazette* is sponsoring. Students at the school were invited to submit entries. The subject was the statue at the park, the one on horseback?" He stopped to look at her.

"I'm aware of the Homer Frost statue. I'm not surprised it's been allowed to deteriorate all these years. At one point

I thought of doing something about it, but as it glorifies war, I decided to not get involved."

He nodded and continued: "As I was saying, the *Granite Cove Gazette* aims to create publicity and, at the same time, raise money—" He stopped when she placed her hand on his knee.

"Cal, I know about the contest." Her grip tightened on his knee. "Are you saying Nathaniel has won?"

He attempted to cross his legs. "Uh, not exactly. They haven't chosen a winner yet. The controversy, you see, is about Nathaniel's entry. Some people—school officials— think it might be too... too violent."

She withdrew her hand from his knee and sat up straight. "How typical an attitude from this provincial town. It makes one understand how the witch trials came about. Anyone with an original perspective is considered a danger." She looked at him with narrowed eyes. "Exactly what are the school officials proposing?"

"Let's see." He glanced at his notepad, stalling for time. "Well, Nathaniel could withdraw his entry. That was Ms. Fedderbush the principal's suggestion."

"Never!"

Hyacinth got to her feet, shoving the chairs aside. "I'll take the school committee to court if they infringe upon my son's freedom of expression. Nathaniel is a gifted young man, while the little minds of Granite Cove are closed. Violence? That's not violence, that's *exuberance*." She thrust her fist into the air.

"Ma'am, please sit down," Cal said, watching her warily. He wished he'd obeyed his impulse to come back and talk to both parents. "I'm sure this can be worked out.

You and your husband can review your options with Ms. Fedderbush."

Her nostrils flared. "Options? I'll give them options. Tomorrow I'm contacting the ACLU. After that, I'm calling Fox News and telling them the Salem Witch Trials are being reenacted five miles away in Granite Cove."

Cal got to his feet. "Nothing's been decided yet. Ms. Fedderbush and the school psychologist want to have a dialogue with you and—"

"Tell them to dialogue with Spencer Farley, our attorney, whom I'm calling as soon as you leave."

She marched to the bottom of the stairs and waited, her arms locked across her chest. Before heading up, Cal said, "Tell Pastor to call if he has any questions." Outside, he sank into the driver's seat with a sigh and wondered at what point everything had gone wrong.

At four o'clock that afternoon, Yvonne opened her desk drawer and removed her rubber galoshes. Amid much panting and pulling, she managed to tug them over her espadrilles.

"You leaving early?" Stewart asked, sounding hopeful.

"I am. We have rehearsals tonight, and I've got to prepare Mother's dinner before the home aide arrives. The silly girl can't heat food in a saucepan. She uses a microwave, and Mother hates the microwave."

"Why is that?" Rose asked, picking up the conversation when Stew showed no inclination to continue.

"She claims it gives food a metallic taste, and she could be right. Mother is sensitive to many things. She wants to be tested for gluten."

"That's a crock," Stewart said from behind his computer.

Yvonne looked up. "I beg your pardon?"

"What I mean is, gluten allergy's a hoax perpetuated upon the American people by the media."

"That's a rash statement coming from a newsperson."

Rose, the harmonizer, rushed to change the subject. "How's the play coming along? I've been meaning to get over there and take photos."

Yvonne, at the coat rack, lowered her poncho over her head and said from inside its folds, "My dear, how fabulous. Why not come around seven thirty? We'll have taken our break."

"Oh, tonight? I didn't mean tonight."

"What's wrong with tonight?"

"Let's see..." Rose's mind was a blank. "Well... I guess I could come tonight."

"Wonderful. How could I function without you?" Before turning to go, she gave Stewart a withering glance.

When the door closed behind Yvonne, Rose sighed and Stewart chuckled. "McNichols, you walked right into that. Will you never learn?"

"I had no excuse. Yvonne uses her mother when she wants to get out of doing something. All I've got is a dog." She gulped the last of her tepid coffee. "I could mention Kevin, but Yvonne knows he performs at night. Oh, well, I was planning on taking pictures anyway."

"Try to get a picture of the lovers climbing into the chief's SUV." He paused and added, "Oh, I forgot. They're not meeting tonight."

"How do you know?"

He shrugged. "Because I can interpret human behavior. For instance, when it's nooky night, Yvonne doesn't eat onions that day. She gets a takeout sandwich at Mega Mug and there's no onions. That's the tip-off."

"I can't believe the chief would risk exposure in a city-owned parking lot."

"Of course not," Stewart scoffed. "They go someplace private. The cops know all the secret places in this town."

"I still find it hard to believe," she said, though she didn't. How else to explain Yvonne's erratic mood swings?

"I'm sure Cal knows about their affair," Stewart said, "but he'd never tell you."

"I'll have you know that Cal tells me everything, or mostly everything."

"Not this. It's the way cops are wired. They don't squeal on each other."

"That's a good policy," she said, giving him a direct look.

Before leaving the house, Rose helped a half asleep Chester climb up on the sofa. "I don't know what you have to be so tired about," she complained. "I'm the one who's putting in the long days." In response, he groaned and rolled over, exposing his belly. His snoring was the last thing she heard when she closed the door behind her.

She stood in the driveway and stared next door. Her neighbors to the right were having a party. Their circular driveway was lined with bumper-to-bumper SUVs like a row of army tanks. Party noises drifted out on the night air, a cacophony of manic voices. On the lawn, the wind had blown over an illuminated reindeer. It lay on its back as if defeated, its legs in the air.

She started the Jetta and shivered when the heater blasted cold air. She hadn't wanted to go out on such a night. All day she'd looked forward to a quiet evening at home, reading the latest M.C. Beaton mystery. If Kevin stopped by later, she'd planned to open the bottle of wine the Phippses had given her. Each departing party guest had received a pastel bag containing a bottle of wine and a box of Swiss chocolates. Upon examining Betty Ann's bottle, Tiny had pronounced it "good shit."

The minute Rose opened the doors to the auditorium, she knew something was wrong. The stage was empty and the footlights turned low. In the dimness she spotted a cluster of people, some standing, some seated in the front row.

They looked up expectantly. "Oh, it's just Rose," Florence said.

"Thanks for the cheery greeting," Rose said, walking down the darkened center aisle.

Chipper attempted a smile. "Sorry. We thought you might be Nathaniel."

Rose looked around at the downcast faces. Yvonne paced before the stage, scratching her forearms. Milton sat sprawled, staring at the ceiling. Several of the actors were draped across the side access stairs.

"So, where's Nathaniel?" she asked.

"He's dropped out upon his mother's insistence." Yvonne said. "Hyacinth heard about the controversy at the middle school and she's retaliating." She resumed pacing. "Oh, I wish the chief were here. He'd know what to do."

Florence snickered. "Yeah, he'd force the kid to return at gunpoint."

"If that's your idea of a joke, it's not funny," Yvonne said. "Victor Alfano is a brilliant strategist."

"Don't get your undies in a twist," Florence snapped back. She moved to stand next to Rose. "What's a strategist?" she muttered.

"It's a... oh, I don't know. Don't mind Yvonne. She's worried about the newspaper's reputation. We're the ones sponsoring the contest."

"Yeah, but folks know you're just trying to raise money for that statue."

"Maybe we can get another Tiny Tim," Chipper said dispiritedly.

"Not at this late date," Yvonne said. "This is all my fault. The poster contest seemed so worthy, getting the young people involved. Who knew it would go so wrong?"

"No," Chipper said, "it's my fault. I should have gotten an understudy for the role of Tiny Tim. I used poor judgment."

"You're both wrong," Rose said. "It was my error. Betty Ann's stepson identified Nathaniel as the anonymous artist. I should have kept quiet."

Florence threw her hands in the air. "You folks quit your bellyaching and listen to me. I've got an idea." She hitched up the long white nightgown and climbed onto a seat. From there she surveyed the group, her hands on her hips. "While you've been yammering on, a face kept appearing in my head. It's that artist that everyone's so gaga about, the Spanish guy in the beret. He's supposed to be a big deal in the art world. Why don't we let him decide whether Nathaniel's poster is art or not. If he says it's art, that'll put a stop to those worrywarts at the school."

A silence fell over the group as they considered the proposal. Yvonne was the first to speak: "I think it's a wonderful idea. If Manuel del Toro says Nathaniel is talented, I'm sure Hyacinth will be mollified. But how can we be certain he'll appreciate Nathaniel's work?"

Florence grinned. "Because the guy's sweet on Rose. If she asked him nice, I'll bet he'd say whatever she wants him to say."

Yvonne turned to Rose. "You could take him to lunch at the Gingham Dog, compliments of the *Gazette*, of course."

"And buy him a few martinis," Florence said. "I saw how he was tossing them down at the Phippses' party."

"You must wear something alluring," Chipper added. "You're free to check out our wardrobe department."

"Thank you all for volunteering my services," Rose said. "If you don't mind, I'll have to think about this."

"I say we're on the right track," Florence said. "Hyacinth is always claiming her son's a genius. If Manuel says he is, no one at the school department's gonna doubt him. After all, the guy's an artist from Europe."

"Is he really?" Rose asked her.

Florence shrugged. "Who knows? He's not from around here."

The auditorium doors burst open and the group turned, hoping to see the missing Tiny Tim. Instead it was Dorothy Dunbar, her nose red from the cold. She headed for the group, carrying a large box from Dunkin' Donuts.

"What's this?" Chipper said, taking the box from her and setting it on the edge of the stage.

She unbuttoned her long coat. "I was just leaving the nursing home when Pastor Chitwick took me aside. He told me about the situation here and asked if I would deliver these to you. He says he regrets how things have turned out."

"Is he going to let Nathaniel return?" Florence asked, removing a blueberry donut from the box. Other cast members followed.

"I can't answer that," Dorothy said. "From what I gather, it's up to the boy's mother."

"In that case, we don't have a snowball's chance in hell," Yvonne said, and quickly added, "Excuse my language. I'm quite upset. We've been rehearsing the play for weeks and may have to cancel."

Licking powdered sugar from her fingers, Florence said, "It ain't over til it's over. Give Rose a chance to go to work on that artist."

"She'd better do it quickly," Yvonne said. "Next week is dress rehearsal."

When everyone turned to look at Rose, she rolled her eyes. "Okay, I'll see what I can do."

Chip leaped to his feet and clapped his hands for silence. "If I could have your attention. I think the chaplain's arrival is a sign. Those who are religiously inclined might call it a blessing. In any case, we should continue our work here. We've gone too far to turn back." The group broke into applause and he said, "Let's get to work. Chorus, I need you on stage. We'll rehearse the first two songs."

As the group moved onto the stage, Yvonne called to Rose, "We'll talk tomorrow, first thing."

Rose headed for the exit. At the auditorium doors, she spotted Dorothy approaching, her coat collar turned up. Rose held the door for the chaplain and said, "I'm glad I got a chance to see you. I have a few of your sister's personal items: a notebook, a couple of framed photos. They were collected from her desk at the shredding plant."

Dorothy placed a hand on Rose's forearm. "You're very sweet, but I'm afraid they would open old wounds. Dionne and I had made our amends. Some issues simply cannot be bridged, and one must know when to let go." She managed a smile. "I tell those whom I counsel that time is the greatest healer. Now I must take my own advice."

Before going to her car, Rose stopped at the girls' bathroom off the lobby. She ran water into a basin, feeling like a giant bending over the low sink. She washed her fingers, sticky from the lemon doughnut she'd eaten.

At the front entrance door, she buttoned her coat and pulled on her gloves. When she stepped outside, she glanced around the darkened parking lot. About ten cars were in the first rows. She'd parked behind them.

As she walked briskly to the Jetta, a car slowly approached her from behind. She remembered Stewart's gossip about the chief waiting in the back lot. She felt alarmed: Had the man mistaken her for Yvonne? How awkward it would be when he realized his error. Then she recalled Stew's final analysis: Yvonne had eaten onions; no chief tonight.

She resumed walking. As the car moved closer, bright headlights flashed. She shielded her eyes from the glare, quickening her step. Was it Cal, spying on her again? The engine suddenly roared and the car shot forward. She leaped ahead and fell, sprawling on the icy pavement. At the same time, the car raced out of the lot, its tires screeching. She struggled to her feet in time to see it speed away.

Inside the Jetta, she found antiseptic wipes in the glove box. She dabbed at her raw, skinned knee. She'd torn a gaping hole in her favorite jeans. Fortunately, torn and ripped jeans were in vogue.

With shaking hands, she put the key in the ignition and wondered if she should call Cal and report the incident. What could she tell him? She had gotten no license plate number. She didn't know the make or model of the car. She wondered if the driver had even seen her in the darkness. Or had someone deliberately tried to run her down?

CHAPTER FOURTEEN

It was midmorning on Friday when Yvonne pushed her chair away from her desk and glanced at the clock. "I believe I'm ready for mug-up. Let's hope Stewart has made enough coffee."

Rose laughed at Yvonne's use of the waterfront term for coffee break. It confirmed that her editor was in a good mood. This had surprised Rose, who had feared that Yvonne would be distraught over Nathaniel's absence from the play. Instead the woman was acting unflappable, like her idol, Katherine Hepburn. Rose wondered how long the good mood would last.

She'd no sooner hung her jacket on the back of her chair that morning when Yvonne appeared at her elbow, a slip of paper between her fingers. "I spoke to Myrna Phipps and got Manuel del Toro's number. He uses the public phone at Harbor House, where's he's staying. I imagine that as an artist he prefers the colorful characters who live there."

Rose was familiar with Harbor House, a boarding house for drifters, loners, and alcoholics. The late Rusty Favazza, a former golden boy turned drug addict, had been a resident. Reflecting upon life in the ramshackle Harbor House, he'd said, "If you don't bother nobody, nobody bothers you."

Yvonne handed Rose the paper. "This is the number of the phone in the hallway. Mrs. Phipps said you have to let it ring several times before anyone answers."

Rose nodded and pocketed the number. Next she devoted her attention to finishing her housekeeping hints column for the next week's issue. Before she had a chance to do a spell-check, Yvonne said, "It might be a good time to call before Mr. del Toro begins his day."

Rose nodded resignedly and picked up her desk phone. She punched in the numbers on the slip and waited. After a dozen rings she was about to hang up when a woman answered: "Yeah."

"Excuse me, but could you tell Mr. del Toro that Rose McNichols wishes to speak to him?"

The woman dropped the receiver and cursed. It banged against the wall as she shouted, "Manny, telephone!"

Yvonne, watching Rose hunched over the phone asked, "What's happening?"

Before Rose could respond, a voice boomed from the phone: "This is Manuel del Toro. Who is this?"

"Mr. del Toro, this is Rose McNichols, the reporter from the *Granite Cove Gazette*. We met at the Phippses' party the other night."

"Ah, yes, the lovely Rose, always scribbling in her book. Do you know what I thought, meeting you that evening?"

"What's that?"

"That you were a rose among the thorns."

He laughed at his joke, no doubt forgetting he'd already said it, and she joined in. When the laughter subsided she said, "I have a favor to ask of you—"

"I don't mind when beautiful women ask favors."

She gave a brief account of their dilemma. "So you see, Mr. del Toro, the play cannot be performed without this young man's participation. And since everyone respects your artistic opinion, we thought you might evaluate his work. If you approve, we're hoping the boy's mother will let him return to the play and the school officials will be satisfied."

"It sounds like you have too many cooks stirring the broth. You Americans make complications. When you visit my country, you bring too many suitcases. At the beach, the families are like beasts of burden trudging across the sand. I am exhausted to watch them." He sighed into the phone. "But if I can help my lovely Rose, I will do what I can. Would you like to visit me here? I'm making sangria in my room."

"Well, I was hoping to take you to lunch at the Gingham Dog. It's a restaurant and 'B and B'. Are you familiar with it?"

His laugh was like a bark. "I am familiar. It is where I first stayed when I arrived at your town as a guest of Senora Phipps. A charming inn but too many rules. The bar closed at one in the morning. In España we are going out at that hour." He chuckled. "At Harbor House they do not care how many guests I entertain in my room."

After a short discussion, they settled upon a day to meet for lunch. "Do you want me to pick you up?" she asked.

"I cannot refuse a lovely woman's invitation, *por favor*."

They said their good-byes and hung up.

"Well, that's settled," Yvonne said. "Do you think we should tell Hyacinth? She'll be thrilled at the thought of an internationally famous artist evaluating her child's work."

"Wait a minute," Rose said. "Manuel agreed to evaluate Nathaniel's poster. There's no guarantee he'll adore it."

"Well, of course he will." She stared at Rose over her glasses. "That's the whole point of the lunch."

"What if he thinks its disturbed?"

"Then do as Florence suggested—buy him another drink. Do whatever it takes to get a glowing opinion from the man."

"Why don't we take up a collection and offer him a bribe?" Rose couldn't keep the sarcasm from her voice.

Yvonne smiled. "That won't be necessary if you use your feminine wiles."

"Yvonne, I can't believe you'd make such a sexist remark."

Yvonne swiveled in her chair to face Rose. "Lest you forget, we're talking about a very vindictive woman. Hyacinth Chitwick can sue the town for defamation of character. Chief Alfano has already spoken to the city solicitor about the situation. For some reason, Hyacinth has it in for Granite Cove. She needs little excuse to file a lawsuit."

Rose thought of the threatening letters Hyacinth had received, which had added fuel to her fire, and wondered if she had received any others. When she'd learned that Rose had confided in Cal, Hyacinth said nothing more about her mail. Although Rose felt guilty for leaking the information, she knew she'd done the right and lawful thing.

Now she addressed Yvonne: "You're saying that no matter what Manuel thinks of Nathaniel's work, I'm to somehow convince him it's brilliant?"

"Brilliant's too much to hope for. It's enough he admits the boy has talent." She gazed at Rose, her expression earnest. "I know you can do it, dear. He'll be charmed by your youthful spirit and gracious manner."

"I'm *not* going to bed with the guy, if that's what you have in mind."

Yvonne looked shocked. "Rose, how vulgar. I was merely suggesting that you enjoy a pleasant meal with Mr. del Toro. From what I hear, the man loves his martinis and brandy. Keep his glass filled. You won't have any trouble influencing him. Let's not forget that our play is also in jeopardy. It would be ghastly if we had to cancel. Chipper and the cast have put heart and soul into this production."

"I can't believe you don't have an understudy for Tiny Tim."

"Remember, this is community theater. There are few understudies. It's hard convincing parents to allow their children to participate, with rehearsals taking place at night." She paused. "Not only that; although Nathaniel may be too robust for the role, no one else auditioned for the part. Chipper said if worst comes to worst, he could play Scrooge. Florence, who's thin and wiry, could be Tiny Tim." She rubbed her forehead. "But could makeup transform a sixty-two-year-old woman into a ten-year-old boy? What about that voice?"

Rose imagined Florence shrieking, "God bless us, every one," and got to her feet.

"First things first," she said. "We'll get Manuel to go along with our way of thinking. Then we'll tell Hyacinth that a *world-renowned artist* thinks her son is a genius. Following that, we'll inform the trolls at the school department that Nathaniel is no psychopath, he's a budding Picasso."

"Oh, bravo, dear." Yvonne reached out and grasped her arm.

"Who are you seducing now?" Stewart asked Rose. He'd been quietly barricaded behind his desktop monitor. Now his voice startled her.

"These cold winter nights, I snuggle up with Chester," she said.

"That's not what I hear," he muttered, rising from his desk.

She ignored his remark. Out of the corner of her eye she watched him move to the wooden coat rack. There he struggled into a worn sheepskin coat with wooden barrel buttons. Following that, he wrapped a long striped scarf around his face and neck. Finally he pulled a tweed golfer's cap over his head.

She and Yvonne watched in fascination. At last Yvonne said, "Where are you headed, all bundled up like that?"

His voice emerged from layers of wool. "I'm walking over to St. Rupert's Church."

"Is there some special service going on?"

He scoffed at that. "I'm interviewing the farmer who rents the Nativity livestock to the church. He's got a place up in Kingston, New Hampshire. Drives down once a week to check on the animals."

"My, that has the potential for a lovely story, but I don't see the sports angle. Shouldn't Rose or Coral be interviewing him?"

He tugged the scarf away from his mouth. "The guy used to be a rodeo champ, touring all over the country. Now he's retired and raises sheep, goats, llamas…"

"I'm always amazed by the stories we uncover in this village," Yvonne said. "You've got a nose for news, Stewart. I've mentioned that to Mr. Curley several times."

"Right." He headed for the exit.

After he vanished out the door, Yvonne said, "Speaking of potential, there's a case in point. Stewart's ancestors represent some of Boston's finest families. Blood doesn't come any bluer than that." She shook her head.

"That's what I've heard," Rose said.

"Yet with all that potential, why is he so—"

"Nerdy?"

Yvonne sighed. "I was going to say unprepossessing, but I suppose nerdy will do."

Rose turned back to her computer. "You said it yourself, Yvonne. Too much blue blood, not enough red."

Rose took a late lunch in order to stop and see her dad. It had been a week since she'd spoken to him, which was unusual. Most times he'd call her, claiming loneliness. Now, since neighbor and geriatric fitness queen Jeannette had entered his life, the calls had lessened.

Rose's feelings about the new relationship were mixed. On the one hand, she was happy for him. When she was on deadline, she felt guilty for cutting their conversations short. On the other hand, now that his calls had all but ceased, she felt threatened.

After years of being number one in her dad's life, she couldn't accept being in second place. Jeannette had better get that through her curly white head.

She decided to stop at Stella's and pick up her dad's favorite sandwich. The sausage, tomato, and Velveeta cheese with mayo was on Doc Moss's forbidden list. Next on the list were her dad's two other favorites: fried clams and chocolate-covered cherries.

Nonetheless, when she'd dutifully followed the doctor's dietetic guidelines, her dad had been indifferent. "You call this a burger?" he'd asked, lifting the whole-wheat bun to peer inside.

"It's a vegetarian burger, Dad. It's made with portabello," Rose explained.

"Porta what?"

"Portabello mushrooms."

He sniffed the faux burger. "Huh, smells like a Porta-Potty."

Stella's Sausage Kitchen was an anomaly in a seacoast fishing village. A no-frills establishment known for deep-fried meats, its parking lot was always filled. Not only was it a locals' hangout, the tourists flocked there too.

Rose found a parking spot near the base of the three pigs. As often happened, someone was being photographed in front of the trio. The four-foot-tall pink plastic pigs, set on a riser, were Stella's pride and joy. They'd become Granite Cove icons and a landmark. People giving directions said, "When you see the pigs on your left, Main Street is your second right."

The middle-aged man spotted Rose getting out of her car and sheepishly lowered his camera, as if caught doing something risqué. His subject, a woman of about the same age, waited.

"Would you like me to take a picture of both of you?" Rose offered.

The grateful pair nodded. The man handed her the camera and joined his companion in front of the three grinning pigs. Rose snapped their photo. The couple had joined the legion of tourists who'd been photographed with Stella's pigs as a backdrop. The porkers' popularity rivaled that of Gloucester's statue of a fisherman at the wheel, and Salem's House of the Seven Gables.

Inside the '50s era knotty pine eatery, Stella stood behind the grill brandishing a giant spatula while keeping watch on everything. A transplanted Southerner with hair the color of scrambled eggs and arms like Popeye's, Stella had a rough exterior that hid a tender heart. Once she accepted you, you joined the regulars. According to Cal Devine, Stella had "the best bullshit detector on the North Shore."

Stella greeted Rose as she stepped to the counter. Rose mentioned her encounter with the tourists outside. "The chamber of commerce ought to have postcards of your pigs. It'd be a lot better than the current offerings."

"I didn't know they even sold postcards," Stella said, scratching her back with the spatula.

"It's a pretty sorry lot. They sell four basic cards: the Homer Frost statue, a seagull in flight, a fishing trawler tied at the wharf, and a recipe for clam chowder. Who'd want to visit Granite Cove after receiving such boring postcards?"

Stella looked thoughtful. "That's a good idea about my pigs, but I can't make the suggestion. Dot Biddle runs the chamber, and she don't like me. We had a dustup not long ago when she wanted to have a luncheon here for the Colonial Dames. I said 'fine' until she started fussing about the menu. She wanted to know about gluten and trans-fats, and could I substitute this and that. I finally said she could kiss my grits if she expected me to turn my kitchen upside down for a bunch of old prunes."

"I guess that didn't go over too well," Rose said.

"Nope," Stella said. "It means my pigs won't be decorating any postcards in the near future."

"It's too bad," Rose said. "New cards would be good for the town's image."

"I hope they hold off a bit. I'm thinking of getting the pigs glazed, to keep the salt from corroding 'em. One of my customers, a car appraiser, said that's the problem with living in a seaside town. The salt air does a number on everything."

"Without a doubt," Rose said. "My mechanic said the Jetta's undercarriage is rusted out. He warned me not to haul anything heavy."

The advice had given her pause when she and Kevin had double dated one night with Betty Ann and Tiny. Kevin sat in the front passenger seat while the well-upholstered Zagrobskis occupied the back. Rose thought it best to not mention the mechanic's warning. Nonetheless, it had been a relief when she finally dropped the couple off at the end of the night.

"Think if it as an investment in your business," Rose said. "The glazing would also be a tax deduction."

Stella pointed the spatula at her. "Good idea. I'll ask Spencer Farley when he comes in for breakfast tomorrow. He's my lawyer."

He's everyone's lawyer, Rose thought. Lately the distinguished-looking attorney had been avoiding her. Not that she was surprised. His wife, Martha, had spent time in the women's prison in Framingham for an aborted attempt on Rose's life one summer night. The situation made for awkward conversation. On the other hand, if Rose found herself needing legal advice, she wouldn't hesitate to call Spencer. He'd known her dad back when the Farleys owned a marine supply store and her father was a steady customer. Not only that, Spencer never charged Rose for his help. Thus she didn't hold "Mad Martha's" behavior against him.

Now she put her key in the ignition. At the same time, a Granite Cove Police cruiser eased in next to her. Cal hopped out. She lowered her window, catching him looking at the grease-stained bag on the passenger seat.

"Dad's lunch," she explained. "I'm going to visit him."

He rested a forearm on her window. "Tell him I promise to take him fishing this summer. We talked about it last year."

"Are you getting a boat?"

"This is stripers. We fish off the rocks."

"I'll tell him, but you'd better mean it. He doesn't get out much and looks forward to it." This was true, although since Jeanette had entered her dad's life he hadn't been complaining about a lack of company.

"I promise," he said. "Your dad and I go way back."

"I know." She felt her cheeks flush and automatically looked away.

He tapped her shoulder. "I've been meaning to talk to you about Marilyn's Pie Palace. It's about Florence's niece."

"Kristal? What about her?"

He straightened and glanced around the lot before answering. "Remember I asked if you'd heard about anything funny going on over there?"

"Uh-huh."

"Well, we're pretty certain Kristal's been turning tricks."

"*What?*"

"The action takes place outside, in the cars. It involves the guys from the shredding plant down the street. When they come in at night they use code words when placing their order, such as 'hold the nuts' and 'deep dish.' After finishing their pie and coffee, they go outside, where Kristal joins them. There's a half dozen guys involved."

Rose shook her head in disbelief.

He continued: "Maybe you can speak to Kristal before someone busts her. It'd be rough on her aunt, Florence."

"It would kill Florence," Rose said, "and Marilyn as well. She's worked so hard to build that business. Something like that would destroy her good name. How'd you hear about it?"

"Someone dropped a dime on her."

Rose thought for a moment. "Was it a woman? Someone who works at the shredding plant?"

He looked away. "I don't know. I didn't take the call."

She met his eyes. "Cal Devine, you can't lie to me. Was it Emma Ubbink, Director of Outreach Shredding Services?"

He shrugged. "I wouldn't know."

"And you wouldn't tell me, either."

"I've already said too much. Listen, I'm doing this for Florence. As far as I'm concerned, Kristal deserves what's coming to her. In any case, you didn't hear it from me."

"Hear what?" She gave him a wink and a wave and drove out of the parking lot.

As she drove away, she thought about Cal's disclosure: Marilyn's Pie Palace, home of the Holy Night Pie, involved in sex for sale. And why should she be the one to intervene? She barely knew Kristal and suspected that any intervention, no matter how well-meaning, would not be appreciated. People like Kristal tended to learn the hard way.

Yet she couldn't expose Florence to the shame of such a scandal. The woman didn't deserve that. Rose would have to speak to Kristal and leave Florence out of it. However, speaking to Kristal wouldn't be enough. The girl had to be caught before she'd pay attention.

As Rose drove along Ancient County Road, a plan formed in her mind...

Auntie Pearl's Helpful Housekeeping Hints

Dear Auntie Pearl:

Lorna and I met in midlife. She'd been divorced, while I'd never married. The first year of our marriage was wonderful; we were compatible in every way. When we bought a house in the suburbs, Lorna said she wanted a cat. She'd always lived in apartments that didn't allow pets.

Before long, "Prissy" entered our lives. As Lorna had never had children, this cat became her child— and a spoiled one at that. Lorna didn't allow Prissy to go outside, because of coyotes in the area. Yet she didn't want to deprive Prissy of the opportunity to roll in the grass and chase butterflies. Lorna hired a company to install a special pet fence. Although it was expensive I said nothing, wanting to please my wife. However, now I can't fit the lawn mower through the opening in the fence. Consequently our yard is an overgrown tangle of grass and weeds. Lorna claims cats prefer junglelike conditions.

I was willing to put up with this and other restrictions, such as Lorna refusing to go away for an overnight without the cat. But lately she's gone too far. Recently Lorna took Prissy for her monthly checkup. The cat doesn't like to ride in a carrier, so Lorna put my favorite Irish mohair scarf inside. Prissy peed on it.

I've told my wife she'll have to choose between the cat and me because I can't see the situation improving.

Had it in Harwich

Dear Had It:

No doubt Prissy hadn't been exposed to the scarf before your wife put it in the carrier. Cats are like children: they crave the familiar. When using a carrier, it's best to include a towel or pillowcase, something that smells like "home." At the same time, it's a good idea to sprinkle catnip on the item (crush it between your fingers first to release the full scent). Recently a new product for this very situation has come on the market. It's a pheromone spray that is calming to cats. Do an Internet search to find it.

Follow my instructions and you'll have a contented kitty the next time Prissy visits the vet.

Signed,

Auntie Pearl

CHAPTER FIFTEEN

Rose had just stepped into the Gingham Dog restaurant when Oliver, the bow-tied manager, signaled to her. "Mr. del Toro wants you to call him." He handed her a slip of paper with the phone number of the Harbor House.

"I'm supposed to meet him here." She glanced at her watch. "Right about now."

"I believe that's why he called. Something about needing a ride."

"My phone's in the car," she said, turning to the door.

He indicated the front desk. "By all means, use our phone."

She dialed the number. Once again a surly woman answered and bellowed for Manuel. Rose heard laughter and then, "This is Manuel del Toro."

"Manuel, this is Rose McNichols. I'm at the Gingham Dog."

"Oh, my lovely Rose. I am in what you call a 'pickle.' My driver has abandoned me and I have no way to meet you."

She said she would pick him up, instructing him to be outside in ten minutes. After hanging up, she explained the situation to Oliver and asked if he would hold the reservation.

"Of course we will. No need to rush."

She thanked him and went out to the parking lot, wondering why she ever volunteered for such an undertaking. Ten minutes later she pulled into the potholed parking lot of Harbor House. As always, the ramshackle building appeared about to topple into the sea. A lone seagull perched on the chimney. The wraparound porch was missing several slats. Through the gap she saw a rusted aluminum lounge chair covered in snow. She scanned the entrance: no sign of Manuel.

With a sigh, she shut off the motor and got out of the Jetta. She hadn't asked Manuel his room number. Now she felt in her pockets: no phone number. She must have thrown it away. She approached the entrance and called Manuel's name. The old Victorian house was eerily quiet. The only sound was that of the plastic webbing on the lounge chair snapping in the breeze. She finally climbed the ice-crusted stairs to the porch.

The front door opened into a narrow foyer. A wooden lectern held a battered registration book so old it had probably recorded Winslow Homer's stay. She peeked into what must have been the parlor. Mahogany panels covering the walls were dull with age. A chandelier's crystals were yellow. Against one wall a once-elegant Queen Anne sofa sagged with resignation.

She heard laughter and moved into the dim hallway, knocking on the first door on the left. After a moment, it opened a crack, revealing a milky blue eye and a springy beard that jutted out as if it couldn't be contained.

"Excuse me," she said. "I'm looking for Manuel del Toro."

"He's upstairs," the occupant barked and yanked the door shut.

"Thanks," she said to the closed door.

She climbed the stairs and, at the top, looked down the length of a long corridor lined with doors. A woman's high-pitched laughter came from a room whose door was partially open. Rose approached slowly and peeked inside.

Sunlight streaming in from a tall dusty window illuminated the room's occupants. Manuel, shockingly bald and wearing a black motorcycle jacket, sat on a twin bed. On the other lounged two fortyish women who at first glance looked like twins. All three clutched red plastic glasses.

"You've got company, Manny," one of the women said, spotting Rose outside. She sounded none too pleased.

"I hope it is not my wife," he joked, rising to his feet and swinging the door wide open. "Ah, it is my sweetheart, taking me to lunch."

He beckoned Rose into the room, where he introduced his guests. They were sisters Lana and Grace Masucci, his new friends. As Manuel introduced Rose—"a brilliant writer"—the sisters, lounging on the bed, looked her up and down. Rose in turn studied their platinum teased hair and artificially tanned faces. Both wore low-cut jerseys, one turquoise, the other pink, over tight jeans. Cowboy boots, pink for Lana and silver for Grace, completed the ensembles.

Having decided that Rose posed no threat, Grace leaned forward and said, "Let's see your nails." Before Rose could pull away, the woman grabbed her hand and studied it, clucking her tongue. "Honey, these are so bad we'll do them for free."

Rose mumbled something about keeping them short for typing.

"Come to our booth at the convention tomorrow," Grace said. "We'll fix you up."

Rose stuffed her hands into her coat pockets and asked what convention she was referring to.

"The nail convention in Salem, New Hampshire."

Before Rose could reply, Manuel, who'd been mixing drinks at a rickety wooden dresser, handed her a glass. "Sangria," he said. "Take off your coat and sit down." He tossed clothing and books off the bed, clearing a space.

Rose glanced at her watch. "Manuel, we have a lunch reservation at the restaurant."

He refilled his own glass from a tall pitcher. "First I want you to hear how I met my new girlfriends." He collapsed on their bed, burrowing in between the pair to rest his head against the wall.

"Is he a character or what?" Grace said, snuggling against him. "We're trying to talk Manny into visiting us in Providence."

"Tell her how we met him," Lana said, tilting her head back to drain her glass.

"Hey, take it easy with that stuff," her sister warned. "We're going out to dinner tonight. I don't want you passing out on me."

"Tell Rose the story," Manuel said, grinning.

"Yes, do," Rose said, taking a discreet sip of sangria and another glance at her watch.

"Okay," Grace said. "You see, my sister and I own three nail salons in Rhode Island. Business has been good, even with the recession. So, we decided to go to the annual convention of salon owners, held in Salem, New Hampshire."

Lana sat up abruptly, sloshing her drink. "My dumb sister thought it was Salem, Massachusetts—"

"Shut up. Next time, you make the reservations." Grace turned back to Rose. "I had to book the hotel, so I used one of those online travel agencies. I'd never done it before and things got a little screwed up when I filled in the information. For some reason, they thought I meant Salem, Massachusetts when I wanted Salem, New Hampshire.

"So, anyway, we got to our motel late and checked to see what was open in the area. We saw the Sacred Cod in Granite Cove served food until eleven. We get directions and go there and have dinner. After that, we sit at the bar for a nightcap. Lana here asks the bartender what's the best route to get to the convention center, and he doesn't know what she's talking about."

Grace continued: "My sister pulls out the convention brochure and hands it to the bartender. He studies it and says, 'This is for Salem, New Hampshire.' So I go, 'That's right. We're staying in Salem, New Hampshire, at the Hawthorne Hotel.' He gives me this look and goes, 'The Hawthorne Hotel is in Salem, Massachusetts.'"

Lana shook with laughter, splashing her drink over her shirt.

"At least," Grace said, "Salem New Hampshire isn't too far away. It's maybe another hour. We thought of checking out of the Hawthorne Hotel and getting a motel up there but it was late." She grabbed Manuel's hand. "And then we met this crazy Spaniard and decided to stay put."

Lana leaned her head on Manuel's chest. "Now we have to get up an hour earlier to drive to New Hampshire."

Rose told them it could be worse; they could have ended up in Salem, Oregon. She set her drink on the night table and got to her feet. "Manuel, I told the restaurant manager we'd be right back. They stop serving lunch at three."

He struggled to his feet. "You Americans, all you think about is the clock. Very well, I will not keep them waiting." He addressed the sisters, saying he was leaving for his date. Rose held her breath for fear Grace and Lana would decide to join them. Fortunately the sisters had to return to their hotel.

"I wanna do my nails before we go out," Grace said.

Manuel looked around the room, his hand clutching his scalp. "My beret! I can't go without my beret."

"You wore it when you went to the bathroom," Grace said. "Maybe it crawled into the toilet."

Lana whooped with laughter. "I need a smoke," she said, pushing herself up from the bed.

"On the porch," Manuel said. He had returned from the bathroom wearing the beret and the toupee, which he adjusted in the mirror.

When Lana teetered from the room, Grace said, "She better not get drunk."

Back at the Gingham Dog, Oliver dismissed Rose's apologies with a wave of his hand. He ushered them to a corner table in the dining room where a few diners were still seated. The white tablecloths, dark wooden furniture, maroon walls, and gingham curtains created an atmosphere of genteel civility. Hanging everywhere were artists' interpretations of Eugene Field's celebrated Gingham Dog poem.

Oliver lit a candle on their table and handed them menus. "Would you like a cocktail to start?"

Rose ordered a cranberry juice and vodka.

Manuel asked, "Do you have Louis the Fourteenth brandy?"

"We have Louis the Fifteenth. Will that do?"

Manuel nodded and slipped out of his leather jacket. Under it he wore a striped French sailor's jersey and a red bandana knotted at the neck. He didn't remove his beret, and Rose surmised it was attached to the toupee. When he slung his jacket over the back of his chair, she spotted a silver flask in the pocket.

She opened her menu. "Shall we place our order before the kitchen closes?"

"I don't have to look," he said. "I want the mussels. They are not as good as those in Puerto Banus, but they are decent."

"I forget you're familiar with this place. You said you stayed at the 'B and B'?"

"Until they asked me to leave."

"Oh, that's too bad." She paused, waiting for him to elaborate.

"Manuel was too much for them," he said, winking. He glanced around the room. "Here there are many old people. At night their canes go clomp, clomp on the stairs. They have many complaints: My visitors, they said, were too noisy. I was told not to entertain after midnight." He rolled his eyes. "In Spain, we go out at midnight."

Oliver arrived to place their drinks on the table and ask if they wanted to order. Rose said she'd have the grilled shrimp over couscous, while Manuel ordered mussels. When the man walked away, Manuel said, with a jerk of his head, "That one banished me from the bar one evening."

"Oliver? Why was that?" Rose took a sip of her drink. It was a perfect mixture of vodka, lime, and cranberry juice.

"He wanted me to be like the other guests, the old people with their droopy faces, asleep in the lounge." He winked. "That is not Manuel del Toro."

"That's a good quote," Rose said, taking a notepad from her bag. "By the way, are you represented by any local galleries?"

"Senora Phipps has a friend in New York who is interested. I have shunned the marketplace but lately have been thinking it is time to try the American way." He leaned forward to clasp her hand. "When I go to New York, will you come with me?"

"Oh... I don't think I can. You see, I'm in a steady relationship." She eased her hand away.

He looked puzzled. "What is that?"

"It's when you've got a significant other in your life."

"Significant other?" He reached for her hand again. "Don't talk foolishness, my lovely. Manuel knows what he wants. He wants to lock loins with *you*."

She tugged her hand away. "Let me ask you some questions."

He slumped back in his chair. "You Americans, all you do is ask questions. You should concentrate more on what is in your heart"—he pressed a hand to his chest—"instead of what is in your head." His abrupt movements caused his beret to slip forward. The thick bangs of the toupee now covered his eyebrows. "I would like a brandy," he said, his voice loud in the quiet dining room.

The few remaining diners turned to peer at them. Rose felt her face flush. Manuel, who had seemed fine when they entered the restaurant, now appeared more than tipsy.

Oliver materialized from the other room. "Your food will be out in a moment."

"I want another brandy," Manuel said. "Make it two."

After the man retreated, Rose leaned forward. "Take it easy, Manuel. We've got time."

He glared. "These little people did not know who they were dealing with when they banished Manuel del Toro."

"Do you mean when they banished you from the bar?"

"When they told me to pack up and go. Senor Phipps sent a driver in the middle of the night. He took me to the Harbor House because nothing else was open." He stared into his glass. "I am going to talk to your Spencer Farley."

"I'm sorry to hear that," Rose said. She dug into her tote, producing a folder, which she set on the table. "Manuel, I'm going to the ladies' room. In the meantime, I'd like you to carefully examine the drawing inside. It's the one we discussed earlier."

"The young man who is being persecuted?"

"Something like that. Study it and tell me what you think." She got to her feet. "I'll be right back."

He gazed up at her with unfocused eyes. "Don't be long, my little avocado pit."

Giving him a smile, she left the room. She didn't want to rush Manuel's evaluation, so she took her time. The ladies' room was small and feminine with wallpaper of pink and yellow dahlias. After using the toilet, she washed her hands in a small porcelain sink. A stack of thick paper hand towels embossed with the restaurant's logo were on a shelf above the sink. She stuffed a wad of them into her purse. Before leaving, she applied plum-colored lipstick to brighten her winter pallor. Gazing into the mirror, she said, "Little avocado pit."

When she returned to the table, their food had arrived. Manuel, sipping a fresh drink, stared fixedly at the drawing which, Rose noted, he held upside down. Silently she slipped into her chair and gazed appreciatively at her plate. Plump skewered shrimp lay on a bed of golden couscous. She squeezed a lemon wedge over them and dug in.

After a few minutes Manuel lowered the drawing and looked at her. "You say this is a young man?"

"Yes, he's thirteen."

He tapped his right eye. "He has got the vision, this boy."

"The vision," she repeated, spearing another shrimp.

"The boy's composition is primitive," he said, "but his grasp is mature." He nodded with satisfaction and drained his brandy. "And now you want Manuel del Toro's opinion?" He lay the drawing on the table.

"Oh, yes, please." She leaned back in her chair.

"Tell your school officials they have the brains of a donkey." His voice, already loud, rose. "Tell them Manuel del Toro says this boy has passion."

She grinned. "That's wonderful, Manuel. So you don't think it's too... violent?"

He slammed his glass on the table, causing the plates to rattle.

"Violent? Have you seen Picasso's masterpiece, *Guernica*? It is violent because the man had passion for his subject. He could not hold back what was in his breast." He pressed a fist to his chest. "It is the fools with donkey brains who should be stifled. The artist must never hold back." He shouted, "Never!"

CHAPTER SIXTEEN

"You don't think your dad will marry this Jeannette, do you?" Kevin asked, settling back into the booth at Mega Mug. He and Rose were having lunch. All around them were holiday shoppers, their bags stacked on tables and at their feet. Over the buzz of voices, Christmas carols played, the same selection as last season and the year before that.

Rose scooped whipped cream from her hot chocolate and licked the spoon. "Marry her? God, no."

"What makes you so sure?"

At that moment Muriel arrived with their food: a tuna melt for Rose and a fried clam roll for Kevin. Rose had questioned ordering clams in December. "They'll be frozen," she pointed out.

To which Kevin had shrugged. "Frozen, steamed, or fried. I like clams all ways."

She elaborated upon his question: "How do I know they won't marry? For one thing, Jeannette's a widow who gets a nice pension. According to my dad, her husband had a good job with the state highway department. She's not going to give that up in a hurry."

Kevin shook the plastic ketchup bottle. "She might if she's madly in love."

Rose stared at him. "Kevin Healey, are you trying to get a rise out of me?"

"No, I'm trying to get ketchup from this bottle." He grinned. "You're cute when your feathers are ruffled. But seriously, at their stage in life maybe your dad and Jeannette want to make a commitment. They realize love's more important than money."

"That's ridiculous. You've been watching too much daytime TV. That's totally impractical."

"At their age, they might not be practical minded. They come from an era when couples got married before... you know, before getting between the sheets."

Sipping her cocoa at that moment, Rose gasped. She coughed and pressed a napkin to her mouth.

"Are you okay?" He pushed the water glass toward her. "Take a sip."

"I swallowed too fast and it's hot." She drank and set the glass firmly on the table. "In the first place, Jeannette is ten years younger than my dad. She says she was a hippie in her day, and as you know they invented free love. In the second place, I don't want to contemplate my dad's romantic situation—which, by the way, is nonexistent."

He took her hands in his. "Okay. I was just trying to get a rise out of you."

"It worked. Now knock it off."

"Didn't I say you're cute when you're agitated?" He glanced at the wall clock. "Now I've gotta go home and pack up my equipment. I've got an early holiday party at the AOH hall in Peabody. "You said you had something important to tell me."

"I'll make it brief." Between bites of her sandwich she told him about Florence's niece, Kristal, and Cal's suspicions about the goings-on at Marilyn's Pie Palace.

"You're saying Kristal's been servicing the guys from the shredding plant? And Marilyn's not suspicious? What about Florence?"

She shook her head. "Florence is proud of Kristal for recovering from drugs and now holding down a job. She'd be crushed if she knew."

"So, what do you plan to do?" he asked.

"I thought of warning Kristal, but coming from me it would carry no weight. She'd probably think I'm jealous."

He nodded. "I'm surprised Kristal's smart enough to organize a little side business."

"I suspect someone else set it up for her and took a cut."

"A cut? You mean Kristal's got a pimp?"

Rose leaned back in the booth. "I have my suspicions, but it's not important. The person who organized everything is no longer in the picture. That's one reason why I believe Kristal's come to the attention of the police."

"You think this person was paying hush money?" he asked.

"I don't know. But you're right about Kristal. She couldn't have set it up on her own. I doubt if we'll ever know the whole story..."

"You're being secretive, babe. Did the pimp leave town?"

"In a manner of speaking, she left permanently."

Suspecting that Emma Ubbink had tipped off the police, Rose had dropped in on her at the shredding plant. The visit was ostensibly to get more information regarding a potential contract with the newspaper. Realistically, there was little hope a contract would come to fruition. Mr. Curley had rejected the idea. If the *Granite Cove Gazette* was keen on shredding old newspapers, he said, they could visit the senior center. At the end of every month, a shredder was available for public use.

"I'm not lugging stacks of dirty newspapers," Yvonne informed Rose. "If Mr. Curley isn't worried about a fire hazard in our basement then I'm not worried."

Following a brief conference in Ms. Ubbink's office, Rose had paused at the door. "It's a pity the police have learned nothing about Ms. Dunbar's death. She left many unhappy people behind. Matter of fact, I understand she was close to a waitress at Marilyn's Pie Palace."

Emma's eyes widened behind the cat's eye glasses. "She did spend a fair amount of time over there."

"Yet she never gained a pound," Rose said. "In fact, she had an excellent figure."

Emma was quick to respond. "I hardly think Dionne was eating pie at Marilyn's."

Rose turned to her. "What do you mean?"

"I can't repeat information that would reflect poorly on this company," she said primly. "As a newsperson, you understand the need for confidentiality."

Rose stepped closer and lowered her voice. "Are you hinting there was something underhanded going on at Marilyn's?"

Emma's eyes glinted. "I think before long certain matters will come to light."

When Rose told Betty Ann about Emma's remark, her friend said, "She acts like she's protecting the company's image, but that's bullshit. She'd love to see Kristal get busted because then Dionne's name would be dragged into it. Emma Ubbink's the kind you have to watch out for: a goody two-shoes with a viper's soul."

Now, Kevin grabbed the check from the table. "This one's on me, babe. Merry Christmas."

"If I'd known that was my present, I'd have ordered dessert."

"No time for that. I've gotta get ready for tonight. So, what do you want me to do, make an anonymous call to Kristal?"

"Uh, I was thinking of something with a little more impact."

"Drive by her house and yell 'slut'?"

Rose placed a hand over his. "Actually, Kevin, I've given this some thought. I was hoping you'd pose as a customer, a john. That way you could warn her directly."

He drew his hand away. "You want me to solicit Kristal Swekla?"

"I want you to *pretend* to solicit her. When she goes out to the parking lot, you'll warn her. She'll think you're just a kindhearted cop. It's Christmas, after all. Cal told me the code words used by the shredding guys. Kristal will think you're an insider."

"Let me get this straight: You want me to impersonate a cop *and* solicit Kristal Swekla?" When she nodded, he got to his feet, tossing bills onto the table. "Babe, that's nuts."

With a quick good-bye, he was across the room. Rose watched him hurrying for the exit. Kevin would need more work. She'd sprung it on him too quickly. As she gathered her things, she spotted Viola Hampstead and Dorothy Dunbar occupying a booth against the wall. They also were making preparations to leave. She grabbed her coat and rushed to intercept them.

The women looked pleased to see her. "I should have guessed you were here," Dorothy said. "I saw Kevin leaving a few minutes ago."

"He was in such a hurry, I thought the place was on fire," Viola said, chuckling. "Did you try to pin him down to a date?"

"Pin him down?" Rose asked.

"You know, to a wedding date." She cupped a hand around her mouth as if imparting a secret. "If you ask me, he looks like the kind who's in no rush to get to the altar."

Rose attempted a smile. "No, Kevin's got an early gig in Peabody. He had to get ready."

"I understand the Christmas play will go on as planned," Dorothy said. "I was so delighted to hear that."

"I think the whole town is happy," Rose said. "It's something to look forward to."

"Edith is catering the party after the show," Dorothy said. "I'll be helping out that night."

"I didn't know they'd planned a party," Rose said. "It's a great idea."

"The Chitwicks are hosting," Dorothy said. "They're so proud of young Nathaniel."

When Rose returned to the office, Yvonne called to her. "This came in the afternoon mail," she said, waving a sheet of paper. "It's an invoice from the Gingham Dog for two hundred seventy-seven dollars."

Rose examined the bill. "I had no idea each glass of cognac was twenty-five dollars. Manuel ordered the top shelf. And if I knew, what was I supposed to do, tell him to stick to beer?"

"I wasn't complaining, dear—"

"Because that lunch was worth every penny," Rose said. "What price do you put on your job, and the newspaper's reputation? Not to mention *A Christmas Carol* will now go on."

"Please hear me. I wasn't complaining. As a matter of fact, Hyacinth is dropping off a press release. It's regarding Nathaniel's winning the poster contest and Mr. del Toro's praise for the boy's work. She wants a photo of her son and the artist together. I told her it was a marvelous idea."

"Are you taking the photo?" Rose asked.

"I've asked Stewart. He's a better photographer." Yvonne patted Rose's head as one would a spaniel's. "You were our angel of mercy, Rose. Don't think twice about the bill. I hope you enjoyed yourself."

"I did, until we got kicked out."

Yvonne gasped. "You got kicked out of the Gingham Dog?"

She nodded. "Manuel gets feisty when he's had a few. The dining room manager asked him to be quiet. That kindled his resentment about being evicted when he first moved to Granite Cove."

"Oh, dear. I hope he didn't use vulgar language."

"It was in Spanish," Rose said. "I don't think anyone could understand it."

Yvonne shook her head. "I'll make it up to you. I'll have you over for dinner some night. Mother is always eager for new Scrabble players."

"Oh, thanks…. Maybe after the holidays."

The elevator doors opened onto the third floor hallway of the Granite Cove Senior Housing Building #3. Rose anticipated having a visit with her dad without attracting his friend Jeannette's attention. Approaching the woman's door, Rose was glad to discover it was closed. The only time Jeannette shut her door was when she was gone.

Rose had known dorm mates like that in college, social beings who loved having people drop in at any time. They always needed to know what was going on around them. Facebook, she thought, was created for such people. Rose, who'd kept her dormitory door closed, had been accused of being a hermit by more than one roommate.

"What if I'm in my underwear?" she'd asked in her defense. Her reasoning fell on deaf ears. To the extroverted students—and college dorms were full of extroverts—a closed door was a personal insult.

Now she crept past Jeannette's unit and rapped lightly on her dad's door. She could hear the sound of canned laughter from inside. She turned the knob and the door swung open. Her father was dozing in his recliner. She tiptoed to the TV. As she lowered the volume, he woke up.

"What? Oh, it's you, Rose." He struggled to get out of the chair.

"Don't get up, Dad. I'm just going to put this sandwich in the fridge."

He yawned. "What'd you bring me?"

"The usual, your favorite from Stella's."

"Doc Moss says I'm not supposed to have fatty foods."

"He's been saying that for three years. You're realizing that now?"

"Well, at some point I've gotta start doing what he tells me."

She stopped to look at him. "Is there something you're keeping from me? Has your heart been giving you problems?"

He looked sheepish. "Nah, nothing like that. Matter of fact, the nurse who visits on Wednesdays, Sandra, said my blood pressure's good."

"I'm glad to hear it. I thought you didn't like Sandra or the health center. You always said it's a waste of time."

"It's only once a week, and Sandra's okay. I bring her a jelly donut and she treats me fine."

Rose attempted a smile. "It sounds like someone's gotten through to you, something I've never been able to do."

"Maybe it's not too late for this old guy."

The words, coming from a confirmed pessimist, were unnerving. She peered at him. "Did Sandra put you on a new medication?" Following her dad's stroke, the nurse had recommended antidepressants.

"Nah, you know me. I don't trust pills." He glanced into the kitchen. "Any coffee left? I could use a cup."

"Do you want decaf?"

"Are you joking? Decaf's for sissies."

She smiled and moved to the tiny kitchen. She would drop the subject of his health. After all, wasn't that what she wanted, for him to take an interest in it? Yet it was annoying, knowing she'd tried for years to get him to change while Jeannette had worked her magic in a matter of months.

While the coffee brewed, she opened the cupboard. Hanging among the cups was an unfamiliar tall white mug. Printed on the front were the words *I Love My Maltese*. Under that was a photo of a curly haired white dog with black button eyes and nose. She removed the mug from the hook, poured her dad's coffee into it, and carried it to the living room.

"I've never seen this before," she said, handing him the Maltese mug.

"Oh, that's Jeannette's. She must have left it here."

"I see. She's got a Maltese?"

"Used to. We can't have pets here." He sipped his coffee. "Matter of fact, she said she'd have moved here sooner but she had to wait for Snowball to pass. He was sixteen and failing. Said she loved that little mutt."

"That was kind of her," Rose said.

He nodded. "She's like that."

Rose turned the subject to the upcoming play. "I thought you might like to come with Kevin and me. Betty Ann and Tiny are also going. From what I hear, it sounds as if all of Granite Cove will be there."

"Sure, I've heard about it," he said. "There's a poster in the club room. I wouldn't mind going."

"That's great, Dad. We'll pick you up early so we can get good seats."

"You don't have to do that. I can meet you there. Jeannette doesn't mind driving at night."

"Oh. Do you think she'll want to go?"

"You bet. She loves music and plays. I don't want you and Kevin to come all the way out here to pick me up."

"We don't mind, Dad. It's no trouble."

"Nah," he said. "You go early and save us a couple seats. Get them close enough so I can hear."

"Fine. I'll meet you there."

She watched uneasily as her father drank his coffee from Jeannette's mug. The rules of the game were changing, and she was powerless to prevent it.

Rose slowed the Jetta and leaned forward to see past Kevin, who sat next to her. She peered into the long front window of Marilyn's Pie Palace. Fluorescent lights cast a greenish glow over the plastic-covered seats. Inside, Kristal Swekla leaned on a customer's table, one hand on her hip.

"Kristal's a porker," Kevin said.

"Not really," Rose said defensively. "Anyone would gain weight being around pies and frosted donuts all day." She studied the girl. "She's not wearing a hairnet. That means Marilyn's not there. Let me park and we'll go over our plans one last time."

Kevin groaned. "You've had some crazy schemes over the years, but this is the craziest. I could get in big trouble. What if my brother found out? He could lose his job because of me." Kevin's brother Seamus, the oldest of eight siblings, was a state trooper.

"Don't be ridiculous. You're not going to get into any trouble. Even if you did, it wouldn't affect Seamus. Look at Billy Bulger, a state senator while brother Whitey was out executing people. It didn't prevent Billy from climbing the career ladder."

She eased the car into a space to the right of the dumpster, away from the handful of cars in the lot. "Why are we having this conversation again?" she asked. "You're saving a young woman's life, not to mention her elderly aunt's. If Kristal gets busted, think what it would do to Florence, her guardian. It would kill her, Kevin."

"Wait a minute," he said. "Kristal's in her late twenties, isn't she?"

"Something like that." She turned off the ignition and the lights.

"Then she's too old for a guardian."

"Florence may not be a legal guardian, but she acts as one because Kristal doesn't have two brain cells to rub together. If Kristal chooses to ignore your warning, then at least we've tried." She turned to him. "Any questions? Do you remember what you're supposed to say?"

He sighed. "Yeah, something about crushed nuts—"

"Kevin, be serious for a minute. You don't want Kristal getting suspicious. Remember, you're the newly hired man at the shredding company. You walked over from the plant. Kristal won't question it. She'll use her car. Remember, when placing your order you tell her one of the guys at the plant sent you. This guy told you to order 'the banana split pie and hold the nuts.' Can you remember that?"

"Banana split pie and hold the nuts," he repeated.

"I almost forgot." She leaned across him and opened the glove compartment. The interior light glinted on a small, shiny metal object. She handed it to him. "When the time comes and you're both outside, flash this. It's a little tarnished."

He immediately handed it back. "No way. That's a badge. Wearing a badge is impersonating a cop. That's a federal offense."

She rolled her eyes. "Kevin, it's my dad's from when he was a fisheries inspector. Kristal's not going to study it. For one thing, it'll be dark. For another, she'll be in a state of shock. You whip out your wallet and flash the badge. You warn her about an impending bust. Tell her she's being watched."

"Won't she be suspicious when I don't arrest her?"

"She will be grateful. You can mumble something about it being the holiday season, or something like that. Don't go overboard."

He gave her a dubious look. "What if she recognizes me? She might have caught my act at the Sacred Cod."

"I thought of that." She reached behind her seat and pulled out a tote bag. "I got these from the college wardrobe department." In the dim glow of an outside light she removed a shaggy dark wig and pair of black-framed glasses. "Your own mother won't recognize you in these."

He gave the wig a baleful look before slipping it on. "I suppose it doesn't matter whether I wear a disguise or not. Impersonating a cop's bad enough."

"You are not impersonating a cop," she said, tugging the coarse hair over his ears. "You're impersonating a fisheries inspector." After that she took a black stocking cap from the bag. "Here, put this over the wig. The lenses are clear glass. You won't have any trouble seeing."

He slipped the hat and the glasses on. "Can you turn on the light? I want to check this out."

"Too risky," she said. "When you get inside, you can visit the men's room to adjust the wig or whatever you have to do. Now give me your wallet. I'll attach the badge." He sighed and reached into his pocket. After securing the badge, she said, "You might want to practice flashing this in the men's room so it feels natural."

"Flashing in the men's room," he said. "What next." He sighed heavily, his breath making a vaporous cloud. "Okay, let's get this over with. The wig's itchy as hell."

"Now remember, I'll be parked up the road between here and the shredding plant. Wait for Kristal to go back inside and come to the car."

"What if she watches where I'm going?"

"The road is pitch black. She's not going to see you. Besides, she'll be too upset."

He scratched his head. "I hope this rug doesn't have fleas."

"And remember, Kevin, don't get in her car. At that point, pull out your wallet and flash the badge."

"Gee, thanks, babe. You think I'd jump in the car with her?"

"No, it's just that she might be very... persuasive."

"When you work in bars you get chicks coming on to you all the time. I can handle it." He kissed her before opening the door. "Wish me luck, babe."

The dome light reflected on his heavy glasses.

"You're a champ, Kevin."

He slid out of the car and shut the door. After a moment's pause, he strode across the lot. Rose started the Jetta and backed out of the parking space. She drove slowly toward the exit, all the time watching the lanky figure with the loping gait. Hands in pockets, Kevin strode purposefully to the entrance and threw open the double doors. Inside he looked around and without hesitation headed for a booth.

Auntie Pearl's Helpful Housekeeping Hints

Dear Auntie Pearl:

I'll soon be attending the graduation of my godchild at a location that's a three-hour drive from my house. My sister, who lives in that area, expects me to stay overnight at her house. She will also be attending the event. As I don't intend to drive back and forth the same day, staying with my sister makes sense. The problem is her mother-in-law, Shirley, who has recently moved in with her. The last time my husband and I visited, for Thanksgiving, the woman's habits were deplorable.

Auntie Pearl, Shirley is obviously suffering from dementia, yet my sister and her husband refuse to face the issue. During Thanksgiving dinner, Shirley gnawed on a turkey leg while wearing a T-shirt and men's boxer shorts (my sister says Shirley insists on being comfortable). While we were trying to enjoy the pumpkin pie, Shirley left the table and returned with a jar containing her gallstones! Periodically she'd give the jar a little shake.

Needless to say, we are not eager for a repeat performance. My husband insists on staying at a motel for the night. I'd like to do this, but my sister will be insulted if we don't stay with her. I'll have to make a decision soon. What should we do, Auntie Pearl?

Perplexed in Peabody

Dear Perplexed:

I found your remarks about the gallstones interesting. You see, my mother also kept her stones in a jar, a souvenir from a hospital stay. In fact, when I was a girl it was quite common to hear about gallbladder surgery among people of Mother's generation.

Today when my readers inquire about "gassy stomach," I refer them to my tried and true antidote: apple cider vinegar. It's the closest thing I know to a universal cure, so versatile is this substance. Apple cider vinegar is nature's antibiotic, killing harmful bacteria in the gut. It neutralizes fats and restores the body's pH balance, thus keeping gallstones at bay.

Apple cider vinegar—one tablespoon dissolved in a glass of water—is cheap, and best of all, you don't need a doctor's prescription. Tell your sister about the marvelous properties of this elixir, and tell her Auntie Pearl sent you!

Signed,

Auntie Pearl

CHAPTER SEVENTEEN

The poster in the middle school lobby greeted theatergoers as they entered: *The Granite Cove Players Presents: 'A Christmas Carol' by Charles Dickens.*

Betty Ann stood next to Rose in the ticket line. Behind them were Tiny and Jonah, the latter's face concealed inside a black hoodie.

"Nathaniel Chitwick did that." Rose said, pointing to the illustration on the poster. "Chipper held his breath wondering what the boy would come up with."

"The kid could have drawn body parts strewn across the snow," Betty Ann said. "Why would Chip take such a chance?"

Rose lowered her voice. "Just between you and me, it was Hyacinth's suggestion that Nathaniel do the illustration. She held all the cards."

"I see," Betty Ann said. "It was an offer Chip couldn't refuse." She peered at the poster, displayed on an easel. Under the play's title, which was printed in Olde English script, was a street scene in muted grays and black. A solitary street lamp illuminated two figures viewed from behind: a man in a top hat with a child perched on his shoulders. The small figure sat upright, his crutch held aloft.

"It's kind of depressing," Betty Ann said, "but at the same time the two characters are sweet. It suits the era and the season."

"I like how the eye is drawn to the one point of color, the yellow in the street lamp," Rose said. "Chipper was happy to have something he could display without creating controversy."

"Maybe Manuel was right; the kid's got talent."

Rose tapped Jonah's shoulder. The boy had retreated further inside his hoodie until only the tip of his beaked nose was visible. When he turned to her wordlessly, she pointed to the poster. "Did you see Nathaniel make this in class?"

Jonah shrugged. "I saw him. He copied it from a book."

"I certainly hope not," Betty Ann said. "That's plagiarism. People can be sued for that."

"That's right, son," Tiny said, joining in. "It's a serious offense."

"Can you go to jail for it?" Jonah asked, showing interest.

Tiny nodded. "In some cases I'm sure you can."

"Awesome," the boy said, pulling a cell phone from his pocket. "I'm calling the cops."

When Jonah began tapping numbers, Tiny grabbed the phone from his hand. "Don't be an idiot," he said. "You weren't about to call the police, were you?"

"Why not?"

"Because citizens don't waste cops' time with stupid calls. Police have important work to do."

"Oh, yeah? Ms. Fedderbush calls them all the time. She called Monday when she saw a poisonous spider in the teachers' room."

Tiny folded his arms across his chest. "In the first place, there are no poisonous spiders in Granite Cove. For one thing, it's too damn cold. I'm sure what Ms. Fedderbush saw was a common house spider. But even if it was a dangerous spider, which I doubt, why's she calling the police? Don't you have janitors to take care of bugs and stuff?"

Jonah nodded. "She told the janitor, but he doesn't pay any attention to her."

"Wonder why," Tiny muttered.

Warming to his topic, Jonah continued: "Me and Skye play cool pranks on her. Skye's got some awesome fake spiders and lizards that look real. We slip them under hers door." He flashed a rare grin.

"That poor woman," Betty Ann said, shaking her head.

"Who's Skye?" Tiny asked. "Is he a new kid?"

Jonah gave him a withering look. "It's a girl, Dad."

"Maybe she'd like to come for dinner some night," Betty Ann said, giving Tiny a meaningful look.

"Get real," Jonah said, turning away.

The auditorium was filling up quickly when they entered. Inside, they relinquished their tickets to a pair of students posted at the door. A fresh-scrubbed young man handed Tiny a program, saying, "In the front are listening devices for the hearing impaired, sir."

As Tiny glared at the boy, Betty Ann took his arm and led him away.

"Was that punk trying to be funny?" he asked.

"I'm sure he says that to everyone over thirty," she said, moving down the aisle. "Let's sit here in the middle."

"Leave two seats on the aisle," Rose said, "for my dad and Jeannette."

They removed their coats and settled themselves, attempting to get comfortable on the hard wooden chairs. The choir, standing onstage before the curtain, sang Christmas carols; Mrs. Buckle pounded the piano keys with gusto.

"Where's Jonah?" Tiny said, looking around.

Betty Ann, who'd noticed the boy slinking off, said, "He's over there, sitting with Norris."

"With who?" Tiny attempted to turn in the narrow seat.

"Relax," she said. "Norris is his tech friend from computer class."

"Remind me to speak to Jonah when we get home. If he thinks he can sneak off behind our backs anytime he wants—"

She patted his arm. "It's a miracle he agreed to come tonight. Leave the kid alone. He wants to be with his friends." Grateful for a respite from her stepson, Betty Ann hoped he'd stay put. Now she looked around the auditorium. "This is exciting. I feel a buzz in the air." She tugged at Rose's sleeve. "Aren't you going to take photos?"

"Nope. Stewart's doing that. I see him near the front. He wouldn't attend unless Yvonne got him a free ticket and admission to the party afterward."

Rose was suddenly engulfed in a fog of Opium perfume. She turned to see Jeannette hovering above her. The older woman wore a red velvet headband in her silver hair and turquoise shadow on her eyelids. Rose's dad, in his best button-down flannel shirt, stood behind Jeannette.

"Rose dear," she said, taking her hand. "I'm afraid your father and I must sit closer to the front. I hope you don't mind."

Rose glanced behind Jeanette. "Hi, Dad."

"What?"

"I'll talk to you at intermission." She tapped her watch.

"What?" He cupped his ear. "This crowd's noisy."

Jeannette patted Rose's cheek. Then she straightened and escorted Rose's father down the aisle.

"So that's the new girlfriend," Betty Ann said, slipping on her glasses to study the pair. "She looks fit."

"She's more like a friendly neighbor," Rose said. "But she's kind of old for headbands, don't you think?"

Tiny, leaning across Betty Ann, said, "Your old man's doing okay for himself."

"She's just a friend who doesn't mind driving him around," Rose said, hunkering down in her chair.

"I'll bet he doesn't mind either," Tiny said with a wink.

"I hope this thing starts on time," Rose grumbled.

It was a packed house when the lights dimmed and the curtain rose to reveal a darkened bedroom. The room contained a fireplace, a four-poster bed, a bureau, and the La-Z-Boy recliner covered with a quilt. The windowpanes were etched with frost. When Florence entered in a long nightshirt and tasseled bed cap, the audience chuckled. To her credit, she never glanced their way. Immediately a knocking sounded offstage.

"I'll bet I know who that is," Florence said in her best imitation of an old man. "It's my clerk, Cratchit, wanting to leave early just because it's Christmas Eve." She crossed the stage to answer the door, muttering, "Bah, humbug."

Moments later, Milton Krazner as Bob Cratchit entered. He wore a frayed top hat and waistcoat. He removed his hat, shivering in the chill of Scrooge's house.

"What? Are you sick?" Scrooge glared at the man.

"Just a bit feverish, sir. 'Tis the season."

"I suppose you've come to ask if you can leave early," Scrooge barked at him.

"I promised my boy, Tim, that—"

"Nonsense," Scrooge said. "I don't believe in Christmas foolishness. Get back to work. You're lucky to have a job that puts food on the table."

As Bob Cratchit turned to leave, he sighed. "Barely enough."

Scrooge was not content to let him go without a lecture. He scolded the weary Bob Cratchit, waggling a finger in his face. After the employee had left the stage, Scrooge prepared for bed, muttering angrily. After a final look out the window to make sure Cratchit was indeed toiling at his desk, Scrooge extinguished the candle and climbed into bed.

On the darkened stage, a clocked ticked. A wintry moon cast a pale light into the shadowy bedroom. The wind howled, causing the shutters to bang. In his bed, Scrooge slumbered on until a sudden loud banging interrupted the silence. He let out a cry and sat upright.

Scrooge wasn't the only one startled by the noise. The audience, having been lulled into a state of tranquility, jumped in their seats. Somewhere a child cried. Betty Ann clutched Rose's sleeve.

"Who in damnation is that?" Scrooge demanded.

The response was a mournful "Ebenezer!" accompanied by a clanging of chains. Scrooge, who'd crept toward the door, stopped in his tracks.

"Go away!" he shouted, and scurried back to bed.

"Ebenezer Scrooge," came the reply, accompanied by moans and clanking of chains, which continued until Scrooge, more angry than frightened, swung open the door.

The unkempt visitor stood barefoot in a torn nightshirt. Strands of long, stringy hair fell in front of his sunken eyes. He wore ropes of chains that dragged on the floor as he shuffled into the room.

Scrooge backed away. "Who are you? Go away! Leave me alone."

The unwelcome visitor introduced himself in a hollow voice. He was Jacob Marley, Scrooge's business partner in life. Shaken, Scrooge moved closer, shining a lamp upon the ghastly visage. "But you can't be. Jacob Marley is dead."

Betty Ann, transfixed by the encounter, whispered, "Who's the ghost? He's great."

"Dean of students at the college," Rose whispered back.

"Shh!" Tiny shushed them.

In an eerie voice, Marley warned Scrooge that he would be visited by three spirits during the night.

"Spirits? I don't believe in spirits," Scrooge said. When the figure retreated, he slammed the door and paced the floor. After a few moments he crept to the door and flung it open. Marley had vanished. Perplexed, Scrooge sat upon his bed and attempted to explain what had occurred. "A bad dream," he muttered. "Must have been something I ate... a spoiled potato, perhaps."

The arrival of the first spirit, the Ghost of Christmas Past, created a ripple through the auditorium. The childlike figure appeared to glow in his voluminous white robes. He addressed the figure cowering under the blankets: "Ebenezer Scrooge, I am the Ghost of Christmas Past, here to take you on a trip." When Scrooge protested, kicking his legs wildly, the spirit said, "Come. Do not be afraid."

When Scrooge reluctantly took the visitor's outstretched hand, bright swirling lights filled the room. A frightened Scrooge gazed about him, wide-eyed. When the lights ceased, the ghost crossed the room and, with a dramatic flair, slid open the bedroom door. Inside, sitting on a love seat, was a young woman in a brocade gown, her head bent over her embroidering.

"Belle!" Scrooge cried, and attempted to rush forward.

The ghost grabbed the sleeve of the old man's nightshirt, restraining him. "She can't hear you."

"We were to be married," Scrooge said, staring at the woman who continued sewing. "I loved her."

"Do you remember what she told you when she broke the engagement?"

Scrooge shook his head, looking away.

"She said you loved money more than her."

Scrooge covered his face. "Take me back. I've seen enough."

After more swirling lights, Scrooge appeared in his bed, asleep. The room was dark, a pair of candles providing illumination. A hush fell over the stage until a faint sound of sleigh bells was heard.

Before long their jingling filled the theater along with booming laughter and blaring trumpets. For a brief moment the stage was plunged into darkness. When the lights came up, a majestic figure, his chest bare under a long red velvet coat, stood looming over Scrooge's bed. He wore a white fur hat and tall buckled boots.

The old man pulled the blanket to his nose and stared up at the sight. "Who... who are you?"

The voice was commanding: "Mr. Scrooge, I am the Ghost of Christmas Present. Come with me." He gave a bow and stood aside, hands on hips. In the candle's glow, the taut muscles of his broad chest glistened.

Betty Ann nudged Rose. "Who's *that?*" she whispered.

"The college wrestling coach," Rose whispered back.

In response, Betty Ann fanned her face with her program.

Like his predecessor, the ghost slid open the bedroom door. This time a scene of domestic gaiety greeted them. The Cratchit family members were gathered around a table. In the center was a platter holding a meager roast and a few potatoes. Milton Krazner, as Bob Cratchit, furtively tugged his vest over his belly. "This is a wonderful feast, Mother," he said.

"I hope it will be enough," said Mrs. Cratchit, a frilly white cap covering her curls. She cast a worried eye over the young people standing around the table.

"Of course it'll be enough," said Tiny Tim. "And what does it matter anyway? We've got each other, and that is all that counts."

"You're a good lad, Tim." Bob Cratchit hugged the boy to him, causing the crutches to crash to the floor.

"Maybe Mr. Scrooge will give you a raise this year, Father," said Mrs. Cratchit. "You haven't had one in three years."

"Hush, Mother," he said. "I'm lucky to have a job in these hard times."

"That's because you work harder than anyone, and Ebenezer Scrooge knows it."

He shook his head. "My dear, I won't have you speaking ill of Mr. Scrooge on Christmas Day."

Tiny Tim raised a glass. "A blessing on Mr. Scrooge."

The other children followed suit, though without enthusiasm.

Looking on, Scrooge said to the ghost, "I hadn't realized the Cratchits were so... lacking."

"That's because you've never visited your employee's home, nor taken any interest in his life."

Chastened, Scrooge asked, "And what will become of Tiny Tim?" He hugged himself and stared at the family tableau.

"You'll find out tonight," the ghost said, his tone ominous.

With that, the curtain slowly descended as the audience applauded loudly.

Betty Ann got to her feet. "Thank God for intermission. I've gotta pee so bad I'm knocking over anyone in my path."

"I'll go with you," Rose said.

Betty Ann glanced at Tiny. "You'll be okay, honey?"

He looked up at her. "Are you afraid I'll be abducted?"

"I just thought you might want to join us. They're selling soda and candy in the lobby."

"It'll be too crowded. If you can manage, I'd love a box of malted milk balls. In the meantime, I'll keep an eye on Jonah and Norris. If they get up, I'm following them."

Betty Ann and Rose joined the mass of people moving toward the door. They found themselves abreast with the Chitwicks, heading in the same direction. Hyacinth wore a plum-colored wool cape fastened with an elaborate pin. The pastor wore his red fuzzy Santa hat. Rose congratulated them on Nathaniel's performance.

Hyacinth nodded. "He definitely has a career in the arts, whether it's theater or fine arts."

"Are you enjoying the production?" Betty Ann asked.

"Experienced objectively, yes," Hyacinth said, nodding. "On the other hand, Dickens perpetuates the myths about spirits by presenting them as stereotypes. For example, the moaning and wearing of chains." She sighed. "I realize it's merely entertainment, but it's difficult to accept."

When they arrived at the doors, the Chitwicks headed for the snack bar while Rose and Betty Ann made for the bathroom.

"Can't she talk about anything besides ghosts?" Betty Ann muttered.

"Excuse me," Rose said. "The word is *spirits*."

"Whatever. I felt like saying 'Lighten up, lady. It's only a play.'"

"Maybe you'll get a chance to tell her at the party."

"Didn't I tell you? We're not going, because Jonah isn't going. Tiny doesn't want the kid home alone."

"Does Jonah know that one of the merchants donated a nativity scene made entirely of chocolate?"

"I tried talking him into it. Somehow I couldn't make a Lutheran church theater party sound exciting to a thirteen-year-old. Not only that, I've got to be at work early tomorrow. The residents are having their annual holiday bazaar."

They reached the door to the bathroom. "You mean I have to go to the party alone?" Rose gave her a mournful look.

"I thought Kevin was joining you," Betty Ann said.

"He said after his gig, but that could run on. Besides, I think Kevin's on the same page with Jonah. Lutheran Church parties aren't high on his list of priorities." Before Betty Ann could respond, Rose held up a hand. "Don't worry about me. This is a working night. I'll review the play and cover the after party."

"Okay, kid. When you file your story tonight, tell them Betty Ann Zagrobski said this play's the most exciting thing to happen to Granite Cove since Mayor Froggett got caught with the school crossing guard in the DPW garage."

"It wasn't the garage," Rose said. "It was the shed where they keep the city sweeper."

"Whatever. Just spell my name right."

CHAPTER EIGHTEEN

Rose and Betty Ann, trailed by Tiny and Jonah, followed the theater crowd to the doors. Outside, people stood in clumps despite the cold and talked excitedly about the play. Rose hung back in order to ask Jonah if he'd enjoyed it.

"Decent," he said.

"That means he liked it," Betty Ann informed her.

Rose said good-bye, giving her a hug. Rather than wait around for the parking lot to empty, she'd decided to leave her car in the school lot and walk the distance to the church for the after party. This she explained to Betty Ann. "It'll be nice after that overheated auditorium."

"Are you sure?" Betty Ann fumbled inside her voluminous pocketbook. "In that case, take my flashlight."

"Never mind," Rose said. "It's not that far."

She continued to rummage in her bag. "Maybe not, but there's that big intersection where no one will spot you crossing. You need a flashlight."

"I have a flashlight." It was in her glove compartment, and Rose remembered the last time she'd used it. Once again she had an image of the shiny black boots against the blood-tinged snow. She shook her head. "I'm forty years old, B.A. I'm not likely to dart mindlessly across the street."

"I'm not worried about you; I'm worried about the crazy Mannory Way drivers this time of year. I don't want you becoming another hit-and-run."

Rose closed her eyes. "How many times do I have to tell you? That was no hit-and-run. That was deliberate—a murder."

"Okay, whatever," Betty Ann said, giving up her search. "Are you sure we can't drop you off?"

"No way," Jonah whined. "I've gotta get back. I got homework to finish. You said we'd leave right after the play."

Betty Ann scowled at the boy. "You've never once wanted to get home to do homework. Here we offer Rose a ride after she was good enough to buy our tickets tonight. Did you remember to thank her?"

"He'd better remember," Tiny added.

Not wanting to get in the middle of a family feud, Rose turned, giving the Zagrobskis a wave. She hurried across the parking lot to the sidewalk. It felt good to leave the milling crowd behind, and she savored the silence.

A few holiday shoppers were still out, visiting the handful of stores that remained open late. She looked at the store windows as she passed. Audrey's Nails 'n' Things had an interesting display: the nails of the plastic hands in the window sported holiday designs with sparkly snowflakes and holly. Rose continued up Main Street until she reached the busy intersection.

After scooting across, she headed up the hill to the church. Halfway she stopped to admire the illuminated crèche on the lawn. The figures of the Wise Men cast long shadows on the snow. Nestled inside the stable and sharing space with the Holy Family were Farmer Hobbs's livestock:

two sheep and a goat, resting on the straw. The donkey was nearby in a wooden stall.

Hearing Rose's approaching footsteps, the goat trotted over to the fence. Rose slipped off a glove and rubbed its muzzle. The animal pressed closer, poking its head through the wooden rails to sniff her pocket. She reached inside and found a stick of dried red licorice.

"Here you go," she said, before the goat yanked it from her hand. She watched him chewing the candy, his jaws moving side to side. She hoped no one had spotted her. Every year the *Granite Cove Gazette* published a plea for residents not to feed the Nativity animals. Every year the plea was ignored as folks surreptitiously slipped them treats.

Now she pulled her glove back on over freezing fingers. She resumed climbing the hill. At the same time, a stream of cars drove past, slowing at the top to turn in at the church entrance. Although Yvonne had claimed the post-theater party was for "cast and family," It looked as if half the audience was arriving. She hoped Edith wouldn't run out of food.

When Rose reached the top, she paused to look at the moon. It was high in the night sky, a slim, bright crescent. Yet it wasn't the only night light. Hovering over the tops of the evergreens that lined the road, a sulfurous glow muted the surrounding stars. It was reflected light from the Mannory Way extravaganza. If that wasn't bad enough, on weekends twin spotlights swept across the sky, visible from all over the village.

The church basement had been decorated with holiday flair. Streamers of red and green crepe paper crisscrossed the ceiling; tall cardboard candy canes brightened the walls.

Rose was among the first arrivals. As she stood at the bottom of the stairs, a member of Young People's Worship approached. The girl was dressed in green tights, red vest, and stocking cap. She snatched Rose's coat from her hands.

Rose looked around the room. The other early birds had migrated to the buffet table where Edith, her hairnet askew, arranged platters of sandwiches. She turned to chide the eager mob, telling them to back off until she gave the signal. Soon she was joined by Dorothy, carrying a large fruit mold. The chaplain, like Edith, wore an apron decorated with red poinsettias.

Rose slipped her notepad from her bag. She approached Edith and asked if Florence would be working that night.

"It's up to her," Edith said. "This is her night, and I've got Dorothy. Should be enough. Besides, Pastor said there won't be more than seventy-five or so." She cast a wary glance at the throng clattering down the staircase.

Rose turned to see the Chitwicks, Nathaniel in the middle, descending the stairs to a smattering of applause. The boy stopped and grinned, raising clasped hands over his head.

Before long the basement filled with celebrants. People stood in groups watching the newcomers descending the stairs. A few stalked the food table, which Edith covered with a clear plastic cloth. At one end sat an enormous punch bowl.

As the buzz of conversation grew louder, Florence appeared on the stairs, her cheeks red from the cold. A raucous cheer went up as she descended, looking both embarrassed and pleased. At the bottom, she bowed and grinned at the crowd.

Rose spotted Stewart at the buffet table easing a sandwich from under the plastic cover. Typically, he wouldn't start working until Yvonne arrived. Rose reached inside her bag for her camera. She circled Florence, snapping some shots of her surrounded by well-wishers.

"Will this be a new career for you?" someone asked Florence.

She considered the question. "I tell ya, it was a lot of fun, but I'm kinda old for leading roles."

"Then you're not giving up your job for Broadway?" Rose joked.

"Speaking of my job," she said, looking around, "I better go help Edith. This is one hell of a mob." She scurried through the crowd to the kitchen.

Moments later, Milton, wearing his top hat from the show, made his way down the stairs. When the crowd cheered, he tipped his hat. He was followed by two of the actors who played ghosts, now wearing street clothes.

Bringing up the rear were Chipper and Yvonne, arm in arm. The crowd moved to the stairs to loudly applaud. Finally, the members of the choir descended singing "Joy to the World."

When they finished, Florence emerged from the kitchen wearing an apron, like her coworkers. She shook a rope of sleigh bells and shouted, "Food's on!" Dorothy and Edith removed the plastic table cover. Under it were trays heaped with sandwiches, a glazed ham, a fruit mold, Swedish butter cookies, and loaves of nut bread. In a massive punch bowl, cherries and orange slices were afloat. At the opposite end of the table, a vat of haddock chowder simmered over a Sterno heater.

Rose, who hadn't had dinner, realized she was hungry. Before she could join the throng, someone grabbed her arm. She spun around. It was Betty Ann, wearing a big smile. "I was sacked out on the sofa," she said, "thinking of you here alone. What kind of person abandons her best friend at Christmas? Not only that—I wouldn't miss Edith's chowder for anything." She gazed at the simmering pot.

"Is Tiny with you?" Rose said.

"He's home watching Jonah. The kid'll get in trouble if he's alone for one minute. Tiny told me to have a bowl of chowder and head right back."

Rose laughed. "What kind of trouble can you get into at St. Rupert's?"

"Don't laugh. He doesn't trust other men. He thinks they're all trying to get in my pants. Speaking of pants—" She lifted the hem of her purple tunic and turned in a semicircle. "Do these pants make my butt look huge? I got them from a plus-size catalog. What do you think?" She turned again.

"B.A., you look great. I don't know what you're worried about. "

She smoothed the tunic over her hips. "You know, I'm seriously considering gastric bypass surgery."

"Don't even think about it," Rose said. "You know Beth, the intern who does our layout after hours? She claims her aunt had the operation and lost forty pounds—"

"I'd kill to lose forty pounds," Betty Ann said.

"Just hear me out. After the weight loss, the aunt developed a gambling problem. She began driving to Foxwoods Casino on weekends, leaving her husband at home. She hadn't been much of a drinker before, but almost overnight she became a boozehound. She met guys at

Foxwoods and started having affairs. One year after the surgery, Beth's aunt, who'd been a Sunday school teacher, had become a compulsive gambler and an alcoholic nymphomaniac. After her husband left her, she entered treatment. The doctors said her former cravings for food didn't go away when she had the surgery. They turned into compulsions for gambling and alcohol. Ditto the sex addiction." Rose paused for breath. "I guess it's the old adage: You can't fool Mother Nature."

"Are you saying Mother Nature wants me to be forty pounds overweight?" Betty Ann asked.

"I'm just telling you not to be hasty. But seriously, you're a sexy woman. Your husband thinks you're a mantrap."

"Tiny thinks I lead them on. I can't help it if I'm a natural flirt. He came home early last week and intercepted a message from Lester Phipps. You know how he invited me to tour his mother's fancy assisted living place? Well, he called my house and Tiny heard the message."

"It's not inappropriate," Rose said. "After all, you're an activities director. Maybe Mr. Phipps wanted to help you get a job there."

"Maybe he does, but he ended the message with a request that I wear something slinky. Those were his words: 'something slinky.' Tiny was furious. So now he thinks I'm leading guys on."

Before Rose could respond, her cell phone buzzed. She dug it out of her bag. "It's Kevin," she said. "I've got to call him."

"Call after you've eaten," Betty Ann said, moving to the food table.

"I'd better talk outside. Hyacinth doesn't allow cell phones."

Dorothy, overhearing this, motioned to Rose. "Come in the kitchen, dear. You can talk in the pantry, if you don't mind the smell of onions."

Rose thanked her. She called to Betty Ann that she'd be right back.

In the dark pantry, Dorothy pulled the cord to a light bulb suspended from the ceiling. Its dim glow illuminated walls of shelving that held giant cans of corn, beans, and peas. Sacks of onions and potatoes sat on the floor. A high shelf held a row of tall coffee pots.

After Dorothy closed the door behind her, Rose glanced warily around the shadowy room. *A perfect place to bury a body*, she thought, noting the earthen floor. She quickly dialed Kevin's number.

"Hi babe," he said. "I'm watching *The Grinch that Stole Christmas*."

"I thought you were meeting me. I'm at the church party."

He moaned. "I'm beat. I did a corporate holiday party at the Cummings Center this afternoon." Before she could admonish him, he added, "And my leg is still bruised from the other night. I oughta take out a civil complaint against Kristal Swekla."

"I'm sorry, Kevin," Rose said. "I shouldn't have gotten you involved."

According to Kevin, helping Kristal had been a thankless—and painful—task. Not only had the girl failed to appreciate the warning given outside Marilyn's Pie Palace but she'd become furious: "She was sweet as pie, no pun," Kevin said when recounting the story to Rose. "Right up until I showed her my badge. After that I thought she was going to tear my head off. When I warned her we were wise to her little side business, I thought she'd take a swing at me. I backed up, but she's coming at me, swearing like crazy. I saw it coming, the kick. You develop reflexes when you work in bars. I managed to turn away in time so she only bruised my leg."

Rose pondered his words. "I can understand Kristal being suspicious when you placed your order inside the restaurant. After all, the guys use a code. Maybe it changes from week to week. But how did she know you weren't a cop? She was taking an awful chance, kicking you like that."

Kevin shook his head. "I don't know, babe. Kristal's got a couple screws loose, no doubt about that."

Now he yawned and asked, "Why don't you come over here when you finish up at the church?"

"I can't. Chester's been in all night. I have to let him out." They exchanged good-byes, and she returned to the party.

Back in the church basement, Betty Ann, plate in hand, was talking to Chipper and Yvonne. Rose moved to the end of the food line. As she waited, the choir sang "O Christmas Tree," one of her favorite carols. By the time she reached the table, many of the platters were bare. The chowder urn, likewise, was empty. She managed to grab a couple of ham slices and a piece of date bread. Finally, she ladled sherry punch into a glass. She looked around for Betty Ann. Stewart, his camera slung around his neck, was in a corner. He furtively scooped food with a plastic fork, his eyes darting around the room. Betty Ann, however, was nowhere in sight.

Rose was finishing her punch when she spotted someone she'd been wanting to talk to. Emmett Quigley was the owner of Quigley's Stationery Store, a long time Granite Cove establishment. The gray-haired man wore his standard outfit of a shapeless white turtleneck and worn tweed sports jacket. Mr. Quigley, Rose thought, could very well hold a clue regarding Hyacinth's anonymous letters. She hurriedly applied a coat of lipstick and approached the man.

"Hello, Mr. Quigley. Do you have family in the cast?"

"Nope." He grinned, displaying horse-like teeth. "I donated the paper for the program tonight. "

"That was kind of you," she said, giving him a warm smile. "How's business?"

He shrugged. "No complaints. I got rid of a lot of the old inventory. Now I'm stocking more greeting cards and personalized items, along with office supplies."

"You've stayed relevant," she said, "by knowing what people need."

"You have to stay relevant or close your doors." Grateful to have Rose's attention, he continued. "Every year I attend the New York paper and gift convention to see what's new. Today it's not businesses we cater to, it's the young people. They've got the money. When I was their age, I delivered newspapers just to buy bubble gum and comic books. Kids today come in, they've got their own credit cards. Seems like there's no limit, either. 'Course, I'm not complaining. If not for the kids, we wouldn't survive." He grinned, flashing his equine teeth. "Just between you and me, if I see another Hello Kitty notebook, I think I'll scream."

She laughed and leaned closer. "You know, I've always wanted to write a story about how the digital age has affected the stationery industry. For instance, do you still sell supplies for manual typewriters—ribbons and such?"

He nodded, taking a gulp of his drink. "As long as our customers need 'em, I'll carry 'em."

"Really? You're saying there are Granite Cove residents still using the old typewriters, manual and electric?"

Mr. Quigley's Adams apple bounced in response. "Yup. I still stock them. Special order, you know."

"How many people are we talking about?"

"There's two. One of 'em's that bird writer, Karl Loopstock, an expert on finches. Your newspaper did a story on him and his bird books a few years ago."

"Yes, I remember that. Who's the other customer?"

He drained his glass and looked away. "I'm not comfortable saying. Heck, it's fine to talk about old Karl 'cause everyone knows he likes the old-fashioned ways. He's always writing letters to your paper about how computers are ruining society."

"That's true." When Yvonne failed to publish one of Mr. Loopstock's letters, the man called the newspaper, enraged. "So why can't you give me the name of your other customer? Is it top secret?"

He chuckled and shifted his weight. "Let's say I don't think she'd want me blabbing her business around town."

"I understand perfectly, Mr. Quigley." Out of the corner of her eye she spotted Dorothy moving through the crowd carrying a tray laden with glasses of sherry punch. Rose reached over and grabbed two, handing one to her companion. She said, "As one of the town's leading businessmen, you have to be discreet."

"It's not really a secret. It's just that, well, you're not the only one who wants to know that information."

"Really? Why would anyone care who's using an old typewriter?"

He leaned closer and lowered his voice. "The Granite Cove Police, that's who."

"Really? I wonder why." Her tone was casual.

"This is not for publication, young lady." He took a big swallow of his drink. "Apparently there's someone in town who's sending poison pen letters written on an old Smith Corona." He gave her a stern look. "Keep that under your hat."

"Certainly. It must have been difficult for you, forced to release that information. I know how loyal you are to your customers."

He looked pleased with himself. "Well, I didn't."

"What do you mean?"

"For one thing, I didn't like the way Chief Alfano went about it, coming into my store, demanding to see my customers list. I told him I'd have to examine my files and get back to him. In the meantime, I asked my lawyer, Spencer Farley, what to do. He said the chief needs a court order for that.

"Tell you the truth," he continued, "if Chief Alfano had asked me nicely, I might have given him the information. I just didn't like his tone. We're a third generation business in this town and we don't take guff from anyone." He chuckled. "You know, I didn't lie. Chief asked if anyone had placed an order for a typewriter ribbon and I said no one had." He winked at her. "They don't have to order them 'cause I keep a couple in stock."

"You're clever, Mr. Quigley. It's why you've earned your customers' loyalty." She gazed up at him. "If you tell me this person's name, I'll make contact and describe the story I plan to write. I'll mention the many authors, including a couple of Nobel Prize winners, who still use traditional typewriters."

"Oh, this lady's not an author," he said. "She just likes doing things the old ways. Lots of folks like that."

Rose reached into her bag and removed her notepad and pen, which she handed to him. "You write her name and I'll get in touch. After that, you and I can set up a date for our interview."

He drained his glass and handed it to her, taking the notepad and pen. Turning slightly, he wrote on the pad, closed it, and handed it back.

She flipped it open and glanced at the name he'd written.

"Yes, I see. Thank you, Mr. Quigley. I have to go now."

Auntie Pearl's Helpful Housekeeping Hints

Dear Auntie Pearl:

I'm an attractive, successful professional woman. People seem to think I have it all, but it's not true. I've never had a long-term relationship. Alone again on Christmas Eve, I will build a fire in the fireplace, hang my stocking on the mantle, and play my favorite holiday song, "I'll be Home for Christmas." As I watch the logs burn down, I'll wonder: Will I ever find my special someone?

Lonely in Lexington

Dear Lonely:

I'll bet you're one of these homeowners who throw away grease-stained paper towels, the ones used to absorb fat when cooking bacon or hamburgers. Did you know these sheets make excellent fire starters? A fistful of dryer lint is also useful for this purpose. Often when dealing with a reluctant fire, a couple of sheets of greasy paper or a bit of dryer lint will make the difference between a flicker and a roaring blaze.

Try it and you'll have cozy fires to warm you throughout the New Year.

Season's greetings!

Auntie Pearl

CHAPTER NINETEEN

Rose worked her way through the partying crowd until she reached the door to the church school. It was unlocked. She flicked the light switch before entering the room. After a quick survey, she spotted a brightly painted trunk on the floor; she knelt before it.

Inside were art supplies. She grabbed a black marker and a sheet of white poster paper and wrote on it with big bold strokes. Then she rolled the thick paper into a cylinder and fitted one end into her pocket. Finally she turned out the light and stepped out of the room. The back entrance stairs were nearby. She raced up them.

She didn't have to walk far to reach her destination. A single light was on upstairs in Viola Hampstead's tall, narrow house. As Rose made her way up the driveway, passing Viola's Honda, she felt she was being watched. She stopped at the front door and knocked loudly. No sound came from inside. She peeked inside, through the lace curtain at the window. A cat on the stairs spotted her and flew up the dark staircase. Rose rapped again, stamping her cold feet on the mat. The house was still, as if holding its breath.

After a moment, she conceded that Viola wasn't going to respond. She moved to the driveway, stopping under an upstairs window. This, Rose knew, was Viola's bedroom. The dim light emanated from inside. Behind the sheer curtains a shadowy figure moved.

Now Rose unrolled the poster paper from her pocket. Next she removed her small LED flashlight from her bag. She aimed its beam at the poster, where she'd written in thick black marker: OPEN THE DOOR.

She shouted "Viola!" into the cold night air. At the same time, she held the poster in one hand and the flashlight illuminating it in the other. She held them both high until her arms got tired. Still there was no response from above. Viola Hampstead was stubborn, Rose thought. She turned the paper to the other side where she'd written: I'LL TELL POLICE. Again she held it aloft, lit by the flashlight's beam.

This time she didn't have to hold it long before the shadowy figure at the window moved. A light appeared above the front door and Viola called, "You may as well come in."

Rose, nodding to herself, put the paper away and moved to the front door where Viola stood shivering in the night air. She wore a corduroy bathrobe over a nightgown and her head sprouted spongy pink curlers.

"I thought you'd never ask," Rose said, stepping inside the warm house.

She followed Viola into the front room. A tuxedo cat, its paws tucked under it, gave her a scornful look. Rose sat on the sofa and unbuttoned her coat. She noticed that Viola, who'd moved to the end of the room, didn't offer to take it.

"I won't be long, Viola. It's late, and I apologize for coming over. But I think you'll understand why I had to come—"

"Would you like some sherry?" Viola said, interrupting her.

"No, thanks."

"I'm having some." Viola left the room, moving toward the kitchen.

Rose waited, feeling the cat's incriminating gaze upon her. She looked around the immaculately preserved room. Even the Canada Mints in the glass bowl were dust-free. Now she rubbed her cold hands together, wishing she'd accepted Viola's offer of sherry. She had automatically refused, fearing Viola might slip something into her glass. Rose wondered whether her paranoia was justified. Was she being sensible or silly? The latter won out.

"Viola, I think I will have some sherry," she called.

Before long, Viola returned carrying a tray with a filigreed decanter and two decorative glasses, which she placed on the coffee table. A paper doily lined the tray. Viola poured and handed Rose a glass. She poured one for herself and sank onto the opposite sofa next to the contemptuous cat. Giving Rose a guarded look, she asked, "What is it you want to know?"

Rose had decided to tell the woman outright. "I learned something tonight from Emmett Quigley. I think I know the identity of the person who's been sending Hyacinth Chitwick poison pen letters."

Viola sipped her drink. "Have you gone to the police?"

"First I want to know why. If I'm satisfied with your answer, I may not have to report what I know to Cal Devine."

Viola finished her sherry and set the glass on the tray. She looked at Rose and said calmly, "You ask why, and I'll tell you. No doubt you won't understand, but I don't ask for understanding. The fact is, if not for Hyacinth, I'd be with Walter Chitwick today. He only stayed with her because he's a man of God.

"I'll give you the background," Viola continued. "Almost fifteen years ago, Hyacinth started a prayer group for those in need of healing. At the time, my husband and I were trying to have children, as I mentioned before. I decided to join Hyacinth's group. After all, it was right next door.

"There were a half dozen of us meeting once a week in the Chitwicks' basement. As a group, we prayed about the members' health problems: one woman's emphysema, a man's bone spurs, someone's gall bladder—and for me, my husband's infertility. His urologist had claimed that Karl's sperm count was low. Hyacinth instructed the group to visualize the sperm multiplying and growing stronger." Viola reddened at this, staring at her folded hands.

"Before long we learned that Hyacinth was pregnant. We added that to our prayer list. I began to enjoy the meetings. It was relaxing, praying with others. It was winter, and Pastor Chitwick would walk me to my door to make sure I got home safely. I loved this brief time with him. He's a wonderful, kind man. He made me laugh—a contrast to my gloomy Karl. After saying goodnight to Walter Chitwick, I'd come inside. Karl would be upstairs in his work room, tinkering with his radios." She shook her head. "Why I ever wanted to have a child with him is a mystery.

"One night—it was around this time of year—I showed up for prayer group as usual. Pastor met me at the door, surprised to see me. Hadn't anyone called to tell me about the cancellation? Apparently Hyacinth's mother had fallen that afternoon, and Hyacinth had driven to New Hampshire to be with her.

"Maybe Pastor saw the disappointment on my face, because he invited me in to see their tree. He'd just returned from St. Rupert's Christmas party, where the sexton had given him a bottle of homemade schnapps. Then he asked me to join him in a Christmas drink. 'It's the least I can do to make up for your inconvenience,' he said.

"We sat in the living room, where Pastor talked about his childhood. His parents had been missionaries in Samoa. It wasn't until he went to college in New England that he experienced a traditional Christmas. I told him about being six years old and finding ribbon candy in my stocking. My family had little money, and this was a treat. I hid it under my pillow, but the next day the dog found it.

"To my embarrassment, I wept while telling him that story." Viola glanced at Rose. "The schnapps was awfully strong. In any case, Pastor put an arm around me, comforting me. I was aware that he and Hyacinth had stopped having relations after she learned she was pregnant. Hyacinth confided this to the group. She felt that an unborn child feels threatened by the sex act."

Viola sighed. "I guess you know where this is leading. After more schnapps, Pastor kissed me. It was magical: the twinkling lights of the Christmas tree, the snow falling at the window, the two of us alone in the house. Making love seemed the most natural act in the world. At one point I even called him 'Walter.'

"Later, walking me home, Pastor was unsteady on his feet. He slipped on the ice and fell, laughing. I helped him up. I hated to return to my house. Karl was in bed but I stayed up, sitting in the dark and looking out the window, wondering if Pastor was thinking about me." She leaned forward and refilled their glasses.

"Hyacinth returned the next day. The following week, when I showed up for prayer group, Pastor wasn't there, so I walked home alone. He wasn't there the next week either. When I tried talking to him outside his house, he'd rush inside.

"Eventually I dropped out of the group, but not before discovering I was pregnant. Hyacinth took credit for this." Viola made a wry face. "How I longed to tell her it was her husband who was responsible, not *her*.

"Three months after Nathaniel Chitwick was born, I gave birth to a baby boy. When Karl left us, I didn't mind very much. My son, Warren, was my consolation. I knew that at some point I would tell Pastor that Warren was his son." She stared into her glass. "Two months later, the baby died following surgery for intestinal blockage. I was alone, and my resentment for Hyacinth grew. I knew Pastor had strong feelings for me, yet he'd never leave his wife. I watched him from my upstairs window. I pretended we were together, living happily.

"When I thought how Hyacinth stood between us, I'd feel a burning anger. That's when I made the first phone call. The letters came after Dionne's death."

"What about Dionne?" Rose asked. "What do you know about her hit-and-run?"

Viola leaned forward to pluck a piece of lint from her slipper. "What makes you think I know anything?"

"Because that night I saw you at the window. When I screamed, every light went on up and down this street. Your house remained in semi-darkness."

She reached for her glass. "I loved the Dunbar sisters, Dionne and Dorothy. During the time I cared for their father, I thought of those girls as my own—"

Rose interrupted her. "Viola, what did you see at the window that night?"

Viola looked beyond Rose. "I saw a woman, who later turned out to be Dionne, leaving the Chitwick house on foot and heading up the street. The sidewalks weren't shoveled and she walked in the road. She was dressed all in black, a foolish choice for walking at night. Not long after that, a car came creeping along. I figured the driver was drunk because no headlights were on. I was frightened for the woman walking in the street.

"When the car got closer, bright headlights flashed. I felt relieved, thinking the driver had finally spotted Dionne. The next thing I knew, there was a thump and the headlights went off. I could make out the cloud of exhaust, but it was too dark to see anything. Soon I heard the sound of the shredding barrel rolling in the snow as if it were being pushed and not rolling randomly.

"Seconds later, the car's engine roared and it sped off with the lights off. The road was pitch black. I didn't think much about it. I assumed Dionne had continued on her way. I figured the driver had come from Mannory Way and knocked the barrel over. Those people race up and down the street. They have no respect for the holy season."

"What happened next?" Rose asked.

"Not long after that, I heard you screaming about someone lying in the road. It wasn't until the next day I learned it was Dionne." She dabbed at her eyes with a wadded tissue from her pocket. "That poor, dear girl."

Rose sighed. "Viola, why didn't you tell this to the police?"

She looked startled. "Because I'd be in the spotlight. They'd look into my affairs, don't you see? They could link me to the letters. I'd never draw that kind of attention to myself."

"All you had to do was tell your story," Rose said. "What you saw from this window."

"And have Victor Alfano's suspicious eyes boring into me?" She folded her arms across her chest and sat back in her chair.

The two women talked until Rose glanced at her watch. It was late and she had to get her car from the middle school parking lot. All in all, her visit had been beneficial. She'd gotten Viola's promise to cease sending anonymous notes. However, Viola had balked at confessing her misdeeds to Hyacinth. "She'd call the police," Viola said. "She'd love to see me banished from the neighborhood."

In the end, Rose settled for Viola's promise to stop the letters. After all, the woman had no choice now that her little secret was out of the bag. Still, it was hard to feel angry with Viola. Rose hoped she never found herself so alone and bitter.

However, Rose planned to tell Cal what Viola had seen at the window the night Dionne was killed. Perhaps now the authorities would give credence to Rose's story. Although the chief claimed to be actively working on the case, precious little had been uncovered regarding the mystery car.

When Rose left Viola's warm house, it felt as if the temperature had dropped another ten degrees while she'd been inside. Shoulders hunched, she dodged the hills of snow piled on the sidewalk. As she approached the downtown, a car silently pulled up next to her. A window slid down to reveal Dorothy Dunbar, waving.

"Quick, get in. I'll give you a ride."

Rose opened the passenger door and climbed in. "Thanks. I'm on my way to get my car. It's in the middle school lot." She sank into the warmth, loosening her scarf from around her neck. Dorothy's stole hung from the rearview mirror. On the dashboard was a metal statue that Rose assumed was a saint, judging by the long robes and sandals, the figure's raised arm.

"Where are you headed?" she asked Dorothy.

"Back to the church. I gave old Mr. Mumford a ride home. He left the party prepared to walk home downtown. It's too cold tonight for anyone to be out walking," Dorothy chided.

Rose mumbled something about leaving the party to get some fresh air. It was the only excuse she could come up with. It had been a long night. She was anxious to get home to Chester and her flannel pajamas.

"How much longer will you be staying in Granite Cove?" she asked.

"Not long, unfortunately. The realtor's drawing up a purchase and sale agreement. If all goes well, the condo will be sold by Christmas."

"That's too bad," Rose said. "You've fitted right into the community. This town really took to you, Dorothy."

"You're sweet." She reached over and squeezed Rose's hand. "I considered staying on, but living at Dionne's place, well, it's hard. I couldn't stop thinking about her death: run down in the street and stuffed into a shredding barrel like so much trash."

"You knew about that, the shredding barrel?" Rose practically jumped in her seat. She stared at Dorothy in surprise. She was certain the police hadn't released that bit of information. After all, they didn't believe it.

Dorothy frowned and stared at the road. Finally she spoke, her voice cautious. "I think I heard someone mention it—Chief Alfano, perhaps." She glanced at Rose. The former pleasant expression was replaced with a wary look. In the dim light of the dashboard, her eyes were narrowed, her mouth set.

"Yes, you probably did," Rose quickly agreed. "That Chief Alfano's a regular chatterbox. Always telling department secrets." She attempted a laugh that sounded more like a croak.

They rode on, a charged silence filling the air between them. Rose felt a fluttering in her stomach. *Say something,* she thought, *something normal and casual.* But nothing came to her. Her mind felt squeezed. The tension in the car was a physical force.

After what felt like an eternity, she spotted the middle school ahead. "There it is," she yelped, jabbing her finger at the windshield. "Just drop me off outside, and thanks so much. I really appreciate the ride, 'specially on a night like this." She was babbling and couldn't stop. When the car continued gliding through the dark street, she said, "Excuse me, Dorothy? You just passed it."

Dorothy frowned and said nothing, her hands gripping the steering wheel.

"I have to let my dog out," Rose said, her voice strained. "He's old. He might pee in the house, or do worse." When Dorothy ignored that, Rose panicked: "Let me out!"

She forced herself to look at Dorothy. The woman seemed to be in a world of her own, as if Rose were not even there. Rose wondered if she'd been drinking. Keep your head, she thought. She tried to swallow. Her mouth was as dry as the bucket of sand in her trunk. She must think.

She looked out the window. They were leaving the downtown area and its deserted streets. Ahead was the sloping lawn of St. Rupert's Church. Rose took a deep breath. Her hand shot out and grabbed the steering wheel, tugging it toward her.

Dorothy grunted and pounded Rose's hand with her fist. Rose hung on, the two struggling for control of the wheel. The car fishtailed on the snowy street. It hopped the sidewalk, missing a light pole by inches. With a loud crack it crashed through the church's wooden fence and came to rest in the center of the lawn. Rose had an image of animals in the headlights, scattering to all corners.

Stunned by the impact, she fumbled with her seat belt. Dorothy looked around, dazed. She'd banged her head on the steering wheel. Blood ran from her forehead.

Rose turned the door handle and pushed. She was about to leap out when Dorothy whipped her chaplain's stole from the rearview mirror and wrapped it around Rose's neck. She tugged. The woman was surprisingly strong. Rose struggled, kicking her feet. The material of the stole bit into her neck. She was aware of Dorothy reaching for the dashboard. Out of the corner of her eye, Rose saw Dorothy raise an object over her head. But before she could bring it down, Rose punched her wrist. The object fell from her hand, its sharp edge grazing Rose's scalp. Now Rose managed to work her fingers under the stole. As the two struggled silently and fiercely, the door opened and the car flooded with light.

"Knock it off!"

Peering in at them was a man in a Santa hat. One half of his face was painted green, the other red. He was bare chested, his belly covered with red and white stripes like a bloated candy cane.

"You gals just broke this fence. Don't move. I'm calling the cops."

Rose pointed at Dorothy, who'd slipped the stole from around her neck. "Grab her," she yelled. "She tried to strangle me." With that, she leaped out of the car, pushing the man aside.

He staggered back, almost falling in the snow. "You stay right here," he bellowed.

But Rose took off, running through the smashed fence, down the hill toward the center of town. Her elegant new boots, useless for running on snow-covered streets, slipped and skidded. She ran in the center of the street. There was no traffic at that hour, no cars on the road.

At one point she heard the sound of pounding hooves behind her. She turned and gasped at the sight. The painted man wasn't alone. Running abreast was the Nativity donkey followed by the goat and two sheep.

At the bottom of the hill and diagonally across the street was the fire station. Firefighter Gene Furcolo was outside taking down the flag when he glanced across the street. What an incongruous sight for that sleepy fishing village: a painted man—half red, half green—whose belly shook like a tub of Jell-O, ran alongside a herd of livestock down Chapel Street hill. In the front was Rose McNichols, reporter for the *Granite Cove Gazette,* leading the pack.

CHAPTER TWENTY

Edwin Mumford lived in a Victorian house on a downtown street that at one time had been entirely residential. The homes were large and set comfortably apart. Following a zoning change, a few small businesses had cropped up: a welding shop, a framer, a gutter company. Likewise, the house next to Mr. Mumford's was a group home for special needs adults.

Rose knocked on the door of the mustard-yellow house. From inside came the drone of a vacuum cleaner. She rapped again, louder. The door opened and Gertrude Rust, a woman Rose recognized from the senior center, appeared. Gertrude shut off the heavy canister vacuum cleaner and opened the storm door. "Yes?"

"I wonder if I could have a word with Mr. Mumford," Rose said. "I've left messages, but he hasn't returned my calls. It'll only take a minute."

Gertrude chuckled. "Reason he didn't call back is he refuses to use the answering machine." She swung the door open. "Come in, quick. He hates a draft."

The housekeeper stepped aside as Rose entered the foyer and looked around. Her glance took in the polished tabletops, the sparkling windows and freshly vacuumed carpet. Gertrude was thorough, Rose thought admiringly.

Mr. Mumford, like many elderly widowers, was no doubt a fussbudget.

"He's in the library reading, but knowing him, he's probably sleeping. I fixed him a good breakfast when I arrived," Gertrude said. She indicated a room diagonally across from the foyer. "Go in and see him. Remember, his bark's worse than his bite." With that, she tapped the switch of the vacuum cleaner with a sneakered foot and the machine roared to life.

Rose entered the dimly lit library. Just as Gertrude had predicted, the old man was asleep in a chair by the window, his mouth agape, the newspapers on the floor. She glanced around, drawn to the shelves lining the wall. Old books with torn jackets shared space with stacks of *National Geographic* and *Time* magazines. On one shelf was a trio of hefty volumes: *The History of Granite Cove, 1750 to 1965*. She lifted one of the musty books and opened it. The author was G. Wainwright Pemberton, no doubt one of Stewart Pemberton's ancestors. Rose made a note to ask Stew, back at the office.

"Looking for something?"

The voice startled her so much she almost dropped the book. She quickly put it back and turned to face Mr. Mumford. "I was just admiring your library. I'm Rose McNichols, reporter for the *Granite Cove Gazette*. We've spoken on those occasions when you've dropped off a letter to the editor."

"Oh, right. Not that my letters did a bit of good. People just keep on making the same mistakes. It's like I tell my neighbor: this village is too good for its citizens. They can't appreciate the natural beauty. All they want to do is build, build, build. Stick in a Walgreens wherever there's space."

He indicated a nearby armchair. "Have a seat. What can I do for you? I hope you're not asking for money."

She sank into the armchair's sagging cushion. "No, I'm not collecting for anything. I'm interested in taking a peek inside your garage, if I could—"

"My garage? Why do you want to look in my garage?" He stared at her, his beaked nose reddening.

"It's your car, Mr. Mumford. I just want to take a look at the front, near the grille. You see, there's a chance someone may have used it without your permission."

"No one's used my car. I don't drive it and don't let anyone else drive it. It's only insured for me. Maybe you heard I had to give up my license temporarily. I did poorly on the eye exam. However, someone from the church offered to take me to the Mass General Hospital. They've got eye doctors there who prescribe special glasses. I'll be able to drive again." He attempted to get to his feet. "You can tell whoever's interested, the car's not for sale."

Rose rushed to help him before he fell. "I'm not interested in buying your car, Mr. Mumford. I just want to take a look at it. I can't see much through the little window in your garage."

"No need for that, young lady. The car's not for sale." He peered at her, his eyes glittering. "Did my son Elliott send you?"

She shook her head. "No one sent me—"

"Because you can tell him I expect to be driving that car come spring. The chaplain, Dorothy, is taking me to the eye doctors in Boston." He rubbed his thumb and forefinger together. "My son just wants to make a little money off his old man. Thinks he can fool me." He motioned to the door. "You can see yourself out."

With a sigh, Rose took her exit.

In the dining room, Gertrude was dusting a wooden sideboard the size of a submarine. She stopped and motioned to Rose, leading her into the front hallway. "Don't pay no attention to him," she said. "Like I mentioned, his bark's worse than his bite."

Rose shrugged. "I just wanted to check out his car, that's all. He's got the garage locked."

"And he keeps the key in his pocket." Gertrude shook her head. "They get like that, suspicious. He seems to think his son's gonna sell the car from under him."

"Mr. Mumford mentioned Dorothy Dunbar taking him to the eye doctors in Boston. Do you know anything about that?" Rose asked.

"She came to give him Communion a couple times. She was good to the old fella." She shook her head. "I can't believe the stories I'm hearing. She'd never assault anyone. Those cops got the wrong person. My sister's nephew is on the auxiliary police force. He claims there's no evidence against Dorothy Dunbar."

Rose ignored this and asked, "Do you know if she ever drove Mr. Mumford's car?"

The woman chuckled. "He won't let anyone drive it." She glanced at the library door. Mr. Mumford stood there, peering at them. Gertrude said to Rose, "You'd better go now before he pitches a fit."

On Friday a light snow was falling when Cal pulled the cruiser to the curb outside Edwin Mumford's house. Rose, sitting next to him, said, "I really appreciate this, Cal. Consider it a friendly visit to an elderly man, a well-being check."

"I'm telling you now, honey, if he refuses to show us the garage, I'm backing off. Dorothy Dunbar is no longer under investigation. I have no official reason to be here."

"Humor me, Cal. And if Mr. Mumford offers resistance, ooze on the charm, something that comes naturally to you."

"Why do I let you talk me into these things?" he asked, looking at her.

She felt her face flush and quickly said, "Because I've been your partner in crime since fifth grade, remember?"

He sighed and opened the door. Together they headed up the driveway. Gertrude Rust answered the door, looking from Rose to Cal, clearly flustered. "Oh, my, what's happened now?"

"Can we come in, Mrs. Rust?" Cal said. "This isn't an official visit. I want a word with Mr. Mumford."

She swung the door open. "He's in the library," she said, pointing a feather duster in that direction. "I'd better take you." They followed her and waited outside the door as she entered. "Mr. Mumford, a couple of people to see you. One of them's Cal Devine, the policeman. The other's Rose McNichols, the news reporter."

As the old man stared at the housekeeper, Cal slipped into the room. "Hello, Mr. Mumford. Sorry to bother you, but I'd like to take a look at your garage for a moment. I won't touch your car, if that's what you're worried about." He held up his hands palms raised.

The old man, shocked to see a police officer in his house, continued to stare. Finally he regained his composure. "Do you have a search warrant?"

Cal shook his head. "Sorry, I don't. I was hoping you'd voluntarily show me."

Rose knew the old man wouldn't do that. They would leave the house without learning if Mr. Mumford's car was the one involved in the hit-and-run. Cal wouldn't attempt to get a search warrant based on her hunch. Now she pushed past Cal and approached the old man.

"Mr. Mumford, you know my dad—Russell McNichols?"

He blinked. "I do. When I used to organize the Masons' fish fries, Russ sold us the fish."

"And isn't it true you're also a striper fisherman?" Rose knew this from writing about the fishermen's summer tournaments.

He nodded. "I was, but I don't get around much now. I can't climb in and out of boats ever since the hip replacement." He stared at her. "What's that got to do with my garage?"

"Nothing, really. But it occurred to me that you might like to go along with my dad and Cal this summer. They're going striper fishing off the beach. Dad sits in a deck chair on the sand. He says it's very comfortable." She turned to Cal. "Mr. Mumford can come with you, can't he?"

Now it was Cal's turn to blink. "Of course. Love to have him."

"Cal brings a picnic," Rose added. "His haddock chowder is the best."

Mr. Mumford mulled this over and finally said, "I wouldn't mind that." He dropped his newspaper to the floor and struggled out of his chair. Rose went to his side to assist. The old man reached into his pocket. He held up a key. "The garage door. I'll go with you."

"It's slippery out there," Cal said. "We'll give you a hand."

They moved to the hallway where Gertrude helped the old man into his coat and scarf. "Those shoes aren't worth a damn on that ice," she said. "You two stay on either side of him. He slips, and it's all over for his hip."

"Gertrude," the old man said, "I'm capable of speaking for myself."

The trio made their way down the driveway, Rose and Cal flanking Mr. Mumford, while Gertrude watched anxiously from a kitchen window.

"Tell your son to put some salt on the driveway," Cal told the old man.

"The boy's too busy visiting his country club. Just waiting for me to die," he said, with a note of satisfaction at having so far outwitted his child.

Moments later they arrived at the garage. Cal cupped his eyes and peered through the dusty window. Mr. Mumford slowly retrieved his key from his pocket and fitted it into the padlock on the door. When the lock fell open, he removed it and nodded to Cal.

Cal rolled the squeaky wooden door up. Inside the garage, a large gray sedan filled most of the interior. "Only seventy-five thousand miles," Mr. Mumford said proudly. "Still got a lot of life in it."

"Nice looking vehicle," Cal said.

He entered the shadowy garage, at the same time removing a flashlight clipped to his belt. Rose stood at the entrance with Mr. Mumford. They watched Cal wedge himself between the car and garage wall. When he reached the front, he aimed the flashlight beam over the car's grille. After several moments, he turned off the light and stood up.

Looking at Rose, he nodded his head

.

EPILOGUE

One month later, Rose met Viola Hampstead for coffee at Mega Mug. Viola wanted to tell Rose about her recent visit to Framingham Women's Prison, where she met with Dorothy Dunbar.

"I brought her a book of devotionals, but first I called to see if it was okay. I was told that books had to be paperbacks."

"Why is that?" Rose asked.

"A hardcover book could be used as a weapon." She looked pleased to be imparting insider information. "But if you ask me, when someone's got a mind to it, anything can be a weapon."

"Including a Saint Christopher statue." Rose automatically rubbed the top of her head. Dorothy's intended blow had only grazed her crown, causing Doc Moss to again comment upon Rose's "thick Irish skull."

Viola gave her a sympathetic look. "You should never have gotten into that car with Dorothy."

"How did I know she'd flip out? She's a chaplain, for crying out loud."

"She was pushed to the edge," Viola said. Her cheeks reddened. "I know all about that kind of thing."

"I think Dorothy's resentment went back to when she and Dionne were children," Rose said. "Dionne was the pretty, witty one, qualities people favor. Dorothy probably pretended she didn't mind. Maybe she was unaware she carried such anger."

Viola took a sip of coffee. "You know, as far as her youthful romance with Roger went, we only have Dorothy's word for it. She said she was going to meet him in Florida during her winter break. But had he broken it off with Dionne, as Dorothy claimed?"

"It's what she told me as well," Rose said. "When I interviewed her about Dionne, she launched into her tale of a summer romance that became a great passion."

"Let me tell you, if Dorothy was planning to visit Roger, they must have kept it secret. If Dionne had gotten wind of it, there'd have been hell to pay. That girl was a regular spitfire."

Muriel stopped at their table to fill their cups. When she left, Rose said, "What I find strange is why Dorothy waited all these years to get even."

"Maybe she saw the opportunity—Dionne walking in the road—and impulsively acted on it. What's that quote?" She pursed her lips. "'Revenge is a dish best served cold.'"

"Nothing impulsive about it," Rose told her. "She must have known Dionne would be attending the class. Dorothy had to plan in order to get the car."

"Yes, you're probably right," Viola said. "All the poor girl had was her memories: Roger had loved her, she'd loved him—until he died tragically. She could live with that. Then Dionne started rattling the skeletons. While attending Hyacinth's class, she claimed she received messages of love from Roger." Viola shrugged. "Maybe she did receive such messages, maybe she didn't. Personally, I'm not a believer in the afterlife. But it's just like Dionne to make sure Dorothy heard about it. She had a mean streak, that girl. She wasn't above rubbing salt in a wound."

Rose nodded, thoughtful. "I was there at the mediums class that night. I heard Hyacinth give Dionne Roger's message."

Viola lowered her voice. "Did it ever occur to you that Hyacinth might have been telling Dionne what she wanted to hear?"

"You mean Hyacinth was faking it? But how? She didn't know about Dionne's romance with this guy."

"How do you know?" Viola asked. "When I joined Hyacinth's prayer group years ago, she met with members individually. She said she needed to know us better, to see if we were 'compatible.' That woman is skilled at dredging up secrets. If you ask me, Hyacinth Chitwick should be a spy for the government. She knows where the bodies are buried."

"Why would she care?" Rose asked.

"Because knowledge is power," Viola said, "and Hyacinth loves power."

Rose sighed. "People always surprise me. Take Dorothy, for instance. Her transformation that night of the theater party was frightening. The look on her face when she suspected I knew, it's like she had become another person." Rose shivered.

"She had. I think Dorothy was pushed over the edge. It wasn't enough that Dionne lorded it over her when they were young. That brief summer romance was something Dorothy cherished. Now her sister was out to destroy that."

"It makes me glad I'm an only child," Rose said.

Viola chuckled. "Someone said that families push our buttons because they know where the buttons are located."

"I just wish I knew which sister was telling the truth," Rose said. "Did Roger really break it off with Dionne and plan to meet Dorothy in Florida?"

Viola narrowed her eyes. "Know what I think? That boy was stringing them both along. He had Dionne in one corner and Dorothy in another. Neither sister knew about the other. Isn't it just like a man?"

Rose nodded. "All I know is, Dorothy would have gotten away with her crime if Cal and I hadn't located the car she drove that night. She was clever, choosing old Edwin Mumford, one of those she took Communion to."

"How did she know Mr. Mumford wouldn't suddenly appear in town driving the damaged car?" Viola asked.

"Because his son made him give up his license, although Mr. Mumford refused to sell the car. He always thought he'd pass the eye exam and drive again. Meanwhile, the car sat in the garage, leaving Dorothy free to use it.

"I'm thankful Cal believed me," Rose continued. "No one else did, when I reported that Dorothy had attacked me. According to her story, the car skidded on the ice, crashing through the fence, and the Saint Christopher statue must have flown off the dashboard and cut my head. Even the guy from Mannory Way who came on the scene was no help as a witness. Who'd take him seriously? He was half naked and had been partying all night. Not only that—he'd arrived right after Dorothy tried to bean me with the statue." Rose sighed. "I had no witnesses. As for my accusing Dorothy of trying to knock me out, Chief Alfano declared I'd suffered a head wound and couldn't remember what happened."

"Poor Rose. Good thing you had a friend in Officer Devine. Such a handsome fella."

"Cal's more than just a pretty face," Rose said. "He did some digging into Dorothy's past. He learned she hadn't retired from her job as she claimed. No, she was caught attempting to embezzle from the company."

"How did you happen to suspect Mr. Mumford's car?"

"The night Dorothy turned on me, I saw something in her face that indicated she was capable of anything. And since most crimes are committed by the victim's family, I began to suspect that she was responsible for her sister's death.

"I was stumped by the car, though. Obviously it would be damaged, so it couldn't have been Dorothy's car that hit Dionne. At the same time, I knew the police were thorough in checking out body shops. It had to be a car that was hidden somewhere.

"Then I remembered the night Dorothy picked me up. She said she'd just given Mr. Mumford a ride home from the play. She said he had been planning to walk home. Around that time, I got hold of a list of St. Rupert's homebound parishioners. It was a process of elimination, checking out the ones Dorothy visited when performing chaplain duties. A colleague of mine at the newspaper has a friend at the Registry of Motor Vehicles, and he obtained information on the parishioners' driving status and vehicles."

Rose smiled. "Basically, all roads led to Edwin Mumford. When his car matched the paint chip, it was all over for Dorothy. They found her fingerprints on the rearview mirror."

"She swears she wasn't driving the car that night," Viola said. "She insists that she'd used the car to buy groceries for Mr. Mumford."

"I know she does," Rose said. "At one point she even said the old man had been driving the night Dionne was killed." Rose shook her head. "Even Chief Alfano rejected that. Dorothy's going to need a high-profile criminal lawyer."

"She claims she's being framed," Viola said. "Even now, I have a hard time believing Dorothy capable of such things. That girl's got such... warmth."

"I'd never have believed her capable until she turned on me," Rose said.

Viola finished her coffee and set her cup in the saucer. "It's an awful shame that two sisters should end up like that, one dead and the other in jail." She sighed. "No man is worth that. I don't care how good-looking he is."

"You're absolutely right," Rose said. She glanced out the window. While they'd been inside, the sky had darkened. A squall was predicted for the afternoon. The streetlights were flickering on. "We'd better get home before the snow starts."

Viola wrapped her scarf around her neck. "Tonight I'm spending a cozy evening with my cats. There's a DVD for me—a romance—and some organic catnip for them. All in all, it's not a bad life."

"Sounds good to me," Rose said.

End

ABOUT THE AUTHOR

Sharon Love Cook grew up in Gloucester, Mass., the oldest working seaport in the US. She now lives in Beverly, a coastal town north of Boston with her husband and herd of rescued cats. Please contact her at:

sharonlovecook@comcast.net

Visit her site, home of her illustrations and cartoons:

sharonlovecook.com